# THE MORNING AFTER

I woke to find Dimitri stroking my arm and sunlight creeping through the light-blocking curtains we'd failed to close the night before. Who knew love with Dimitri would be as exhausting as, say, battling a power-hungry werewolf or blasting a few dozen black souls? I snuggled closer, wishing we could spend the day in bed, knowing it was time to meet the Red Skull witches and make our final stand against the demon Vald.

I played with the dark, springy hairs on his chest. "You don't have to go with me."

"Yes, I do."

I lifted my head to find him gazing intently at me. He flashed a cocky grin that made the skin around his eyes crinkle.

What do you say to a guy who'd go to hell and back, just to be with you?

I wrapped my arms around him. "Kiss me."

# ANGIE FOX

# The Accidental Demon Slayer

LOVE SPELL  NEW YORK CITY

*For my parents, Ted and Marie Fox,*
*who pretended not to notice the flashlight*
*I kept under my bed for when I had*
*to read just one more chapter.*

LOVE SPELL®

August 2008

Published by

Dorchester Publishing Co., Inc.
200 Madison Avenue
New York, NY 10016

ISBN 10: 0-505-52769-3
ISBN 13: 978-0-505-52769-1

The name "Love Spell" and its logo are trademarks of Dorchester Publishing Co., Inc.

Printed in the United States of America.

10 9 8 7 6 5 4 3 2 1

Visit us on the web at www.dorchesterpub.com.

# ACKNOWLEDGMENTS

Special thanks to:

Chessie Welker, my first reader and critique partner, for keeping me on track.

Leah Hultenschmidt, who found this manuscript and made a dream come true.

My agent, Jessica Faust—I don't know how she got to be so smart, but I know I'm lucky to have her in my corner.

Harley rider Brad Jones, who answered a slew of "What if?" questions, let me ride along on the back of his hog and introduced me to Harley Boy and Cletus, two of the coolest biker dogs around. Thanks also to Jesse Lane, International Pack Guardian of the Biker Dogs Motorcycle Club.

Chocolate covered thanks to Stephanie Rowe and Sally MacKenzie for showing a newbie the ropes. I hope I can do the same for someone else.

Finally, I'm indebted to my own personal cheering squad— Joanna Campbell Slan, Ann Aguirre, Diane Freiermuth, Theresa Burnham, Candy Calvert and Nancy Herriman, Kathye Marsh, Mary Cooper Feliz, Anja Boersma, Scott Granneman and Aileen Crowe Nandi. You make the journey a lot more fun.

And, of course, to Jim.

# The Accidental Demon Slayer

# Chapter One

When I opened the door to greet my grandmother for the very first time, I'm not sure what I was expecting. I know I hadn't envisioned an apple-shaped woman in a *Kiss My Asphalt* T-shirt, with wind-burned cheeks and a sagging tattoo of a phoenix on her arm. But what I really didn't bargain for was a brief hug, followed by a forceful shove that had me landing firmly on my butt on the cold, black-and-white checked floor of my hall bathroom.

"Let me out of here!" I twisted the bathroom door-knob until I wrenched my wrist. How the frig did this happen? One minute I was answering my door, and the next I had landed booty over tea kettle on tile that was about two weeks overdue for a good scrubbing.

"Buck up, sugar cake." My grandma's chunky silver rings clinked against the other side of the door, and her gravelly voice sounded like she'd spent the last century breathing semitruck exhaust. "This is for your own good."

*My own good?* In what world could she know what was good for me? I'd never even heard from my mom's mom until she'd called me the day before. The next thing I knew, she was flying to Atlanta to meet me. I had assumed that meant air travel, not the hot pink Harley parked in my driveway.

I kicked the door with all my strength. "Ouchie!" I hollered as pain seared my foot. Dang it all. Three years teaching at Happy Hands Preschool and I couldn't even cuss right. I limped in circles, the pointed toe of my simple black heel curled up like an elf shoe.

Why tonight, of all nights, did this have to happen?

Grandma chuckled. "Why, Lizzie Brown—kickin' and a hollerin'. Thank heaven my grandbaby has spunk. I know you're hacked to Hades, princess. But trust me. If I let you out now, you'd wreck all your pretty furniture."

She'd obviously cracked her head on the pavement one too many times. As for ruining my Pottery Barn knockoff furniture, my pathetic excuse for a watchdog would take care of that. Pirate, my Jack Russell terrier, tended to piddle at the first sign of trouble. I pounded against the door until my hands throbbed. Of all the dumb things to do, I had to let a stranger into my house.

*Was I that desperate for affection?*

Probably. My adoptive parents, Cliff and Hillary, meant well. But they weren't exactly warm and fuzzy. They didn't even like to touch each other. So, sue me, it felt good—even if it was a little forced—when my biological grandmother hugged me for the first time.

*"Levitis cadre. Familio, madre,"* she chanted like a deranged monk.

"Cut it out! Today is my thirtieth birthday, and I'm going to be late for my party if you don't open this door. Now!" Let's face it. I couldn't go out much on my salary. Happy Hands Preschool wasn't exactly raking in the big bucks. And the one night out of the year where I could count on all of my friends to be dateless and available, this geriatric biker had to take me prisoner.

She rapped her knuckles on her side of the door. As if I were going anywhere. "Lizzie dear? You have ridden a bike before?" she asked, as if I'd taken Hog 101 in high school.

Had she seen my cream-on-white front room? "Yeah, um. In case you haven't noticed, I'm more of an indoor girl." Not that I was against motorcycles, in theory. But if Grandma thought I was going to hoist my rear end up on the back of her hog, a pothole had knocked something loose in her head.

"Well, Lizzie, the thing is . . ." She paused to find the right words to say whatever it was I was sure I didn't want to hear. She cleared her throat. "Our coven's on the run."

Oh lordy. "You think you're a witch?"

"Am a witch, darlin'. So was your mother. And if I wasn't such a damned good witch, all hell wouldn't be after us. I don't have time to spell it out for you right now, but let me ask: You own any leather chaps?"

Yeah, hanging right next to my white capri pants. "No!"

"Well, that bites," she said. "Life on the road can chafe your thighs."

I gulped. She'd better not even *think* of kidnapping me. That was it. "Pirate! Watchdog! Attack!" He didn't even have the courage to whimper. Useless beast. Last time I was buying him Silky Bones Pet-sicles.

"Less than one minute to go, by my watch. You were born at precisely 6:43 P.M." She rubbed at the other side of the door like she was comforting a spastic kitten in a crate. "I found you just in time."

"Oh yeah, that makes sense." If I could get her to open the door, I could bolt past her and be free faster than I could say whack job. Our reservations were at 7:30. If she let me out now, I could lock her out of my

house, out of my life and, of course, make a mad dash
to my flipping birthday party. I rubbed my temples.
Oh, to be less desperate for a night of fruity drinks and
debauchery.

We were supposed to be heading to Fire, one of Atlanta's newest bistros. I'd slipped into my sapphire
party dress and twisted my inky hair into a stylish updo
for the occasion. Now I could just feel curls escaping.

"Times like these I wish my hog watch had a second
hand." Grandma snorted. "And hey—" She rapped on
the door, clanking her rings. "Try to stay clear of anything flammable."

The woman was delusional. And I still couldn't figure out how she'd locked the door from the outside.

"A few of these little beauties . . ." she said to the
sound of jars being unscrewed. "You know, I would
have been in your life sooner, but we lost track of you.
Never would have recognized you in that Audrey
Hepburn–looking getup."

Audrey Hepburn my rear. I bought this dress on
clearance last week at Ann Taylor. And what was I doing even listening to fashion advice from a senior
citizen in rhinestone-studded skinny jeans? "Why me?
Why now?"

"My spell only allowed me to locate you when your
power had grown strong enough."

*Spell?* I groaned under my breath. This is exactly why
I hadn't searched out my birth parents. Somehow, I knew
my biological family would be a bunch of nut jobs.

And was that incense I smelled?

The pungent aroma of ginger and clove seeped under the door. Oh, no, no, no. "You'd better not be light-
ing things on fire out there!" *Decision made.* I mustered
a few calming yoga breaths and tried to stuff my hair
back into its polished updo. The further I got away
from this branch of my family tree, the better.

"Listen, lady," I said as I struggled to bring my temper down a notch. "I mean, Grandma. Listen, Grandma. Let me out of here and you can whip up whatever spell you want."

*After I remove you from my house and my life.*

I searched under the sink for a weapon and came up with a toilet brush and a bottle of Purple Prairie Clover sanitizing spray.

Was I really going to shoot my own grandmother?

Yes.

"Open the door and let's talk."

She began to hum. It sounded like a church hymn.

"Grandma? Come on, now. Look. It's not just that people are expecting me. *He's* going to be there," I said, as I used my thumb to pop the top off the sanitizing spray. "Hot Ryan Harmon from the gym," I explained, as if she was supposed to know who that was. My girlfriends certainly did. "It's taken me months of flirting on the elliptical machines to screw up the courage to ask this guy out, and you are not going to ruin it for me." I deserved to date once in a while, didn't I?

"Lizzie, you stay away from him. That man is a troll."

"And you know because . . ." Crazy *and* opinionated. What a lovely combination.

I needed this shot at Ryan because—newsflash—I didn't know many single men over the age of four. Hot Ryan Harmon was all I had going.

"Don't take it personally, lover girl." She pulled the door open a crack, her long gray hair swooshing as she shook her head. "Trust me."

I whipped up my sanitizing spray and fired just as she slammed the door.

"Gak!" The air around me erupted with Purple Prairie Clover mist. I breathed in a metallic taste. The room smelled like I'd fallen headfirst into a vat of wild-flowers.

"Ten seconds!"

"Until what?" The flowery spray was going to my head. Bright spots dotted my vision. Stumbling, I smashed my already sore toe into the cabinet under the sink. "Mother Fudrucker!" I braced myself over the sink as my stay-slim rice cake and peanut butter pre-dinner rumbled up the back of my throat.

"Seven seconds!"

Maybe I'd poisoned myself. My tongue thickened, and my head felt like it was stuffed with packing peanuts. The room swirled and my legs buckled. A hot flash seared up my spine, through my limbs. I could have sworn I saw my hands melt into the faux marble countertop. Steam bubbled inside me and rose from every pore.

"You are the Exalted Demon Slayer of Dalea. Or at least you will be in four seconds. Three . . . !"

The place reeked of melted plastic and Purple Prairie Clover. I had to be hallucinating. Standing seemed like too much of an effort. My legs gave way and I slid down the door, my head coming to rest near a forgotten smidge of Extra Brite toothpaste on the floor. The room—no, the air itself—gleamed. The black-and-white tile practically sizzled under my body.

I felt something approach from behind. It gave off a funny clicking sound, like high heels on hardwood. And, phew, it smelled like I'd gone from a bad bonfire straight into the outhouse.

My grandma threw open the door. "Now we—"

The look of terror on Grandma's face made me think missing the party was the least of my worries. Her eager greeting melted into a scream. I turned and immediately wished I hadn't. I choked back a shriek while my heart did the samba.

A shrunken, razor-toothed, man, no—*thing* perched on the top of my toilet bowl. He existed in a swirling gray cloud that clung to his essence like a shroud. A gold ring wound through his flared nostrils until the heavy ball of it rested against rows and rows of spear-like teeth. His hide crinkled, as jagged as desert earth after a drought. It crackled as he tapped a single clawed toe against the white porcelain. Worst of all, his scarlet eyes seemed to have only one target—me.

# Chapter Two

He bowed his head and cackled low in his throat, sending a shiver straight down to my toes. *Run!* My mind screamed in horror. My blood pounded in my skull and my hands flopped helplessly. *Run!* I dug my heels into the tile and managed a pathetic half circle. Oh my God. I was going to die right here on my bathroom floor.

Grandma whipped her hand forward. "Go to hell, Xerxes!" she screamed, sending a wave of energy shrieking over my head. Her turquoise choker glowed around her neck. The air itself vibrated. Xerxes didn't even blink. Instead, he lifted a skeletal finger and pointed it at me. I wanted to cry. *Keep it together.*

Grandma clasped both hands around her necklace. She began to chant, her raspy voice repeating a single word, *"Digredior. Digredior. Digredior."* Xerxes snorted and the acrid smell of sulfur seared the air.

I stared down at my own fingers, steaming on the tile. *Run!* Impossible. It was like my body was trapped in a thick sludge. I fought back a wave of panic. If I couldn't escape, I had to think. I puffed the hair out of my face and focused on the geometric white tiles in front of me. *Be logical.*

Somewhere, there existed a reasonable explanation for what was happening. I just had to find it. Had I inhaled some of the sanitizing spray? Naturally. Yes. That could explain a lot. *Please.* This had to be a warped Purple Prairie Clover head trip.

"This is a hideous side effect," I pleaded with everything I had. Life seeped back into my arms and legs. I sniffed, wiped at the sweat tickling down my face. "Monsters do not, not, *not* exist." My whole body shook as I ventured a peek back at my toilet bowl.

Xerxes hissed, spittle clinging to his blackened lips. Vapor swirled through his fingers and gathered into a thick smoke. It loomed toward me, a wave of ash, boiling upon itself. Stale, dead. My heart slammed in my throat. I fought the urge to gag. This was real.

Grandma focused, heart and soul, on the beast. *"Digredior. Digredior . . ."*

I had to get out of here. Grandma too. Whatever she was saying to that creature, it wasn't working. And just because she was crazy enough to face him didn't mean she deserved to die. My body ached as I inched toward the doorway. I prayed he didn't notice. But who was I kidding? I could taste the dark mist approaching, feel his red eyes burning into my back. I had to turn. Had to look.

Xerxes's claws clickety-clacked as he snaked down from the top of the toilet. Shock drilled through me, pinning me to the floor. Xerxes bobbed his head once, twice. One side of his mouth twisted into a smirk. "Stay, Lizzie," he said slowly, his Greek accent punctuating each word as his dark cloud embraced me.

"How did you know my na—? Hmm." Warmth washed over me. Oddly enough, I found myself smiling at him. *This can't be right.* But darned if all my concerns didn't seem to be—whoosh—falling away.

I stifled a giggle. Time to axe the Cheshire cat grin, if only for Grandma's sake. She'd aged a century in five seconds flat.

Strange. I hated him. He was evil and foul and he smelled like rotten cheese.

But I liked cheese, especially with crackers.

He lowered his head and hit me with the sweetest smile. His cracked skin showed character. It molded to his sleek, muscular frame. I wanted to touch him.

My grandma said something or other.

The pupils of the demon's eyes began to shift like a kaleidoscope. Fascinating. So that's what he was. A demon.

I stumbled. "Would you look at that?" I didn't even remember standing up. I found myself strutting toward him, closing the space between us. "Xerxes, I'll bet you are just the Brad Pitt of the underworld."

Then Xerxes did something quite rude. He shot darts out of his eyes. It's so uncomfortable when you meet someone and five minutes later they invade your personal space. Even more frightening, the shimmery green darts headed straight for my neck. What was this guy trying to do? Chop my head off?

The old lady behind me, whatshername, started wailing.

Not good. I slowed things in order to get a good look at the darts. They shone like miniature glow sticks. I touched one and it sizzled on the end of my fingertip. Warm, but not painful. I pulled it out of the air and it hummed in my hand. I gingerly touched the tip. "Ow!" Sharp as broken glass. "The trick is to grab 'em by the side," I said to myself. I gathered them up like I was plucking tomatoes off the vine.

"Whaddaya think about that, Mr. Xerxes?" I held out a handful of green sizzly things.

The demon seemed almost frozen in time. My grandmother stood with her eyes transfixed, her mouth gaped open.

"Biiiiitttch!" The demon screamed.

Like he was one to talk. "How would you like it if I

tossed magical lawn darts at your head and called you names?" I launched the barbs back at him.

They crashed into his forehead and he exploded into a million flecks of light.

I shielded my eyes as the world ratcheted back into focus. Grandma's scream pierced the haze in my head.

"Ak!" *What had I done?* My arms sizzled from the electricity in the air, and every hair on my body stood on end. The room itself tasted bitter. Grandma and I gaped at each other for about a half a second. Then she snapped her mouth closed and dashed out into the hall.

"This is real," I said to my wild-haired reflection in the bathroom mirror. What a terrible thought.

Grandma hurried back juggling a half-dozen ziplock bags full of heaven knew what. "Get out." She shoved past me, dumped the bags on the floor, and drew a circle on the tile with ashy, gray chalk.

"What?" I choked. Handprints—*my handprints*— burned into the countertop like a brand. I stared at my palms. There wasn't a mark on them. My fingers throbbed like they were asleep. I rubbed them on my dress to get the circulation going again. "Are you going to tell me what just happened here?" I grabbed the bathroom towel to wipe snot, tears and heaven knew what else from my face.

She paused, chalk quivering. "Yes. But first I'm going to slam the door on these bastards. Xerxes only wanted a look at you. There'll be more."

*A look?* I didn't believe that for a second. "In case you didn't notice, he fired green pointy things. At my neck!"

She slipped on a pair of silver-framed reading glasses with rhinestone clusters in the corners. "You're right. He did decide to kill you." She began rifling through a collection of glass vials. "Demons can be impulsive."

She harrumphed. "Like yo-yo grandchildren who touch what they shouldn't." She chose a vial of olive-brown liquid and stuffed it into the front pocket of her jeans. "I don't know what you were thinking, grabbing his fulminations."

"Fulma-what?"

"No time," she said, rifling through her bag again. "But don't think for one second that you're off the hook, slick. I'm gonna ride you 'til next Sunday." She handed me a Smucker's peanut butter jar filled with a canary yellow sludge. "Can the questions. Keep this with you. And for the love of Laconia, let me work."

"Okay . . ." A demon wants me dead, so I get a Smucker's jar. Shouldn't we be running? Hiding? Where, I didn't know, but Grandma's Harley was sounding better by the second. Even if we ended up some place like the Laconia motorcycle rally. My fingers slid over the greasy glass of the jar and I darn near dropped it. What was I supposed to do if another demon showed up? Throw this at his head?

"Ey-ak!" I squealed as she popped open a ziplock bag that smelled like a dead mouse. She ignored my distress and began rubbing tiny circles of mush onto my bathroom floor. "Tell me that isn't poop," I said, as she ground the foul substance into my grout.

"Raccoon liver. Now get out!" my grandmother ordered without looking up from the mess on my bathroom floor.

"Gladly." I had no idea what had just happened and I was not at all opposed to getting as far away from her as possible. I tripped over Grandma's animal-hide bag and what had to be about a half dozen Smucker's jars in the narrow hallway outside the hall bathroom. They were filled with various brackish liquids, plants, and at least one possum tail. Roadkill witchcraft. Fan-frickin-tastic.

I slumped down at the kitchen table and buried my face in my hands. "Face facts, Lizzie. Xerxes the demon just tried to chop your head off."

What would Cliff and Hillary have to say about that?

I didn't know what to think anymore. That thing was real. No question about it. He came for me. And he would have killed Grandma too.

An hour ago, I wasn't even sure I believed in hell. Now it was after. Xerxes probably tracked me like my grandmother had. Worse, he'd gotten inside my head without even blinking. How could I defend myself against a creature who could control me like a Muppet? I had no idea what he—or my grandma—could possibly want from me.

When my grandma had called, I figured she was interested in what I'd been doing the last thirty years of my life. I'd tell her about my friends, my teaching job at Happy Hands Preschool. She'd tell me about herself and her family. Make that my family. At last, I'd learn about my mom, any brothers or sisters, who I was, where I came from.

Now I wasn't sure I wanted to know. I could be dead right now. Killed by a demon in my very own bathroom.

Claws scurried across the ceramic floor in the hallway.

"Grandma!" I leapt from the chair, on instant high alert.

She shot out of the bathroom as I realized my would-be attacker was, in fact, my Jack Russell terrier. Pirate was mostly white, with a dollop of brown on his back that wound up his neck and over one eye. He scampered around the corner into the kitchen, slid three feet and nearly thwacked his head on the side of the refrigerator.

"Pirate." The tension oozed out of me and I about

collapsed on the floor in front of him. He leapt into my arms and licked wherever he could reach. I hugged him close, his wiry hair tickling my nose. "Where have you been, boy?"

His entire body wriggled with excitement. "Alone! Locked in the backyard! Alone! But I dug under the fence. And then I ate through the screen on the front door. And I'm here now! I'm here! What'd I miss?"

My blood froze. "Oh no, no, no." I scrambled away from him like an oversized crab. "There's a demon in my dog!"

Pirate danced in place. "Are you kidding? It's me! I burrowed, I ate screen, I ignored Mrs. Cristople's tabby cat. I'm here to save you!"

Grandma scrubbed her hands on her jeans, leaving an oily smear behind. "Pirate is fine. A little impatient." She grabbed a vial of silver powder from her back pocket and uncorked it with her teeth. "I told you to keep quiet until I had a chance to speak with Lizzie."

Pirate let out a high-pitched dog whine.

"I don't want to hear it," she said, eyeball-measuring a bit of silver powder into her palm. "Now, Lizzie. I have to finish this containment spell or we could have another Xerxes on your toilet bowl." She gave a worried snort. "Or worse . . ." She disappeared back into the bathroom.

I stared at Pirate, who promptly began licking himself.

"Stop it."

He ignored me like he always did.

"Well hallelujah. At least some things don't change."

But, oh God, what had just happened?

I didn't feel any different. I did a quick once-over in the mirror above the living room couch. I didn't look any different. But there had been a demon in my bathroom. And he knew my name. I wasn't up on my demon lore, but something told me that wasn't good.

As for Pirate, I didn't know what to think. I took a deep breath, counted to three. There had to be a logical explanation for all of this.

"Hey." Pirate ran his cold nose along my ankle. "How 'bout you feed me? I swear I haven't eaten in a year. And screen door doesn't count."

I stared down at Pirate, who spun three times and sat.

He cocked his head. "Why the face? Am I drooling? Oh geez. It's the doggie pellets. I think of doggie pellets, I drool."

"What?" I stammered. *What are you?* That didn't sound polite. I rubbed my temples.

*Get a grip.*

"Why, Pirate?" Each word was a battle. "Why are you talking to me?"

"Because," he said, mimicking my stilted tone, "I am hungry." We stared at each other for a long time. "Now."

"This isn't happening," I said. I turned back to the mirror and started shoving my hair back into place. I needed something to be normal. Anything. Even if it was something as trivial as a hairdo.

"Come on, Lizzie." Pirate licked my leg. "Lighten up. And hey, if you don't want to feed me that dry stuff, I'll take the fettuccine from last week. Back of the fridge, to the left of the lettuce crisper, behind the mustard."

Yeah, right. Instead, he got dry kibble and a fresh bowl of water. Then I set about canceling my thirtieth birthday dinner. I didn't know what I was going to tell my friends.

*Sorry, guys. I couldn't wait to celebrate with you.*

*Believe me. But then my long-lost biker grandma locked me in my bathroom, a demon tried to kill me and now my dog won't stop yapping.*

I dialed my friend Yvette and settled for a simple excuse instead.

"A problem with the dog?" Pirate harrumphed after I'd hung up the phone. "You owe me one."

When Grandma finished closing the portal to hell, or wherever Xerxes had come from, she took a chair opposite me. She'd perched her reading glasses on top of her head like a tiara. Slicks of oil smeared her T-shirt and a bit of brown gunk had caught under one of her rings. She folded her hands on my sunflower-print table-cloth. "Would you like to talk about what happened?"

"Sure," I said. She had to be kidding. "Where would you like to start? With the crazy green bars of light or with the fact that my bathroom is now glowing?"

And I didn't mean glowing from a great cleaning job. As I spoke, a purple haze spilled out from the bathroom and into the narrow hall off my kitchen.

"A mange spell. Wards off demons, gremlins, succubi. Good against black magic too." She flicked a small piece of I-didn't-want-to-know from under one of her fingernails. "The black lords don't usually recognize demon slayers so quickly after the change. And they're never this bold." She arched her brows as if I should nod and understand. "But there have been unusual happenings lately."

Lovely. I wanted her to leave. I wanted to forget this whole thing ever happened.

She tsked. "If only your mother were here."

My voice caught in my throat. "Where is my mother?" The day I was born, she'd given me up for adoption. I'd never known anything about her.

She threw me a guilty look. "I suppose I'll have to tell you. But for now, we need to hit the road."

"Where?" I asked, afraid to know.

"Well, we got kicked out of the coven in Westchester. I'll let my buddy Ant Eater tell you about that one." She chuckled to herself. "We aren't always the best houseguests. But hell, life is short. Nothing like the freedom of the open road."

"Open road?" I said, starting to panic a little. Okay, a lot. "I'm not like you. I get carsick, train sick, plane sick. I get dizzy watching the kids swing at Happy Hands."

"Um-hum," Pirate agreed. "Don't forget the time you yarfed up your hot chocolate all over Brian Thompson's toboggan." Pirate studied the look on my face. "Oh, but I didn't like him anyway. He had cats. Three cats. The brown one, I called him Thor, he had pointy teeth. And another brown one, I called him Tuna Breath—"

All the homeless dogs in the shelter that day and I had to pick the motormouth. "Pirate, level with me. What made you start talking?"

"Me? I always talk. Why'd you start listening?"

"Enough!" Grandma clamped my hands in hers. "We're hopping on my Harley whether you like it or not. The coven's holed up outside of Memphis right now. It'll be a good spot to teach you. You need to learn your hexes from your horny toads. Magically speaking."

"I need to get back to normal. I have a job, friends, a cute guy I just cancelled on." I slipped out of her grasp and saw my French manicure had melted away.

"Holy ship anchor!" I gaped at her.

"Like I said, there's a lot you need to know. And Xerxes will be back—with a bunch of bloodthirsty creatures. Time's up, Lizzie. Unless you can come up with a better idea, we need to hop the hog and get out of here."

"I don't think so," I said, eyeing the lumpy remains of my polish. She reached out her hands, but I wasn't about to let her near me again. "Back off. You can't hit town on your Harley, lock me up, introduce me to Xerxes and turn me into Lizzie the road warrior. I deserve some answers."

She sighed. "You're right, Lizzie. The truth is, what you did in there was . . . unique. I know I've never seen it before. Your nail polish was consumed by the demon's vox because, frankly, most things . . . heck, most people would have been. You, Lizzie, are special. Whether you want to be or not."

*Not.* "So most people get hit by the green thingies and they die. Instead, I pluck them out of the air and they ruin my manicure?"

"The nail polish was not of you." She touched her fist to her heart. "This. The power you have inside. This is of you."

"Okay . . ." I said, bobbing my head one too many times. "But you have"—I glanced at my glowing bathroom—"magic. You can handle a demon, right?"

Hands clasped, she leaned across the table. "I run from demons. You can kill them."

I didn't even like to kill June bugs.

"I know it's a lot to swallow. That's why you have to plant your pretty butt on my bike. Other demons will come."

"Why can't we leave each other alone? Live and let live?"

She shook her head. "Doesn't work that way, Lizzie. You come from a line of powerful women. Every third generation, we are honored to produce a demon slayer. You."

But I didn't want to be a demon slayer.

I also didn't want any more demons showing up in my bathroom. Or at sushi night with the girls. Or at the

Happy Hands Preschool where I worked. That last thought chilled me to the core. I couldn't imagine what would happen to my class of innocent three-year-olds. I had to stay far away from them until I could get rid of Xerxes, and anything like him, for good.

"If I come with you," I began, "will you teach me how to get rid of any demon complications, once and for all?" I needed to learn how to have my normal life. Let Grandma have her voodoo-hoodoo. As long as I could get this thing under control enough to teach preschool.

Her bracelets dangled as she leaned toward me, resting her chin on her hands. "I will show you everything you need to know. But I'm not telling you anything else until we get to Memphis. It's not safe."

Not safe? Try mixing me with a Harley.

I pounded my fingers on the table until they tingled. "If I do go with you to Memphis, will you tell me what to do about Pirate?"

I followed her gaze to the Jack Russell sniffing her Smucker's jars. "I'm here to teach you magic, Lizzie. The dog is your problem."

## Chapter Three

"Don't worry, Pirate," I said, shoving a mountain of underwear into a pink plastic overnight case I'd yanked from the closet in my small, loft bedroom. "I have a plan to get us a half-dozen counties away from that Harley."

A quick online check showed American Airlines had a flight leaving in two hours. We needed to be on it. I hated to fly, but when the alternative was driving four hundred miles with Grandma, a talking terrier, and twenty-seven Smucker's jars filled with heaven knows what, I was ready to make an exception. Besides, we didn't need to be out on the open road with demons on our tail.

"What?" Pirate yelped, dropping the Mickey Mouse panties he'd just stolen. "Are you leaving without me? You can't leave without me. I'm your watchdog. I watch out for you. You need me."

"I'm not leaving you," I assured him. "And honestly," I said, scooping up the panties and tossing them in the direction of the bathroom hamper, "you need to tone down the watchdog shtick." His face fell and I found myself working hard to recover. "Not that you aren't great at it. You are. I feel very safe." At least I used to feel safe. "But you have to learn to pick your battles."

Pirate blinked twice, seemed shocked at the thought. "What? You don't think I can handle it?"

With shaking hands, I yanked three pairs of khaki pants from their hangers. "Feel free to protect me from butterflies, the vacuum cleaner, my hair dryer," I said. "But please. No demons."

Pirate considered my advice while I folded two pairs of pants and left the third pair out to wear. "I could take a demon." He twitched his ears, daring me to tell him he couldn't. "You should have seen me today. I wasted the Phantom Menace. Been after him my whole life. And today—whammo! So don't tell me I can't bust a demon. Oh yeah. I can bust a demon."

I tossed an armful of button-down shirts into the case. "The Phantom Menace is from a *Star Wars* movie. Not a real person." Pirate liked to yip at every shadow in the yard.

"He's real," Pirate insisted. "I left teeth marks." He growled and showed me his canines. "Good? Yeah? What about this?" He sprung into a stalking stance and bared his teeth, his whole body shaking. "I'm an animal!"

"And you caught your own shadow."

"No—a phantom. He flies! Likes to watch over the yard. Bet he's after my squeaky frog. Today, he tried to give me something gold and shiny. Completely inedible. So I chomped him."

Technically, Pirate's rubber toys were supposed to be inedible too. I sighed and wrestled a simple white top off its hanger. Normally, I would have ignored a rant like that. Wait, who was I kidding? Normally, I wouldn't be having this—or any—conversation with my dog.

Holy hand grenades, I sure hoped Pirate was imagining things. I didn't want to think of shadowy figures hanging out in my yard. *Watching me.* To be safe, I said, "Promise me, if you ever see Phantom Menace again, you will not go anywhere near him. Understood?"

Pirate attacked his tail.

I eyed the little beast I'd shared my bed with for the last three years. "Pirate." I stroked him behind the left ear and he turned to mush in my hands. "Are you listening to me? Remember what we learned in obedience class? A good watchdog also listens."

"Ahhh . . . anything you say, Lizzie. Just keep hittin' the sweet spot." The instant I stopped scratching, he jumped to his feet and began nosing around the semifolded clothes in my suitcase. "You know, we would have passed that class if that sexy Pomeranian hadn't winked at me. Lost it on that one. Dames."

"Pirate," I warned. "Don't attack any yard spooks. You come get me." He treated me to the innocent doggy look, but we both knew he wasn't fooling anybody. I pulled on a pair of khakis and, yanking down my top, plowed through my closet for the comfortable, lace-up shoes I wore at the preschool.

I plunked down on the bed to tie my shoes and while I was there, gave Pirate a quick rub on the head. "Let's motor. I'm going to try to convince Grandma to head to the airport, but we have to hurry if we're going to make the next flight to Memphis." My stomach roiled at the thought. Flying gave me hives, but all I had to do was look out into the driveway and there sat my courage, with chrome wheels and silver flames painted down the sides.

"Give me a frosty Pet-sicle and I'll tell you where I hid your wedge sandals." He burrowed between two pillows.

I rolled my eyes and attempted to clip the clasps on

my bulging suitcase. "You'd just better hope we can convince Grandma to get off that hog of hers."

"A hog?" Pirate shrieked and pillows flew. He raced to the window behind my bed and shoved his nose against the glass. "Oh, biscuits! I could zoom down the highway, wind in my face. Checkin' out the babes."

So he hadn't processed anything I'd said about bike versus plane. Peachy. I had a talking dog, not a listening dog.

Good to know, I decided, as I tried to force the suitcase shut with the weight of my butt. My socks and underwear bulged out from between the clasps. "I expect you to back me up on this one." I'd tell him later that he'd have to fly cargo.

If we took the hog, Pirate would have to be fastened to me. Grandma had this contraption that was basically a glorified strap-on baby carrier. Pirate would hate it. It wouldn't be fun for me, either. Pirate hadn't had a bath in a week or two, and besides, he tended to have digestive issues.

We had to fly. *Please.* I shoved my clothes farther into the case and tried again.

My Saturn would have been my second choice, but Grandma already told me the demons probably had spotters looking for it. Besides, she was married to that hog. But a plane would be faster. She couldn't argue with that.

"You ready yet?" Grandma charged up the stairs holding a sandwich and one of the apple juice bottles I kept on hand for school lunches only. "Lizzie! Stop farting around."

"You have to be kidding me." The woman expected me to wrap up my life in the time it took her to make a cheese sandwich. All I wanted was a simple, stable life. I liked to have things I could count on—my friends, my job, and even Cliff and Hillary. Heaven knew they'd never change. My spontaneity came from Pirate, and when that miniature problem with paws ran amok, I could just pick him up. Crisis averted. There was a reason I'd avoided people like Grandma.

She shook her head, her long, gray hair tangling over her shoulders. "Time's, up, Lizzie. We've got trouble."

Because we hadn't had enough of it lately.

My stomach dropped. "Don't tell me you blew up my bathroom."

"Worse. Remember my purple emergency spell? It turned blue. Demons sucked the red right out of it. They're coming. Fast."

Yikes! I attacked the case with renewed vigor.

"Stop!" Grandma commanded. "What do you think this is, Spring Break at Daytona Beach? Ain't no suitcases on a Harley. One backpack." She held up a single finger, with a silver snake ring wound around it. "One."

"Let's just fly," I pleaded, hearing the desperation in my voice. "It'll save time!"

She threw her hands out, sloshing apple juice onto the hardwood floor. "I can't protect a whole plane! You want demons camping out on the fuselage?"

Oh my word. We were a human tragedy waiting to happen. I shoved the image out of my mind. "Fine," I said, yanking my school pack from its peg. "This will barely fit a tube top and a pair of socks."

Grandma raised a brow. "Well, won't the truckers enjoy that?"

I packed a change of clothes and a hairbrush, then dashed to the kitchen for Pirate's Healthy Lite dog chow and a spare water dish. The bathroom was indeed glowing an incandescent blue. The haze spilled out into the hallway, carried on an invisible cloud. It had a palpable presence. A demonic one. It crept up to the ceiling and inched down across the floor like a slow, steady breath of evil. Holy h-e-double hockey sticks.

Grandma had already dragged Pirate out front to fit him for his riding gear. I stuffed his food and bowl into my purse, checked the back-door lock and dashed through the living room toward the front door.

"Akkk!" Pirate dashed circles in the yard while Grandma chased him with a black leather contraption that looked like she ordered it straight out of the Ozzy Osborne Pet Gear Catalog.

"Damn it all." She tossed the contraption to me. "You try it. Lucky Bob built it for his late ferret, Buddy."

Pirate went still with shock. "Why late? What happened to Buddy?"

We didn't have time for this. "Pirate! Sit!" I said, summoning up the voice I learned in doggy obedience classes.

"Like hell!" He took off in a dead run.

"Pirate! Ditch the drama before Grandma zaps you in the butt with one of her demon spells."

He dug in his front legs to stop, but his back legs kept going and he flipped over. Pirate popped back up, shaking with doggie indignation. "She's going to tie me up! Look at that thing. It's a doggy straightjacket!"

Grandma loomed over him, fear burning in her eyes. "If we don't get on this bike in two minutes, you'll be wearing your intestines as a necklace."

Pirate released his bladder. I didn't blame him.

Grandma wound her thick hair into a bun and stuffed it under her helmet while I fought to untangle the black leather straps of the carrier. The Harley roared to life. She pumped the engine until the kickback rattled my teeth. "Lord help us," I mumbled as I finagled Pirate's hard little noggin through the ferret carrier. "It's okay, sweetie," I yelled, trying not to breathe in any of the choking exhaust billowing from Grandma's chrome pipes. I hoped Pirate could hear me over the deafening roar. He lashed his head back and forth. I tried to summon the tone I used with my preschoolers. "It's snug, but that just means I can hold you close and keep you safe."

"Bullshit." Pirate yelped, half in, half hanging out of the carrier.

I heaved us both up on the pink Harley with silver flames shooting up the sides. "Hold still," I ordered as I lowered both terrier and carrier over my head. Not an easy task, considering he'd decided to escape. His stubby legs grasped for traction as they dangled out of the baby carrier.

Grandma secured her bag of jars. "Strap him in!" She growled impatiently. "We need to go. Now."

"This is humiliating!" Pirate lamented to Grandma's back as I wedged him in tight and fastened the straps around his tummy, his stubby tail poking me in the stomach.

Grandma reached around to tighten the straps. "Cut the chatter."

I adjusted my helmet and tried not to think about the deep scratch marks that marred its dull, black surface. How many wrecks had this lady been in? Maybe we could stop somewhere for an extra-heavy-duty helmet with a face mask. While we were at it, maybe we could rent a Volvo.

Grandma wore a sleek silver helmet. Hers didn't have a safety mask either. What? Would it have broken some kind of biker code to fly down the highway at head-smashing speeds while wearing full protective gear? She eyed me as she pulled on a pair of riding goggles.

"Hold on to my waist," she hollered over the engine. "Lean when I lean and for God's sake turn your helmet around. You've got it on backward."

My fingers dug into the strap under my chin. I didn't

know how I was going to survive this odyssey when I couldn't even buckle a helmet right. And talk about crummy instructions. *Lean when I lean.* How far? How much? I chewed at my lip. *If we crash, please don't let it be my fault.* I felt so helpless.

Grandma eyed the blue smoke curling out from under my locked front door.

"What if Xerxes tears apart my neighborhood?" I asked, wrapping my hands around Grandma's thick waist. I never really met my neighbors. They never seemed to venture outside of their houses, but still . . . Pirate squirmed, his legs flopping in the air. All three of us lined up on Grandma's hog like a warped version of the Three Musketeers.

"No worries, babe." She reached in her pack for a mossy-looking Smucker's jar wrapped in masking tape. She yanked off a section of tape, shoved it against my face and yanked it back.

It stung like blazes. "God Bless America!" My hand flew to my right eyebrow.

Grandma spit on the tape that held way too many of my eyebrow hairs. She stuck it back against the nasty-looking jar. *"Confuto aggredior!"* She fired the jar at my house and it shattered on the front porch. Glass flew everywhere and greasy slime oozed down my top step and onto my red brick walk.

"They'll be following us now." Grandma gunned the engine, and my back slammed against the safety bar as we peeled out into the gathering dusk.

"Yell if you see Xerxes or any of his hell-raisers," Grandma said at the first stoplight we reached. "We'll make Evel Knievel look like a pussy."

"Urgle." I nodded, stomach churning. Two blocks and my butt throbbed from the vibrations. Maybe in another two it would go blessedly numb.

"What? Why'd we stop? Did someone say stop? Pup-per-roni, we were flying! Wind in my face, wind in my ears, wind in my toenails. Wind whipping all up in my . . ."

"Pirate! If you keep whamming me in the gut with that tail, I'm going to heave." Yeah, blame it on the dog. Nausea climbed up the back of my throat. I fought to ignore the smushed stinkbugs on the windshield. And the gas fumes from the cars surrounding us. And the pulsations that rattled every raw nerve in my body when I just wanted to lie down. Why did I ever think this would work? I could barely ride bumper cars without yarfing all over the place.

Pirate's tail pounded my fragile stomach. "Your problem is you got no sense of adventure. Green light!"

Grandma stomped on the gas and we lurched from zero to five hundred in two seconds flat. The wind stung my face and arms. Pirate flung his legs out in the air. "Eyyah! I'm king of the world!"

"Car!" I screamed as we slammed toward a Toyota Prius.

"Yyy-yes!" Grandma swerved at the last second, zig-zagged between lanes and gunned it out onto the open road.

*I am going to die.* What was worse? The road ahead of us or the demons we left behind? At that moment, I wasn't sure.

Thanks to small miracles, we made it out of Atlanta alive. We zipped over the Georgia/Alabama border near Bowdon and caught the back roads from there. Alabama had plenty of quiet side roads where we could still rumble at butt-breaking speeds without risking detection on the open highways.

In the darkness, the trees on the side of the road formed an army of shadows, breached occasionally by the light from a house. I breathed in the warm night air. It was a moment to savor because—sure as Grandma's Smucker's jars—our luck had to run out sometime.

It almost didn't seem real—the demon in my bathroom, my biker-witch grandma, any of it. And now we were out on the road with no more than a change of clothes and a doggy bowl. This was so not me. I didn't like to leave for the grocery store without a typed shopping list and my color-coded coupon file.

*Worry about things you can control, like . . .*

Darned if I could think of anything.

Okay, fine. I could still have a moment of peace. I tuned out the droning roar of the bike and focused on the good in my life. I nuzzled my little dog, his prickly hair warm against my cheek. It reminded me of when he was a puppy and used to like to curl up on my chest and listen to my heartbeat. I felt myself relax. Pirate too. He fell asleep somewhere after Talladega, his little legs dangling out of the ferret carrier.

Sure enough, trouble found us at a QuikTrip just outside of Jasper. We'd stopped for gas, a clean bathroom and a Rooster Booster Freezoni for Grandma. While she parked herself in front of the self-serve slushie counter, debating the merits of adding a blue raspberry layer to her energy drink, I found a field for Pirate next to the station.

He sprinted across the small meadow, leaping here and there, just for the fun of it. "I was made for the open road. How come we never blew out on a road trip before?"

Because I'd never thought of it. The full moon illuminated my romping dog, as well as the road dust clinging to every inch of my body. Ugh. I smelled like a diesel gas pump. I brushed at the grime on my arms. "We were fine in Atlanta."

"Fine does not mean alive!" he said, hurdling over a

patch of weeds. "Tingly!" He hopped back the other way. "Oh yeah. That's what I'm talking about," he said, continuing his assault on the shrubbery. "Belly scratch!"

"Pirate. Hurry up. Do your thing. Grandma will want to leave sooner rather than later," I said, as I caught her out of the corner of my eye. She'd chucked her Freezoni and jogged toward us with a hotdog wrapper flapping out of her pocket and the look on her face I was coming to dread. Shadows gathered in the skies above the QuikTrip.

Pirate sniffed furiously at a clump of dried grass. "Hold the phone, Lizzie. You guys eat hotdogs while I get dull, dry dog food. And now you rush me in the john."

"Four pixies," Grandma called out before stooping over to catch her breath, "back by the beef jerky. Two more by the weenie machine. Let's move, people!"

Sweet heaven. Pixies? She might as well have told me she'd spotted the Easter Bunny.

Pirate's head popped up from a clump of wild daisies. "Don't pressure me. I can't stand pressure." He circled twice. "Oh look, now I'm all locked up."

Grandma and I made tracks for the bike at pump 6 while I tried to wrap my head around our newest supernatural terror. Someday, when I wasn't about to have a heart attack, she was going to have to sit down and explain all this to me. "Tell me about pixies, Grandma. They're bad?"

"They report to the imps. I thought we'd keep you under the radar, least 'til we sharpened you up."

"Until Xerxes the demon," I said under my breath. "Wait." I gripped her arm. "You smell that?" A faint trace of sulfur floated past. And what else? Burned hair. It smelled like evil. Oh no. I sure hoped I was wrong. "Pirate, now!"

For once, he listened. I stuffed Pirate into the ferret

carrier while Grandma reached for a Smucker's jar. She unscrewed it, revealing a leafy-looking sludge. And was that a deer tail? My hand shot to my eyebrows.

She yanked the top off her silver snake ring. "Here." She forced the severed cobra head into my free hand. Its emerald eyes twinkled under the fluorescent lights of the gas station. Protruding from the ring, which was now basically a snake neck, was a very small, very sharp-looking needle. Grandma plunged it into her chest.

"Ak! What are you doing?"

She winced as it pierced the flesh above her heart. I seized her arm as she flicked one, two, three drops of blood into the jar.

"What kind of lame-ass question is that? Gimme." She took the snake head and snapped it back onto her ring. Dark wet blood stained her *Kiss My Asphalt* T-shirt. "Blood. It's a small death. Makes the spell stronger." She braced the Smucker's jar between her thighs and threw on her helmet. "We're gonna need an ass load of magic to get out of this."

"Ohhh squirrels!" Pirate struggled against the ferret carrier, his legs automatically giving chase.

Not squirrels. My voice caught in my throat. Three— no—at least five shadowy creatures slinked toward us. I scrambled for my helmet, if only to whack them with it. They curled around the gas pumps and past the only other car at the pumps, a white Chevy Nova. "Help!" I called, hoping like heck the Nova belonged to an exotic-animal wrangler.

"Pipe down. Nobody can see the imps but us."

*Imps?*

Lovely. I'd have to thank Grandma for opening my eyes to the wonderful world of magical creatures. Sweat pooled under my arms and chest. The imps' congested breathing grew more and more excited as they drew

closer. Purple eyes glowed from under dark, furry
brows. They had weasel-like faces and the bodies of
thick, hastily constructed people. Dark hair clung to
their bent frames.

*"Confudi!"* Grandma tossed the Smucker's jar and
it shattered between two of them. The air radiated for a
split second and the creatures screeched.

The imps retreated as fast as they'd appeared. Yow.
I let myself breathe again. "You've gotta teach me
about those jars," I said. Maybe I'd try something with
a SoBe bottle or two.

Grandma's eyes widened. "Move!" She shoved both
of us against a gas pump and I felt a wave of energy
crackle past.

I spun to face her, Pirate dangling between us. "What
was that?"

Huge wings beat a blue streak above us. I looked skyward and dread swelled inside me. A monstrous eagle
with the body of a lion circled above the convenience
store. Big as a truck, it screeched and displayed feathers
of red, purple, green, blue. *Impossible.* Oh begonias.
After today, who was I to even think that?

"The Phantom Menace!" Pirate's legs clambered for
him. "You coming back for more? Shake your tail
feather this way. I'll show you more."

The creature blocked out the moon as it plunged
right for us. I scrambled for the hard leather seat of the
Harley. The bottoms of my shoes slipped off the riding
boards as Grandma peeled out of the parking lot. We
were on Route K in a heartbeat, flying so fast it made
my head spin.

"I float like a butterfly, sting like a bee!" Pirate hollered as we sped off into the night. I clung to Grandma
and closed my eyes to keep from being sick. I didn't
know how we were going to outrun that *thing.* My hair
swirled under the edge of my helmet, and I could feel

my face stretching with the wind. Every hill we crested, I swore the bike went airborne for a second or two. Heaven help us.

"Holy shit!" Grandma hollered as we careened around a hairpin turn at a speed I didn't even want to know. The bike skidded, skipped over a dip in the road and slapped pavement again. My fingers dug into her sides when I saw the road ahead. Or make that, the lack of road.

Our stretch of asphalt ended in a small lake. It consumed both lanes of the road and the forest beyond.

Grandma hunkered low and steady over the handlebars. "Hold on!"

"What? Stop!" My gut clenched as we thundered straight for it. A flash flood like that could sweep a car away, much less three idiots on a bike.

There were no detour signs, no road cones. No reason for the water. My toes curled and I clung to Grandma tighter. We were traveling uphill. Water does not run uphill. But this water did.

Pirate fought the ferret carrier. "Oh no. I don't do water. Water is not good." He lurched, just like he did every time I tried to dunk him in a—

"Bath!" he yelled and pitched his body to the left.

"Shiii . . . p!" I screamed, as I lost my balance and toppled into the air.

"Holy hell!" Grandma grabbed us by the doggy sling. The bike plunged into the lake and skidded sideways through the surging water. Depression and rage swelled from its depths. "It's an ambush!"

We lost the bike in a wave of water. I clutched Pirate as we slammed nose over toes into the abyss. Eyes closed tight against the muck, I fought past fleshy ropes of seaweed. It clung to my arms, heavy and stringy.

*Please let it be seaweed, even if we are a thousand miles from the ocean.*

Pirate's flailing leg caught my arm, and I winced as his doggy claws sliced deep.

We broke through to the surface and, blessedly, I was able to touch bottom. Afraid to draw too much attention, I crouched in the water, just high enough for Pirate to keep his head above the churning darkness. The despair of this place surrounded us. Waves of hopelessness and fear tangled my insides. Grandma was nowhere in sight.

Pirate flailed in his carrier. "Oh, biscuits! Calm down. You calm? I'm calm. Oh, biscuits."

"Shhh. You're fine."

"Shit." Pirate shook off as best as he could, peppering me with putrid water. "That's what I said. I said I was fine."

"Look for Grandma."

Pirate tried to wriggle a leg out of his carrier. "Oh yeah, the lady who said she wanted to make my intestines into a necklace? Yeah, let's get right on that."

*Hang tight. Focus.* I scanned the area for demons, witches and anything that wasn't one hundred percent normal. Grandma had called this an ambush. Someone or—I gulped—some*thing* had created this lake in the middle of the road. And they had us stopped cold.

A shimmer spread throughout the water. Goose bumps snaked up my arms. Holy moley. I couldn't believe what I was seeing. "Is it me or is the water glowing green?"

"Oh, man," Pirate said, ready to climb up to my shoulders. "You know I'm color-blind."

An emerald glow radiated from the depths of the water and broke to the surface in a roil of bubbling water. Churning foam sucked at my shoulders. "That's it." Ambush or not, I broke into a run, the waist-high water sluicing off us. We had to get out of here.

In a flash, Grandma appeared at the far side of the lake, at the edge of the woods. Shadows dove at her from every direction. "Lizzie, run!" she screamed before she disappeared.

"Grandma!" I made a mad dash for her. I had no idea what to do, but I had to do something. The air itself vibrated and smoked. It tasted like singed hair.

"Stop! Halt! Cut it!" Pirate yelled. "Wall!"

"Wall?" Then I saw it. It shimmered like a giant soap bubble. There was no time to stop. I felt my toes leave the ground as it sucked us through.

Thick, wet undergrowth tangled around my ankles. I steadied myself, ready for the worst. I clutched Pirate's knobby little body and blinked once, twice. We'd raced headlong into a clearing littered with scores of rodentlike faces staring up at us. Imps. Their glowing purple eyes bounced through the darkness as they scuttled toward us, baring row after row of glistening teeth.

Grandma braced herself at the far edge of the clearing. Heavy iron cuffs bound her wrists and ankles. She struggled to hold them away from her body, despite the weights pulling at each cuff. An eerie tickle crept up my skin when I realized why. Curved snakelike fangs protruded from the cuffs and connecting chains, ready to pierce her skin if she gave in to the weight of her restraints. I wondered what horrors waited inside the fangs.

"Oh, this is just great," she said, breathing heavily with exertion. "I told you to run, not get yourself trapped. Honestly, Lizzie."

She could at least pretend to be grateful. "Ditch the attitude. I'm saving you," I said. *Somehow.* The imps cackled like psychotic weasels as they skulked closer. I rubbed Pirate, who hadn't stopped shaking since we broke through the wall.

"Yeah?" Grandma fought to keep the razor-sharp fangs from plunging into her skin, "Well, if you're going to save me," she stopped to catch her breath, "untie the damned dog and let's get to work."

"Right. That's what I'm talking about. On-the-job training," I said, desperate to mask my fear. I released Pirate. His wiry body slid down mine and to the ground. I had to focus, find my power. If I didn't get this right, I hated to think what could happen to us.

*Focus. Breathe. Find a way.*

They might have numbers on their side, but I'd sent Xerxes to hell and I could send the imps too.

Pirate circled my legs as the imps stalked us from every direction. "Oh, you'd better get your ass back," he said, "you filthy looking, I don't know what you are. You do smell kind of nice. But don't you be testing me. I'll kick you into next Thursday. Don't you think I won't."

I ignored Pirate and reached deep down inside. I was the most uptight, disciplined person I knew, and I had to use that. Whatever raw magic I possessed, whatever had allowed me to drive Xerxes from my bathroom, I'd find it and own it. Now.

"Water nymph at two o'clock," Grandma warned. A dripping, green fairy rose from the marsh at the edge of the lake and skimmed toward us. She might have been beautiful if she hadn't looked so desolate. She was tall, with the body of an underwear model. But her face sagged and her eyes held horrors I didn't even want to imagine. She wore a shift that—ick—looked like it had been crafted from the skin of imps. And, I gulped, she held cuffs, the same kind that bound Grandma.

I dug my fingernails into my palms. *Show no emotion.* Instead, I focused every bit of will I possessed, felt the magic churning inside me. The center of my body hummed with energy. I could feel it right down to my fingertips. I let instinct take over and screamed the first thing that came to me. "Begone!" My own voice tore at the back of my throat as I flung my power into the clearing.

The imps cowered, clung to the ground.

"Begone!" I zapped them again with everything I had. This time, they stood still, studying me. The water nymph had sunk down into a puddle after my first try. Now she drew toward me, curiosity playing on her features. Oh no.

*"Solvo dimittium,"* Grandma hollered.

Hope flared and died quickly. They didn't react to that either.

"Lizzie." Grandma struggled against her chains. "You say it! *Solvo dimittium.*"

"Right." I nodded, resisting the urge to run, which I knew would be useless and stupid and wrong. *Solvo dimittium. Solvo dimittium.* Driving my power to me once again, I opened my mind, took a deep breath and bellowed, *"Solvo dimittium!"*

A slight wind rippled the water nymph's hair. A curl of blue flame sizzled a circle around her water-logged hair before fizzling.

"Shit," Grandma said.

No kidding. "That's it?" My voice hitched as the creatures closed in around me. "What else should I do?"

Pirate brushed past my leg. "You stand there and look pretty. Let me give it a whirl." Pirate stalked toward a scowling imp.

"Pirate, no!" Bravery was one thing. This was something else.

Pirate thrust his tail out. "Suave dimmi-who's-it's, you bug-eyed freak of nature."

The imp shrieked and reared back to attack. Pirate yelped as it leapt onto his back, claws digging into his fur.

"Pirate!" That thing could kill him with one bite. It clambered up his back, heading straight for his neck.

Rage boiled inside me, and I drop-kicked the imp like I was punting a football. Three more took its place. I booted another. Blood flowed down Pirate's back. At least one imp landed hard on my shoulders, clawing rivers of fire down my back. I spun, desperately trying to throw it off, when I spotted another creature circling.

A winged beast the size of a Clydesdale descended upon us. The same breed of creature we saw at the gas station—with the head of an eagle and the body of a lion. A griffin? Tail swishing in the gathering wind, it reached for us, claws outstretched, like a hungry bird of prey.

Pirate broke free and bit the nearest imp. I threw an imp from my shoulders straight at the pair of talons leveled at my head. Grandma screamed something or other, but it was impossible to hear her over the high-pitched yelps of the imps and the screeching calls of the griffin. The flying creature dove straight for the water nymph.

But the nymph was fast. She disappeared into the nearest puddle as the bands on Grandma's wrists and ankles snapped and crumbled away. The imps scurried back to the shadows, save the two dead ones at my feet. "Take that!" Pirate chased the remaining imps to the edge of the clearing.

I stood catching my breath, my back burning. The coppery scent of blood hung heavy over the clearing. I wanted to collapse with relief. Or was that fear? Just because this thing didn't kill me before didn't mean it wouldn't hurt me now. He landed a few feet from me, settling his wings around his body like a bird. He wore a single emerald ring on one of his talons, and his feathers shone in a burst of colors.

Grandma bustled over to me. "You alright?" I nodded. "Well, then." She flexed her hands, working to get the circulation going again. "Hiya, Impetrix Heli—" She paused. "Um, Impetrix. Thanks for saving our asses. Now, with your permission," she saluted him, "we're outta here." She grabbed my arm. "Come on."

"He's just going to let us go?" I asked, hustling behind her.

"If we go quick enough."

I fought the urge to look behind us. Good enough for me.

We exited the clearing, and I couldn't hold back a gasp. The immense lake had disappeared as if it never existed. Grandma's bike lay twisted down a steep embankment off the main road. We scrambled through some mud and pulled the hog upright. Grandma wrenched the handlebars and yanked the seat.

"Hurry," she said quietly.

"So he's . . . ?"

"Trouble." We managed to heave it halfway up the embankment, but the bike was too mangled and heavy.

"Is he worse than the imps?"

Grandma groaned as she hauled the bike with everything she had. I joined her, pulling until I felt my arms stretching half out of their sockets. For every inch we dragged the flipping thing, we sank two in the mud. It was no use.

"God damn it!" Grandma shoved the bike and it fell back into the ditch, nearly taking me with it.

I slid an extra few feet and stared down at the wreck of a bike. It was toast, and we were trapped.

She brought a bloodied hand up to her mouth. "Yeah. In a way, he is worse than the imps."

My nerves quivered. The air felt heavy, *smoky*. I felt it in the pit of my stomach. Maybe my magic was finally kicking in. It was about time. "What is it, Grandma?" I asked. "More demons? Or the griffin?

"It's not that," she said grimly. "It's him." She jabbed a mud-slicked finger at an imposing, olive-skinned man who stood like royalty at the edge of the ravine.

I gripped her hand and felt my pulse leap. "Is he a monster?"

"That depends," she said, giving him the evil eye.

My blood warmed just looking at him. He was striking. If you liked the *GQ* type. He wore a dark, tailored suit cut to fit his broad shoulders. His angled features gave away nothing as he watched us. I felt his eyes, hidden in shadows, sweep over every inch of my body. I blinked twice, studied him. Something inside me felt like I knew him.

That was impossible, I thought with a twinge of desire. If I'd ever met this man before, I would have remembered. He seemed so out of place on this swampy, dirty backwater road. Everything about him was polished, except for the way his thick, ebony hair curled around his collar.

His eyes flashed orange, then yellow. Holy Moses. I stumbled backward in the darkness as his eyes began to glow with a positively arresting, utterly horrifying grassy hue. My body tensed, ready for a fight if it came to that.

"Well, look who likes you, Lizzie." Grandma rubbed at her wrists where the chains had been.

What? The automatic excitement that flared at the idea of a good-looking man finding me attractive fizzled under the dread that it was this emerald-eyed . . . person. Why couldn't any normal guys like me? Oh wait. One of them might have. Tonight, at this very moment, I was supposed to be enjoying a Rum Swizzle with a boatload of friends as well as Hot Ryan Harmon from the gym. A birthday extravaganza with the stunning Mr. Harmon as the ultimate party prize. Instead,

I stood here, at the bottom of a ravine, staring up at this magical enigma.

"Good to see you're keeping your distance," Grandma said, drawing me toward her like an old girlfriend. "That man is nothing but trouble."

No kidding. Yet another supernatural complication I could do without. "So who is he?" I asked.

"Well, sugar beet," Grandma said, giving my hand a firm squeeze. "He's your protector."

# Chapter Four

I gaped at him. *My protector?*

Grandma straightened her shoulders. "I took you without his permission."

I stared at her. "My protector?"

"You're my granddaughter, for goodness sake!" She sniffed as he tossed a climbing rope down the embankment. "Damn that man. He's stickier than a pinecone enema."

He'd stripped off his coat and rolled up his shirtsleeves away from his dark, muscled forearms. "Now we're going to have to let him help us," she said, as if we'd lost a major battle. "Whatever you do, don't tell him about Xerxes. Don't go anywhere alone with him, and don't reveal too much."

Not a problem since I didn't have a clue what was going on.

She threw up her hand. "Stop!" she said, as he prepared to descend to help us. "We're fine on our own."

"Speak for yourself," I muttered. This ditch was taller than I was. Besides, we had to get out of here before more griffins, imps or anybody else showed up. We didn't have time to see if my seventy-something grandma knew how to climb a rope.

Grandma grabbed the line and clambered up. Her boots scratched at the embankment, sending down a shower of mud clumps, weeds and god knew what else. "Show-off," I muttered. But my heart wasn't in it. I was too focused on the sharp-featured man who didn't look at all pleased. His eyes had stopped glowing, so that was something. Still, I couldn't help wondering what kind of person we were dealing with.

My *protector*. I rolled the thought around in my mind. When I reached the top, he took my hand. I'd thought I was warm. He was positively toasty. I detected a trace of sandalwood cologne. His other hand was steady and strong at my back as he led me away from the edge. His very presence cut ribbons of heat down my spine. I tried my best to ignore them. Facts were facts—something brought this man here, to us, at this particular moment. I wondered what he wanted.

"Lizzie Brown," he said, with a slight Greek accent that made my name sound almost lyrical. "Dimitri Kallinikos. It's an honor."

"How did you find us?" demanded my grandma, before I could say a word.

He arched a brow, deliberately unruffled by her tone. "I have my ways," he said, dropping my hand. "Although, as I said, I would have rather gone with you."

Grandma cocked her head up at him. "You weren't invited."

He leveled an icy gaze at her.

Oh, please. The wind whipped through the trees, chilling the night. "We were fine by ourselves," I said. "Really." Was I going to have to separate these two?

But he'd forgotten I was even there.

"I am her protector," he insisted.

"And I am her grandmother." She glowered at him.

Hello? I was standing right here. But if there was one thing I learned teaching preschool, it was how to pick my battles. Let them argue. I'd figure out how to get us out of here. I scanned the sky for griffins.

Pirate scrambled up the side of the dropoff, sending globs of dirt flying every which way. "What'd I miss?" Mud, and worse, slicked his fur.

"Pirate, get over here." I winced when I saw the bloody gashes on his back. He danced away from me when I tried to inspect them closer. "Oh yikes." We had to get out of there.

"Hey." I waved at the dueling duo. "Less talking. More moving." I wiped my hands on my khakis and nodded toward the Harley, crumpled at the bottom of the ditch. I prayed we could get the hog going. It might not be pretty, but we just needed it to work.

Dimitri extracted Grandma's hog with barely a wrinkle to show for it. In the meantime, Pirate had run off to hide. We didn't have time for this.

"Oh, Pirate," I yelled to the forest of trees edging the narrow, blacktop road. "I have a Peanut Pupper for you. Come on, little guy. Mmm . . . what about a Pupper-Mint stick?" I listened for any sign of Pirate among the chirping crickets and other sounds of the night. Traces of magic hung thick in the air. He didn't need to be out there. This place was bad news. It creeped me out that we hadn't seen another car or truck on this road, save the black Lexus SUV parked a little ways down the shoulder. Dimitri's. He'd turned on his emergency flashers and was busy getting something out of the back.

"Come on, Pirate. How 'bout I throw in a Schnicker-poodle?" Heck, I'd toss in a whole bag of them. I hoped he was okay. Right when I was about to head into the trees to search for him, Pirate called to me from underneath the SUV.

"Show me the Schnicker-poodle."

Oh geez.

"Aha. You don't have no Schnicker-poodle. I know the whole Schnicker-poodle act. You pulled that act at the park last week. Schnicker-poodles, my ass."

Dimitri closed the tailgate as I dashed up to him. "My dog is under there." I bent over to look underneath the car and there was Pirate, hiding out behind the muffler.

"He'll come out when he's ready." He eyed me intently. "Won't it be easier if you don't have to force him?"

Yes, but I wasn't going to admit that to Dimitri. "How's the Harley?" I asked, afraid to know.

"Too wrecked to ride." He gestured toward Grandma, twenty yards back on the shoulder. She was alterately coaxing and kicking the mangled mess.

What else could go wrong? I sighed and focused on the man in front of me. I wasn't one for hitching rides with strangers, but since Grandma knew him and he'd saved our butts, we'd have to trust him. For now.

"Think we can hitch a ride?" At least it would throw off our pursuers. And besides, I'd admit it, if only to myself—I had to get out of there. The place was too empty. I rubbed at the goose bumps on my arms.

Dimitri seemed to sense my anxiety. "We'll leave soon as your grandmother is ready." His gaze flickered over my bloody arms as he opened the back door for me. "Wait here." He returned with a white golf towel and a bottle of spring water. I braced my damp, dirty rear on the edge of the backseat and reached for the towel.

"Let me," he said, gently easing me onto the buttery leather seat.

"You'd better not, I mean—" I said, cursing myself for rambling, but I wasn't used to this kind of attention. It was too intimate and frankly, it made me nervous. "I'm stinky and wet and—"

"Brave. When you need to be." He touched the cool cloth to my elbow and I winced. Every stroke of his fingers spiraled right down to my toes. I really didn't need to be here, especially if I found myself wanting to reach out and touch him back.

*Keep it together, Lizzie. He's just trying to keep as much gunk as possible off his nice leather seats.* I flinched as the water stung a particularly deep scratch. His warm palm cradled my forearm. I pushed through the pain until the only thing I could feel was the soft cloth and him holding me steady.

I had to know. "What are you?"

His eyes met mine. A rich brown, sinful as buttermilk chocolate—not green or yellow . . . or orange as they had been before.

He shrugged. "I am your protector. That's the only thing that matters."

I felt my blood run cold. It was a straight question, and I deserved a straight answer.

My whole life, all I'd asked from people was for a little honesty. I snatched the cloth from him and cringed at the stinging pain as I dabbed at my own friggin' arm. No matter what it was, I could handle the truth better than avoidance and downright lies. One by one, they'd let me down—Cliff, Hillary, basically everyone who claimed to have my best interests at heart. And now this guy. I was sick and tired of it.

He sat back on his haunches. "Your grandmother has been less than honest with me."

Boo flipping hoo. "Doesn't feel very good, does it?" I pressed the cloth to a burning scrape.

Grandma was down the road, saying something to her bike. A final good-bye, perhaps. Even the best body-shop repairman would need a boatload of magic in order to put that hog to rights again.

He saw me watching her. "She hasn't told you the whole truth."

My stomach churned at the thought. Actually, in the short time I'd known her, Grandma had been remarkably straight with me. If I thought about it, that was probably one of the reasons I'd jumped on her hog in the first place. That and the demon in my bathroom.

Reluctance swept across Dimitri's features before he resumed his mask of calm. "There's something you need to know. I'd let your grandma tell you herself," he tossed the towel over his shoulder, "but she won't until it's too late."

He placed his hand on my leg, his dark eyes catching mine. "Lizzie, your grandmother is wanted for murder."

Nothing could have prepared me for that. Shock slammed into my throat. I couldn't see her as a killer. I just couldn't. Not without a good reason.

"Murder?" I repeated. *Impossible.* My mind reeled, trying to deny it, knowing very well it could be true. If so, it would explain why she was on the run. "Who did she kill?" A person? A creature? I searched his face. "Is that why those *things* tied her up back there?"

The tiny lines around his eyes crinkled as he frowned. "No," he said, reluctant to say more.

"What? You're going to tell me just enough to worry the snot out of me? Stop being such a jerk and level with me." I clenched my fists. How dare he try and drive a wedge between me and Grandma and then hold out on me. I needed answers. "Now."

He contemplated the darkness, seeming to decide if he wanted to come clean. The muscles in his jaw clenched before he finally answered. "Facing the evil that surrounds us takes strength, focus. Your grandmother has too many of her own problems. Her energy is scattered."

He searched my face. "You need to have a serious talk with your grandmother. Make her explain why she's on the run. While you're at it, ask her how she thinks she can possibly protect you."

Doubt gnawed at me. "We did fine," I said, not even believing it myself. "Those creatures didn't get what they wanted."

He shook his head. "No, they didn't." His eyes caught mine. "Lizzie, I'm afraid those creatures wanted you."

Lovely.

And why, by the way, was everybody after me when I couldn't even fight an imp without getting my butt kicked? My brain felt like it was about to explode. "So tell me. What makes you think *you* can possibly protect me? And why do you even want the gig? What's in it for you?"

He opened his arms, palms raised to the sky. Mr. Innocence. My foot.

"Oh no. That act doesn't fly. I know you have a stake, or you wouldn't be out in BFE in the middle of the night, dragging bikes out of ditches and—miracle of miracles—you also happen to be the only man who can drive us back to civilization." I stared at him and his mock expression of sincerity. If he told me the truth now, I might have at least a thimbleful of respect for the man. But he stood silent. "Fine. Don't tell me." At least I'd spotted his smoke and mirrors from the start, unlike the disaster with my adoptive parents. They let me live a lie for sixteen years.

He gripped my shoulders—warm, demanding. "I suppose this would be the wrong time to inform you that you need me. I know you don't trust me, and that's fine. I haven't earned that yet. But it is crucial that you look to me for guidance."

Fat chance.

Even though Dimitri was a godsend while we were stuck here with a broken-down hog, I didn't hold any illusions about him. He'd probably aired Grandma's dirty laundry in order to chip us apart. It burned me to realize it had worked. I did doubt her. Well, enough to learn more.

Grandma's boots crunched against the loose rocks on the side of the road. She whipped the towel from Dimitri's shoulder and used it to wipe the sweat from her neck. "I'd say she's clean enough, buster."

Dimitri snapped to attention and leveled a steely-eyed gaze at Grandma. He pulled another clean towel from his back pocket. "This one's for your dog. I think you'd better handle him."

Pirate jammed his nose into the highway rocks at Dimitri's feet. He circled, muttering to himself. "You say I never met you, but I know that smell. I could smell a German shepherd drug-sniffing dog to shame, that's how good I can smell."

"Pirate!" This time, he leaped into my arms, my cuts burning with the impact.

Pirate made a show of sniffing the air in front of Dimitri as I touched the damp cloth to Pirate's back. "E-yow!" He scrambled to escape.

It was everything I could do to hold him down. The imps had sliced his back pretty bad. It hurt to look at it. One particularly deep scrape might even require stitches. I cleaned his back as well as I could, pain for my little doggy lodging in my throat. It was my fault this happened. I should have left him in Atlanta.

I looked up and found Dimitri watching me. Something flickered in his eyes. Understanding?

Grandma huffed. "So are we going to stand on the side of the road all night, or are we going to get the hell out of here?" My thoughts exactly.

Dimitri flipped a Milk-Bone to Pirate as my watchdog and I scooted into the backseat.

"Do you have a dog?" I asked.

"Not exactly," Dimitri replied, sparing a glance at my grandma.

The door thwumped closed and silence enveloped us. "I swear this backseat is bigger than my first apartment," I said, eyeing the gray leather interior.

"I still say something smells funny." Pirate devoured the Milk-Bone and immediately began sniffing for crumbs.

Grandma rode with Dimitri in the front seat. If she was a cold-blooded murderer, I wondered what he'd done to get her goat. Something worse? While it was true I didn't know the woman very well, she didn't seem like the type to get offended easily. And while Dimitri might have told me one of Grandma's secrets, both of them still had plenty of their own. Those two were hiding something. Grandma wasn't surprised enough when he saved our butts. Or grateful enough. What did he have on us?

As soon as he started the car, they fell into a heated discussion. I tried to listen, but Dimitri turned up the radio. The only thing I could hear from the back of the car was Mick Jagger belting out "Sympathy for the Devil."

Oh no. Not on my watch. I unbuckled my seat belt and shoved between the two front seats. "What's going on?"

"Nothing!" Grandma huffed. "Except for the fact you need instruction."

"She needs to be safe," Dimitri said, his eyes on the road.

"I can keep her safe," Grandma declared.

"Oh yes," he said, contempt dripping from his voice. "With troll hitmen after her." He paused to let that sink in before he continued. "I wouldn't be surprised if they unleashed the demons."

Um, like Xerxes? Maybe Dimitri had a point.

Grandma shot me a *keep quiet* glare. Oh sure. Why shouldn't I stay out of a conversation—*about me?*

My involvement pretty much ended the conversation. We tried to use the remainder of the journey to rest up. According to Grandma, we'd need it. The hum of the motor was a treat for my aching muscles. Pirate and I were asleep before Haleyville. We curled together in an easy slumber until the SUV started bouncing through a country side road with more holes than Augusta National.

I opened my eyes, my contacts fused to my corneas, and batted a muddy paw out of my face.

"The coven in Nashville would be a wiser choice," said Dimitri.

Grandma huffed. "We haven't been welcome there since Crazy Frieda clogged their pipes with water sprites back in '92."

I stared out the window at a small, main street. This wasn't Memphis. It had to be one of the smaller towns on the outskirts. Worn, turn-of-the-century buildings housed a pawn shop, a barbeque joint and a few junk shops disguised as antique stores. We stopped in front of a bar called the Red Skull. Purple neon snaked up the side of the crimson front door. Beer signs suffocated the windows. The *thump-thump* of heavy-metal music was obvious even inside the car. Large black crows roosted in the twiggy trees that sprouted from breaks in the sidewalk. I could just imagine what we'd find inside.

"Here we are." Grandma patted the seat back as she twisted around to see me. "Home for the next month or so. We live on the two floors above the Red Skull."

"A heavy-metal bar?"

"Buck up, buttercup. The Red Skull is a happening place. Lenny named it after our red hat club." She frowned. "You know, for gals fifty and over."

"I thought you belonged to a biker gang."

"What's the difference?" She sidled out of the car.

"I smell cheeseburgers!" Pirate jumped over the seat and darted out behind her.

"Stay where we can see you!" I called to my dog, who chased the crows out of the trees. The birds beat their wings and squawked in protest.

When Grandma opened the door to the Red Skull, Iron Maiden's "Stranger in a Strange Land" blasted us. She ushered us inside the dark hole of a bar. About thirty bikers, mostly women, crowded the pinball machines and pool tables. Cigar smoke burned my lungs.

"Gertie!" Wild shouts erupted and we found ourselves at the center of a group of leather-clad bodies. I stared at Grandma, who now had a cigarette dangling from her lower lip. Grandma Gertie? It just didn't sound right.

I knew Dimitri stood behind me. I felt him. His presence put me on edge. I didn't know what he wanted from Grandma or from me. The folks in the bar seemed to give him a wide berth. More than one gray-haired rider nodded solemnly to the man behind me before diving at Grandma with a whoop and a holler.

"Pay attention, princess." Grandma slapped me on the back. "This is Ant Eater, Betty Two Sticks, Crazy Frieda . . ." I nodded at the parade of Red Skulls, knowing I'd never be able to keep the names and faces straight. Not tonight, at least. Although I did have to wonder how Crazy Frieda managed to glue rhinestones on the tips of her fake lashes.

Dimitri drew me against his hard chest. Oh my. The man had abs. "I need to see you," he whispered, his breath hot against my ear. "Tonight."

"Not until you tell me why." In the last twelve hours, I'd been taken from my friends, my job, my home. I'd been stalked by imps, a griffin and a demon. Now I was stuck at a Red Hats biker bar five hundred miles from home where a seventy-year-old-plus woman named Ant Eater sat stuffing peanuts up her nose in a disturbingly successful attempt to impress a woman named Betty Two Sticks. I didn't need to be playing games with Dimitri.

The crowd jostled us as Grandma hugged some friends and thumped others on the arm. I did my fair share of handshaking and smiling as I tried to ignore Dimitri and at the same time, hear something, anything these people said above the roar of the music.

Dimitri's warm hand seized mine and pulled me away from the crowd, toward the pinball machines. His dark eyes studied me. "I'm serious. I need to talk to you." His fingers rubbed at the sensitive spot between my thumb and my forefinger. "Leave your bedroom window open."

Well, when he put it that way . . . "No."

"Do it," he said under his breath as Grandma hurried toward us, her posse in pursuit.

I stared up at the massive hunk of man in front of me. "I'll open my window when you come clean about who you are and why you think you're my protector." In the meantime, he could stay outside with the troll hitmen, the demons and maybe a few regular old criminals.

"Thank you, Dimitri," Grandma said, attempting to sidle between us. "But I think your services are no longer needed."

He refused to budge.

"Good-bye, Dimitri," Grandma said, irritation tingeing her voice.

The corners of his mouth tugged into a devilish grin.

He reached down and kissed me, a brief brush of the lips. But still, I felt him shudder, or maybe that was me.

It was over before I knew it. Heck, it was enough, with everyone watching. But he didn't stop there. I went rigid with astonishment as he came back for more. He ran his thumb along my chin, tilting my head back for a kiss that sent molten heat coursing through my body. Claimed. In front of everyone. A wicked heat wound through my body, along with a little hum of pleasure. My first touch of goodness in a horrid night. That jarred me back to reality and I broke away.

What a presumptuous, forward, ungentlemanly—

"Jerk," I whispered.

His eyes burned. "You win," he said, his lips inches from mine. "I'll tell you everything. Tonight."

I touched my hand to my mouth as he pulled away. His mouth curved into a predatory smile.

Dimitri ignored the gaping crowd of bikers, except for one. He nodded to a tall, bald fellow with a *Ride Like You Stole It* tattoo before he turned his broad back and strode out into the night.

# Chapter Five

"I declare," Crazy Frieda checked out my bloodied arms. "Lizzie Brown, you look like you picked a fight with a briar patch."

At least she was kind enough not to mention Dimitri's kiss. I didn't know what to think, much less how to explain it to anyone else. He'd been gone ten minutes and I still found myself stealing glances at the door.

*Don't trust Dimitri,* I warned myself. *Don't trust Dimitri.* Maybe I should write it on my hand so I wouldn't forget.

"You okay?" Frieda cocked her head. Geez, it was like she was the biker reincarnation of Flo from Mel's Diner. Or maybe I'd watched too much *Alice* as a kid. "You don't look so good."

Said the woman whose fashion choices included a paisley dog collar and a canary blonde bouffant. The rhinestones on her lashes sparkled in the glow of a neon tribute to Milwaukee's Best. I did feel rotten, though. The few hours of sleep in the car had been a tease. Even then, I'd slept with one ear open, waiting to hear if Grandma confronted Dimitri. I still didn't know why he wanted to help us. I didn't trust him, even if his kiss made my toes curl.

"I need to talk to my grandmother," I said to Frieda.

"You will, sweetie," Frieda's white plastic hoop

earrings dangled practically to her shoulders. "But first I'm gonna help you out."

Well, what would it hurt? Ant Eater had Grandma in a headlock and didn't look like she'd be letting go anytime soon. Pirate was perched on the bar, sharing a basket of popcorn with Betty Two Sticks. I followed Frieda to the back.

It irked me to admit it, but Dimitri was right about one thing. I needed to learn more about Grandma's past. There hadn't been time before. Now that I was officially hiding out with the Red Skulls, I deserved to know if Grandma had killed someone, and exactly what the members of her coven had done that kept them on the run for thirty years.

Frieda led me to a door marked EMPLOYEES ONLY. "How long have you known my grandma?" I asked. *And is she a murderer?* I wanted to add.

"Oh, sweetie, I've known Gertie since before you were born." She held the door open for me, and I snuck one last look at Grandma. I could barely see her flowing gray hair behind a crowd of bikers. I'd never had that many friends in my life, much less in one room. And the kicker was, Grandma had to be feeling as bad—or worse—than me. My back throbbed, my legs ached. I plucked at my muddied khakis. They were starting to dry stiff and smelly.

"Now, stop that," Frieda said, patting at my arms. "Don't you worry your pretty little head. Come along and we'll get you cleaned up."

We passed through a small industrial kitchen and up a narrow, back staircase. Sticky booze residue clung to the concrete floor. The place smelled like pork rinds and beer.

"Too bad you missed dinner," Frieda said, the heels of her boots echoing on the hollow stairs. She stopped abruptly and I nearly ran into her. "Skunk surprise." She rubbed a manicured hand over her almost flat tummy. "We don't hardly get it, but when we bag one or two, it's certainly a surprise. Phew! You hungry?"

"No," I snapped. "I mean, no thanks. My stomach is still pretty shaken from the ride over here."

Frieda lit a cigarette and the smoky fumes poured into the claustrophobic space between us. The rhinestones on her cotton candy pink nails flickered along with the bare bulb dangling above our heads. "At any rate, we set fire to the Beast Feast as soon as we heard you were coming. Like I could eat another thing. But you're gonna love it."

The smoke burned my lungs. "Beast Feast?" I choked. My mind raced back to the etiquette classes Hillary had forced me to take. I scrambled for a polite—or heck, less than utterly offensive—way to decline. But in no way, no how, no universe was I ready for a heaping helping of roadkill surprise.

Frieda took a long drag off her cigarette and blew the smoke out her nose. "Don't fret if anybody nods off," she said, a few smoke curls lingering above her pink-glossed lips. "We're used to turning in by ten o'clock or so."

"Why tonight? You don't need to be staying up for my sake." I'd never be able to have a real discussion with Grandma in the middle of a party, even if I could talk my way out of a plate full of skunk flambé. Besides, my head hurt. It was after midnight. I needed to get some answers and get my aching butt into bed.

Frieda's eyebrows shot up and practically collided with her poofy bangs. "Oh, honey, it has to be tonight. We can't offer you our protection until we complete the Covenant Rite. Besides, you don't want to miss the Beast Feast reception after the ceremony. Possum pâté, rotisserie raccoon . . ." she said, like she was rattling off the courses at a four-star restaurant. "We've got a squirrel cacciatore

that'll make your head spin. Now chop chop." She clapped
her hands together as best she could with a cigarette dangling between two fingers.

Frieda led me down a narrow hallway. Well-traveled
photos lined the bare plywood walls, jammed into place
with silver thumbtacks. Most had been folded at one
time. Two, often four creases marred the images.

Frieda kissed her hand and plastered it over a gnarled
photo of a bald man with a thick, braided beard. Humor sparked from his heavy lidded eyes and he had the
look about him, like he was getting ready to tell a
whopper of a story. Frieda didn't say who he was. She
sashayed down the hall, her silver bracelets clinking,
all the while humming "Love in an Elevator."

She knocked twice on the wall outside a doorway
draped with a yellow, flowered sheet. "Bathroom's clear."
She pulled the makeshift door aside to reveal an industrial shower. It didn't have a curtain, no real floor even.
The water drained into a metal pipe that pushed up
about an inch out of the concrete floor. "Don't dawdle."
She treated me to a conspiratorial smile. "I was supposed to take you straight into the hole."

"Hole?" My voice caught in my throat.

She gave me the same look she probably used to comfort animals and small children. "It's nice." Her voice
trailed off. "For a hole."

Did I want to know? Probably not. It couldn't be any
worse than what I'd already been through. Could it?

I ducked under the wonderfully strong shower and
let the hot water pound my aching muscles. What I'd
give for a steaming hot chocolate followed by a soft,
warm bed. Or a nice, warm man. I groaned. Where had
that come from?

Oh, who was I kidding? I grew melty just thinking
of Dimitri's kiss.

He'd given me the kiss of my life right in front of an

entire bar full of people, and I'd enjoyed it. I didn't know what was wrong with me. It's not like I was into public displays of affection. But I couldn't get around how heady it felt. I liked a man who knew what he wanted.

Honeysuckle soap sloshed down my body as I lathered my shoulders. It didn't make any sense. We barely knew each other. It was crazy even to think about him. He was a complete unknown, and besides, I knew he wasn't quite human. Dimitri had shown up right on the heels of the griffin who'd rescued us. Coincidence? I wouldn't bet on it. Besides, those eyes of his—I'd have been perfectly fine with green, but orange and yellow? No. I wished I could have remembered what color the griffin's eyes had been.

Add that to my list of questions for Grandma. I washed my hair twice with a half-full dish-soap bottle labeled *Wild Ass Gertie's Homemade Sage Shampoo*. What would Dimitri do if I refused to meet him tonight? Or—my cheeks flushed—what would he do if I *did* let him climb through my bedroom window?

Yow.

When my sore body had enough, I reached for the ancient towel Frieda had left on the peg next to the door. After being so utterly stinking, dirty, clean felt amazing.

"Hey, babe!"

I about leapt out of my skin as Frieda poked her head past the flowered sheet. "Gertie says you lost your luggage. We're about the same size, so I put a few of my things on your bed. Third door on the right."

A draft snuck past Frieda and chilled my damp skin. Oh wow, I hadn't even thought of my backpack since we threw it in one of the saddlebags on the side of the Harley. I clutched the towel around me. I'd lost everything. My wallet, my credit cards. Every stitch of clothing that wasn't in my demon-infested house. "I need to make a phone call. If anyone finds my Visa, they can go on the shopping trip of the century." I hardly used the thing.

"Don't worry. Gertie cancelled everything." Frieda took in the expression on my face and shrugged. "We researched your background as soon as we found you. Social security number, credit history, education, criminal background check, any phobias or complications that could endanger the mission. Standard practice."

How could these people do in-depth background research when they couldn't even buy a shower door?

Everyone had their priorities, I supposed. Doubt crept into the pit of my stomach. Good thing I trusted Grandma or else I would have been very, very afraid.

Frieda patted her bouffant. The steam from my shower wasn't doing anything for her hairdo. "I don't know what Gertie was nattering on about. You talk less than a witness taking the fifth." She tucked a few stray hairs behind her ears. "But never you mind. Just get dressed. I'm going to go check on the ceremonial whosits and whatnots. We don't want Niblet to get away."

Niblet? My fingernails dug into the damp towel.

*Focus on what you can control.*

I checked to make sure there was no one in the hall-way before I tiptoe-ran to my room. At least this one had a door. The space was the size of some people's walk-in closets, and mostly bare. Nevertheless, I managed to trip over a cardboard box poking into the entry-way. I slid it to the side with my foot. A beat-up child's dresser painted white with gold trim stood by the window.

My new clothes were spread neatly on a mattress on the floor: a pair of tiger-striped black leather pants and an orange tank top with a diamond cutout between the boobs. Lovely. To make matters worse, there was no bra in sight. Instead, Frieda had draped a pair of black underwear across the tank top. The tiny wisp of fabric looked like it was designed to fit a munchkin. I clutched my towel and leaned closer. There was some kind of writing on the panties. I gingerly picked up the underwear by the black ribbons on the sides. Eek. My first thong. The front was embroidered with a dainty announcement in pink, scrolling letters: *My vibrator has two wheels.*

No way.

No how.

No.

Grandma burst through the door and frowned at my towel-clad body. "Aww! Frieda told me she let you shower. Dang it, Lizzie. We gotta get you to the hole. Now."

"Oh, I don't think so," I said, holding the panties as far away as I could. "Where are my old clothes?"

She threw up her arms like I was the crazy one. "Out in the trash heap, buried under deer guts and various other entrails."

"I don't care. Go get them."

"Fat chance," she said, meeting my glare head on. "Cripes, Lizzie, stop being dramatic. I know you had a tough day. Hell, I smashed my hog. But these people stayed up to wait for us and now they're staying up later to give you the mystical protection you need to survive the night. So move your keister."

*Survive the night?* Now who was being dramatic?

When I didn't budge, she sauntered over to inspect the clothes. "This ain't bad. Be glad she stayed away from the zebra pants. I've seen those in action."

I tossed Grandma the offensive panties that—let's face it—should have come with a warning label. I didn't want to know where any of these clothes had been, especially the underwear. This was not me. Of course, neither was going commando, so Grandma had better come up with a solution, or at least some underwear that wasn't sold with a brown paper wrapper. "There's not even a bra in here. I wear bras. Most normal women wear bras. And I'm not going to wear someone else's underwear."

"So then why are you bitching about a bra?"

"Grandma!"

She hooked the edges of the black underwear under her thumbs and whistled when she held it up to the light. "Isn't she a beaut? Frieda bought this special in Lubbock. Been saving it for a special occasion." She pointed the thong at me like a finger. "She must have taken a shine to you or she'd never have gifted you with these jockeys. Don't you insult her by refusing."

Oh lord. "But this isn't me!"

"Newsflash, Lizzie. This isn't about you." She dug through the box next to the door. "Here." She tossed me a plain white sports bra. "Buck up. At least you got to shower."

That wasn't the point. "Grandma, listen to me. Before we do anything else, we need to talk."

"You want answers? You'll get them." Hands on her hips, she regarded me like an impatient mother. "This is an important ceremony for everybody. Be downstairs in two minutes or I'm sending the Ant Eater after your ass."

I struggled into the black leather pants while the thong gave me the wedgie of the century. "Oh yeah, Lizzie," I muttered to myself. "Leave your home, your job, your family—dysfunctional as it may be. So you can hop on a Harley and follow Grandma Thong to the freak show of the century." The too-tight sports bra mashed my boobs and showed through the diamond cutout in the orange tank top. Thank goodness. It was certainly better than showing more skin.

Because there was some luck left in the world, the witches had spared my oxfords, stained and smelly as they were. I ignored the wet squish as I slipped my feet into what was supposed to be a pretty comfortable pair of shoes.

I hurried downstairs to the bar and found Grandma next to a hole in the floor where the Pop-A-Shot Basketball game had been. I wished these witches didn't have to be so freakin' literal. The entrance to their ceremonial room was basically a brick-lined hole with a rust-flecked ladder leading down. Voices echoed from deep in the cavern below. I leaned closer, but had a hard time making out any actual words. Musty air tickled my nose. I paused, mustering my courage, when a seventy-something man in a tricked-out wheelchair came barreling toward me. Pirate rode in his lap, his tongue flapping out the side of his mouth.

Sidecar Bob had lost both legs in a biking accident, or so Grandma said. His silver goatee was immaculately trimmed. His hair was not. It stuck out in tufts from his ponytail and basically rebelled against the black hairnet he wore. Bob skidded to a stop and howled like a banshee when I had to jump backward to save my toes.

"You see that? That's what I'm talking about!" Pirate practically tap danced in Bob's lap. I was glad to see Pirate had left his bandages in place. In fact, he seemed to have forgotten about them completely.

"I feel the need . . ." Bob announced.

"The need for speed!" Pirate and Bob shouted together.

I swear Pirate could make friends with a doorknob. In this case, he had great taste. I liked Bob immediately. "You tell me if this mutt gets to be too much for you," I said. "Feel free to send him back."

"Hell no!" Pirate buried himself under Bob's arm. "We were in the kitchen cooking. And eating. That is some fine squirrel. That barbeque sauce isn't bad, either."

I resisted the urge to lecture Pirate about his eating habits. The little guy had been through a lot. He deserved a break. "So, Bob, are you heading down to the ceremony?"

He threw his head back and guffawed. "My old lady would have my head." His belly poked out of the navy gym shorts that seemed horribly at odds with his black leather vest. "Nah. I'm stoking the fires, keeping the Beast Feast warm for when you're done." He scratched his nose. "But I did want to give you something." He glanced at Grandma. "None of the gals will admit it, but you do need it."

"Well, thanks," I said, trying to sound casual, feeling anything but. I yanked at the skin-tight orange top creeping up my stomach.

Bob fished a rubber band from the fanny pack strapped to the side of his chair. "Here ya go. Put your hair back. It gets messy down there."

"Sure," I forced a smile.

"We'll keep the squirrel fires burning!" Pirate said as I clung to the cool, metal rungs of the ladder and made myself descend. A crowd had already gathered below, their whoops and hollers echoing off the subterranean walls.

"Welcome to the Rat's Den!" Ant Eater clapped me on the back, her gold tooth shining in the light of dozens upon dozens of candles. The ceiling hung so low I could have reached up and touched it. The smell of paraffin and candles burning assaulted my nose. Under it, I could smell old brick walls and mildew.

The place needed a serious cleaning. Boxes, discarded barware and old CB equipment cluttered the tiny room. On every surface candles of all shapes and colors crowded against each other. Not smart. I winced as

Frieda brushed past a box stacked with candles and nearly sent it crashing into one of the old beer posters lining the walls.

"Eeeee!" Frieda shimmied up to me. "Oh Lizzie, you are hotter than a two-dollar pistol. You meet Ant Eater?" Frieda indicated her gold-toothed buddy. "Whew, does she have some good stories. This woman—" She paused while Ant Eater guffawed. "This woman will try anything once." She cocked her head and leaned in closer. "And I do mean anything."

"Okay people, pipe down!" Grandma hollered from behind me. She lifted her head toward the open hole. "Bob, you can close 'er up." The trap door above hissed like an airlock. The candles blazed as the light from the bar receded and we were left in semidarkness. "Join hands," Grandma instructed.

I took Grandma's strong hand and Frieda's chilly one, as the crowd of about twenty witches drew back. A fire crackled in the center of the room. Flames curled around a smoke-stained burner on a portable camping stove. A worn, silver pot boiled on top of it. My mouth went dry. If Bob was upstairs stirring the port-braised beaver, I couldn't imagine what they dumped in that pot.

The witches stood transfixed and closed their eyes. I felt the magic build. The only sound in the room came from bubbles frothing in the pot. The air grew warmer, thicker by the second as the candles cast tall shadows on the walls behind us.

Grandma bowed her head and the others followed. "We, the witches of the Red Skull, are bound to the magic that has sustained our line for more than twelve hundred years. In it, we find warmth, light and eternal goodness. Without it, we perish. This night, we welcome into our fold a sister who was lost to us. As we pledge ourselves to her, she pledges herself to us."

My hands grew damp. Oh boy. I wasn't too sure

about that last line. What did pledging myself to them mean? Sure, I wanted answers, but I wasn't ready to *join* the Red Skulls.

Grandma stepped into the circle, holding a monstrous ziplock bag filled with rust-colored pulp. Ant Eater scrambled for my free hand. The witches observed Grandma with bated breath as she popped open the seal and dipped her fingers into the mush. She stood and faced me, her heavy breath tickling my bangs.

"From death comes new life." She rubbed the goo onto my forehead. It felt sticky, wet and it smelled like roadkill. She dipped her fingers again and came at me a second time with the wet, lumpy gloop. "May you see with new eyes." She rubbed it into my manicured brows.

"May you listen to your heart." She rubbed it onto my ears. A rivulet of juice trickled into my ear canal.

"May you speak against the evil that surrounds us."

Oh no. I pressed my lips together, and she slopped the pulp from one side of my mouth to the other. The sweet, meaty fumes scoured my nose, and I almost gagged.

"May we forever travel together as guardians of the light."

She visited each witch, thumbing a portion of the gloop onto their foreheads. I wondered if I was allowed to wipe mine off. The small room, jam-packed with bodies, started to feel stuffy. My tiger-striped leather pants grew sweaty and itchy. A drip of liquid trailed past my left brow and down toward my eye.

Grandma stood in the middle of the circle. "May we see our future as one coven, united in our quest." The witches scurried to the boxes behind them. One by one, they held up dead animal pelts. Foxes, coyotes, deer. Oh my.

The animals had been skinned so that their legs and tails dangled. The witches positioned the animal heads over their own, peering out of the hollowed eye sockets.

Frieda jabbed me in the arm with her fingernail. "Here," she handed me a damp, burlap cloth. "Wipe that raccoon liver off your face. We don't want it staining your deer hide."

"Urgle." I rubbed the rag against my mouth and face until my skin felt raw. I wasn't cut out for this. "What is it with the dead animals?" I cringed as Frieda lowered a deer head over mine.

"It's the circle of life, sweetie." Frieda tugged at the deer's empty eye sockets until I could see, well, barely. The thing had about as much visibility as a Halloween mask and it smelled like old leather and mothballs.

"Don't fret," she whispered, wrapping the deceased deer's front legs around my shoulders while the hooves bumped against my chest. "It's only for show. Ceremonial and all."

Now she tells me.

"Your grandma likes to do things up nice." She stepped back. "There."

"Frieda," Grandma warned.

Frieda slipped back into place next to me. Grandma snuffed the fire under the large pot. A tall, red-haired witch with ruby rings on her pinkie fingers rushed forward with a large platter. It held a crystal goblet with handles on the sides. Grandma ladled a portion of boiling liquid into the cup. It steamed with the heat. The amber liquid continued to boil for a few minutes, sending up chunks of what looked to be meat. Roadkill and crystal. How very . . . them.

I couldn't drink that.

I locked my knees with dread and wondered how I could possibly get out of it.

Grandma held out the cup to the group. "As we drink, we are one." She inhaled the vapors above the goblet and took the first sip.

Frieda went next. She accepted the cup from Grandma and brought it to her lips. Ugh. The chunks looked even bigger up close, with bits of membrane and who knows what floating around.

I wanted to hug Frieda when she passed the cup to the witch on the other side of her. I scratched at my steamy leather pants. She calmly watched the other witches drink from the goblet.

This ceremonial stuff might be no sweat to her. For all I knew, she did this every Saturday night. I didn't. I'd had enough excitement for one day—battling a demon, meeting my mysterious protector and joining a coven of witches. Now was not the time to quaff down a goblet of roadkill surprise. I appreciated what these people were doing for me. And of course I would never do anything to offend them or dishonor their traditions. At the same time, I had my limits.

When the cup came to me, I forced myself to take it. Heat radiated from the swirling brew. I wished it would stop moving. I held my breath and brought it to my lips. The pungent odor of mint rose with the steam.

*I can't. I just can't.*

I tipped the cup, moved my throat and pretended to sip. I felt the group exhale. They'd doubted me too, it seemed. I wiped the excess from my lips and handed the goblet to Grandma, who solemnly drank the remainder.

I wanted to sigh with relief. Maybe now I could be bestowed with my protection and get to bed.

The lights flicked on above us and I suddenly had to squint.

"E-yow," Frieda threw a hand over her eyes. "I hate when they do that."

A tangle of voices rose from the crowd. The show had ended, it seemed, and I wasn't protected.

"Wait a second," I said, grabbing Frieda's wrists by the bracelets. "It can't be over." It couldn't be. "What about my protection? Am I covered?" Grandma hadn't said anything about it during the ceremony, and I certainly hadn't felt anything magical happen after they sealed the door. "Don't tell me I had to wear raccoon liver for nothing."

Frieda giggled. "Relax, honey. You are protected. And just in time. Look, there goes your grandma to meditate." We watched Grandma break the seal and climb out into the bar above the ceremonial room. "The demon that's been chasing us, Vald, we think he knows about you." Frieda shivered. "He's coming." Worry flashed across her face before she forced it aside. "But don't worry. We have you. That potion, it sealed you to us. You don't have to be alone anymore. You have all our magic working for you."

My stomach did a backflip. "Potion? You mean the one with the chunks?" I didn't drink it. Why didn't I drink it? Because I'm an idiot, that's why.

"What can I say? We like our squirrel. But that wasn't the magic ingredient. We use bakki root. Smells like Wrigley's gum."

Of all the ways for me to screw this up, this was, well, this was not good. "I've never heard of bakki root." Maybe we could get some more.

It's magical. Takes forever to grow. Ant Eater is our resident gardener. "Mmmm . . . it tastes like heaven, doesn't it? Gives me a bit of a buzz, too."

I didn't want to ask, but I had to know. "How hard would it be to make some more?"

Frieda giggled. "Sorry. I am buzzed. Believe you me, I'd die for more, but we used up the whole kit and caboodle on you, dearie."

Oh no.

She smiled. "Don't look so upset. You're worth it! Where are we going to find another long-lost demon slayer sister?"

I didn't know if they'd want me when they discovered what I'd done.

# *Chapter Six*

"Beast Feast!" Sidecar Bob hollered down into the ceremonial room. The witches snuffed the candles and stampeded to the exit in record speed.

"Wait. Hold it!" I fought against the current of the crowd, struggling to reach the remains of the protective stew, growing cold on the portable camp stove.

"Bottoms up!" Ant Eater quaffed the last few drops from the silver pot. She wiped her chin as I screamed, "No!"

"Gotta be quicker than that, sport." She wiped down the pot with a blue bandanna.

She had no idea what she'd done. There went my protection, my insurance policy against the demon Vald, who—according to Crazy Frieda—was at this very moment on his way to see us. I had to fix this. "Is there any more? What about that bakki root? Did you save any of that?" *Please!*

She swallowed a minty burp. "'Scuse me." She fanned the air with her hand. "Greedy little cuss, aren't ya? Well, I hate to break it to you, but when it comes to magic, we don't keep leftovers."

Holy hexes.

I had to find Grandma. She'd know what to do, after she kicked me into next Thursday. *Why didn't I just drink the potion?*

The thwump, thwump of heavy-metal music blared in the bar above me, accompanied by the whoops and cheers of the coven. I scrambled out of the hole and nearly fell into a cheap, metal-backed chair with a vinyl-padded seat. Every table in the bar had been lined up to form a massive banquet table.

It would have smelled heavenly—roasted potatoes, onions and garlic—if I hadn't known the other ingredients. The tiny blue-haired witch next to me flopped into the nearest empty place. "Liquid appetizers!" she hollered, as she reached for a pitcher of beer. Two of her friends sidled up, mugs in hand.

A buffet line ten witches deep formed in front of the steaming dishes set out on the bar. Sidecar Bob pulled up to the table with two heaping plates of roadkill surprise. Pirate bounced on his lap, nearly out of his skin with anticipation. "Lizzie! It's people food! And I have a plate. Lookie there. Food! On a plate. For me! Me! I've made it, I tell you. I've finally got a seat at the table!"

Sweet squirrels. My stomach rolled over. "That's roadkill, Pirate."

"Oh, no," Bob piped in. "We wouldn't waste roadkill on a banquet. Roadkill's special magic. It goes straight into a spell jar. This here on the table is hunted meat."

Okay, that was a relief. But still, Pirate should have been eating his Healthy Lite dog chow. Of course that disappeared off the bike along with my clothes. I watched him eat an entire slice of meat in two bites. Pirate loved to eat. And despite his enormous energy and complete willingness to chase anything that moved, he tended to have weight issues. Pirate peeked up from his plate, took one look at me and started to eat even faster.

Lucky for him, his weight was the least of my concerns now. "Bob, Grandma got out of the pit before I could talk to her. Frieda said she was heading off to meditate. Do you have any idea where she might be?" I ignored his disapproving look. "This is serious," I said over the thwump, thwump, thwump of the speaker above us. "I have to talk to her before she gets too involved with whatever she does in there."

Bob sopped up some gravy on a piece of bread and fed it to Pirate. "Listen to this guitar solo," He closed his eyes and felt the music. "You hear that? That's Marty Friedman, the old Megadeth axeman. Oh yeah." He played air guitar against his chest. "Yeet, yeet, yeet!"

"Bob!" I'd tell him where to shove his *yeet*. "This is a matter of life or death."

I really hoped I was exaggerating.

"Where's Grandma?" I asked again.

He hung his head. "Aw, Lizzie. Don't ask me that. The Cave of Visions is sacred ground."

"I wouldn't be asking you if it wasn't absolutely necessary." We didn't have time to haggle. "I mean it, Bob. You've gotta trust me on this one."

Bob rubbed Pirate's back absently as Pirate climbed halfway onto the table and began to lick his plate clean. "Okay." He scratched at his arms. "But if she chews out my ass, I'm sending her after you next."

"My butt is yours."

Pirate leaned too far over his plate and nearly knocked over Bob's beer. Bob snatched up his wobbling brew and took a long swallow, watching me.

Pirate sniffed at his empty plate. "I'm sorry. My manners are rusty. I haven't been using my table manners when I've been forced to eat out of a dog bowl." He sniffed at Bob's full plate. "You don't mind, do you?" Pirate started in on Bob's dinner.

Bob slipped Pirate, and his plate, onto the floor.

"Come on," he wheeled backward, away from the table. "It's out back. Looks like a cheap storage shed. What the hell am I saying? It is a cheap storage shed. We needed to get her someplace quiet, and this bar didn't cut it."

"Thanks." I patted his shoulder as we wove our way through the crowd toward the back door.

"Lizzie." He captured my arm. "Don't go barreling out there. Your grandma's under guard. Approach slowly. Tell them who you are. Be prepared to prove it. Demons can take on many forms."

"Right," I said. I could handle this. I hoped.

The back door clacked on its hinges as I stepped out behind the bar and onto a small patio, crowded with rusting bar chairs. Sheesh. And I thought they'd dumped all their junk into the hole. Crushed beer cans littered the narrow parking lot that led into the alley beside the bar. Tufts of grass and weeds poked up between and around the faded yellow lines. A rusting Camaro sat stranded on concrete blocks.

At the edge of the parking lot, just beyond the Dumpster, stood a plastic storage shed framed by scraggly trees.

Bob nodded to the tall, red-haired witch standing guard. I recognized her from the protection ceremony downstairs. "Go on out. If she can, I'll bet Gertie will be more than glad to hear what you have to say. If not, well, there'll be time later."

Yeah, well maybe. Maybe not.

The chilly night air tore at my hair and whipped the dried leaves and grass into circles. I crunched over a mashed Budweiser can as I made my way to the storage shed. I could see a faint light between the plastic swinging doors and I chose to focus on that, rather than at the hawk-nosed witch standing guard. She hadn't looked too friendly down in the hole and she looked even less glad to see me now.

"Hi. I need to talk to my grandmother." When she didn't move, I added, "It's a matter of life and death." How terrible to realize I wasn't exaggerating at all.

She stood her ground in front of doors imprinted with the word *Yardsaver*. "Leave," she said automatically, "or I'll be forced to have you removed."

An eerie creek sounded from inside the storage unit. A blast of air shot out between the doors, chilling me to the core.

"What was that?" I smelled sulfur, evil. Oh my word, I hoped Grandma was okay in there. "You'd better check on her," I told the tall witch. "Grandma?" I hollered. "Do you need me in there?" Like I could help her, I thought automatically. Wait. It was time to get out of that habit. I could help her. Somehow.

The tall witch blocked me. "No, Lizzie," she said, low and serious. "She's meditating. No one disturbs her when she's out of body. It's dangerous." Her eyes traveled to a spot over my shoulder. "Ant Eater, see that Lizzie makes it back inside. And keep her there."

"What? Oh, come on," I said, as Ant Eater's grip practically wrung the blood from my right arm. "Ow!" Where had she come from? "Look, I made a mistake. We need to straighten this out," I said, as Ant Eater practically dragged me back into the bar. "Damn it." I tried to shake her grip. "Let me go! You don't understand." I tugged at the black, spiked bands crisscrossing her wrist. "I screwed up. Royally."

She dragged me through the back door and bulldozed me against an old-fashioned phone booth. Pain laced through my shoulder blades. I could smell the bakki root on her breath. "Don't you ever push me, bitch." She shoved me again, hard. "I don't care whose grandbaby you are or what you can do. I will fuck you up."

What the frig was wrong with these people? "Okay, okay," I said, trying to catch my breath. Her last slam had knocked the wind out of me. "Are you done? We don't have time for this. I need to talk to Grandma."

She brought her fist back. Holy schneikies! I braced myself, sure she was going to haul off and hit me.

My salvation came in the form of a blonde bouffanted Frieda waving a roasted leg of . . . something. "God almighty, E!" Frieda yanked me so hard my arm about stretched out of its socket. "What the hell are you doing?"

Ant Eater stood there with her fist cocked, breathing heavily. "That bitch almost killed Gertie."

"What?" Frieda exclaimed.

"No!" Never. "I need to talk to Grandma," I insisted. "This is important. Hugely important. I was trying to explain myself out there when this jerk went all Naomi Campbell on me."

Frieda glared at Ant Eater. Then she leveled the same contempt at me.

What the heck did I do?

"Come on," Frieda said as she hustled me out of Ant Eater's reach. I met at least twenty pairs of eyes as the witches stopped their feast to watch the show. Frieda dragged me through the crowd and back into the kitchen.

Industrial pots bubbled with stews and sauces. A rust-stained sink labored under a mountain of dirty dishes. Bob loaded up a fresh tray of barbequed squirrel while Pirate snatched up every scrap Bob tossed down to him.

"I swear I'm gonna kick some ass!" Frieda dragged me toward the stairs.

"You said it. I can't believe the way she manhandled

me. That woman needs professional help!" I tried to catch Bob's eye, but he took a sudden interest in his oven mitts.

Frieda dragged me up the stairs. "Lizzie, I love ya. I really do. But if you pull something like that again, I'll strangle you myself."

Wait, she was on Ant Eater's side? "You've got to be kidding."

She pulled me into a room at the end of the hall and slammed the rough, wooden door. Homemade bunk beds lined each wall, with room for little else. Frieda blinked her rhinestone-tipped lashes, fighting for control. "Lizzie. Oh, Lizzie. You could have killed your grandmama tonight."

I felt myself pale a few shades.

"Sit." She plopped my butt down onto a saggy mattress and, straightening her back, arranged herself next to me. "When Gertie is in a meditative state, any interruption can be dangerous. Fatal." She paused to take a breath. "To see into the evil that surrounds us, she needs to draw herself closer than any of us would ever dare. Any breach, any break in her concentration, well—it would be like walking through the ghetto waving a wallet full of fifties. You're just asking for trouble."

"I'm sorry," I said. "I had no idea."

She patted my hand. "I know, sweetie. Ant Eater does too. She's an overprotective sort."

Overprotective like a Mack truck. "How long does Grandma stay in her trances?" I asked.

"A few hours, a few days—however long it takes." She knitted her brows. "I worry about her. It's not like she goes out to the shed often, but when she does, she usually prepares. Gathers her strength. Tonight, she ran in there like Rambo. At her age, it's just not smart."

From what I'd seen, Grandma hadn't slowed down

since I met her. "I think she might be trying to learn more about the demon who attacked us in my bathroom." Or the imps we met on the road.

Frieda crossed her legs and leaned in closer. "She's trying to get a leg up on Vald. He's pure evil."

I remembered her talking about him. "Vald?"

"He's a fifth-level demon—the worst. Your Great-great Aunt Evie, the last slayer, locked him up in the second layer of hell. He's been trying to break out ever since. As far as we can tell, he's close. I don't even want to think about what he'd try to do to us." She shook her head. "When—" She paused. "Well, that is to say, after an unfortunate incident with your mother, we've been on the run from Vald's minions. He's got a nasty streak and an army of sub-demons."

"What happened to my mother?" From what Frieda had said, it didn't sound good. But still, I had to know.

"Um," Frieda cleared her throat. "Your mother . . . It's complicated," she said, embarrassed.

"Please," I said. "I never met her. I never knew her. But I'd like to know what happened."

"Oh, sugar." Frieda patted my leg, the corners of her eyes growing moist. "Your mamma? It's like this." She blinked several times, as if trying to decide how to word it. Finally she said, "Your mamma didn't quite make the cut."

Call me confused. "What does that mean?"

Frieda squeezed my leg, shooting pain through cuts I forgot I even had. "Truth is, we don't know what happened to Phoenix."

"Phoenix? My mom's name was Phoenix?" Knowing Grandma, she had a tougher name for her Harley. Life must have gotten a bit more rough-and-tumble for Grandma. Heck, she'd been on the run for thirty years.

"Your grandma will explain later."

"But—"

She threw up her hands, "I'm sorry, baby. I've already interfered enough. This is a family matter best discussed with your grandmother."

Point taken. "Okay, then answer me this: What would happen if Vald came back?" It had to be bad or the coven wouldn't have put me under their immediate protection. And Grandma wouldn't have rushed out there tonight.

Frieda worked a bit too long on her answer.

She could sugarcoat it all she wanted. Heck, she could wrap it in cotton candy. I already knew. "He'd come after me, wouldn't he?"

She blinked. "He'd certainly try. But don't worry, honey! That's why we put you under our protection tonight. You're bound to us now!"

Sure. If I'd been smart enough to actually *drink* the potion.

"You okay? Here." She fished a hand down her bra and pulled out an airline bottle of Jack Daniels Tennessee whiskey. She handed it to me and I took a swig.

It burned all the way down to my stomach. *Yeah, Lizzie, drink a shot of Jack but not the uber-rare protection potion.* I was the worst demon slayer ever.

Frieda finished the bottle. "Got some more under the bed. You want to hang out a bit?"

Definitely. I'd have to stop drinking, of course. I could already feel that shot in my dazed head. Out of all the dumb things I'd done today, getting drunk wouldn't be one of them. I needed to be sharp, especially if Vald decided to show up.

Frieda dug through the plastic grocery bags under her bed while I took a look at the photos she'd plastered across the wall beside her bed. Most were of Frieda and various witches I'd seen downstairs. And there were two more of the heavy-lidded man whose picture I'd seen in the hallway. Mr. Love in an Elevator. I wondered what had happened to him.

Frieda handed me a bottle of Bailey's Irish Cream liqueur. Darn. I would have had to waste my shot on the Jack. I rolled it between my hands. I should get to the bed they'd given me, but I didn't want to be alone. Heck, I didn't even want to think. It was hard enough to let go of the fact that I'd faked my way through the protection ceremony tonight. Me, the person who prized honesty above all things. Then again—I yanked the orange tank top down over my stomach—I wasn't exactly myself tonight.

An eerie moan drifted up from the yard outside. I reached for Frieda's bony arm. "What was that?"

"Come on." She led me over to the window. Years of dirt clouded the glass. I tried to yank it open, but it didn't budge. Together, we pried it away from the rotting windowsill. Another moan, louder this time, pierced the sounds of crickets chirping in the night. "Your grandma's having one of her visions."

I looked out into the copse of trees beyond the back parking lot. Purple rays of light streamed from every joint and corner of the Yardsaver shed. Heaven help her. "Grandma?" I gulped.

The red-headed witch knelt in front of the swinging doors, her arms spread against them as if she held them closed. Her even chants floated out into the night air.

Frieda peeked out beside me. "Don't worry," she whispered. "Scarlet has her covered."

Yeah, well I didn't like Scarlet. The snitch. From what I could tell, Grandma needed someone who could think on her feet, not a panicky know-it-all who would rather call the guard instead of having an honest-to-goodness conversation with someone, aka me.

"Come on back, baby," Frieda said. "We'll only distract them."

Scarlet looked pretty intense to me. I hoped Grandma could handle herself. Or if she couldn't, that Scarlet was half as powerful as the griffin who'd come to our rescue at the edge of the lake.

For the moment, I let Frieda lead me away from the window. We each sat on the bottom of a bunk bed, facing each other. It felt like a twisted version of summer camp. If I heard anything strange—anything—I'd be down there faster than Frieda could blink those crazy lashes of hers.

And since she'd mentioned rescuing, "Frieda, what do you think of Dimitri? He said he's my protector, but I don't know. You'd think I would have felt something, kind of like when I met Grandma. Something about her made me feel like I was supposed to be with her."

Frieda handed me an airline bottle of Smirnoff. "Hard to say." She plopped onto her side, reached into a plastic Valu-Mart bag on the floor and withdrew her own little bottle of Jägermeister. "He's helped us out from time to time," she said, unscrewing the bottle. "Done us some favors. But with guys like him, favors always seem to come with a price tag attached." She took a long sip. "E-yahhh." Her bracelets jangled as she wiped her mouth with the back of her wrist. "One thing's sure. He seems to have taken a shine to you."

I tipped my Smirnoff bottle back and forth, watching the liquid swirl. No question about it, that man could get my blood flowing. I didn't know if it was the way he'd looked at me downstairs—like he'd like to devour me whole—or the fact that he probably could. I hadn't met anyone like him. Heck, I hadn't run into many interesting guys at all since college. Happy Hands Preschool wasn't exactly hot date central. It felt good to be pursued. Then again, I wasn't about to lose my head just because some hunka hunka burning male rescued us from the side of the road. "I don't trust him. It's too convenient. He has to want something."

Frieda waggled her brows and I felt my face warm.

"Besides . . . that," I added. Oh lordy, I had to stop thinking about that kiss. I had no business indulging in mildly shocking, utterly delectable forays with my mysterious Greek protector. He belonged in their world. Not mine. As soon as I learned to control my powers, I'd be back to my normal life, and that didn't include men whose eyes flashed yellow and who hung out with griffins.

"I can't believe I saw a griffin tonight," I said.

"Saw one?" Frieda scoffed. "You smooched one."

My stomach squinched. "I was afraid of that."

"Aw, don't be so hard on yourself." She grinned. "I sure wouldn't kick him out of bed for eating crackers."

I tried to mirror her humor, but I wasn't feeling it. Twenty-four hours ago, I hadn't even known griffins existed. My brain needed to catch up with my hormones.

"At least he's not a werewolf," Frieda said, spinning her Jägermeister cap on a pink-glossed nail.

"I'm going to pretend I didn't hear that." I eased back onto my elbows. Even if I could accept what he was, I still didn't know if I could trust him. "Tell me, Frieda. And be honest. What would you do?"

She pursed her lips. "I don't know, honey. I just don't know."

Frieda fell asleep in the middle of her minibottle of Jägermeister. Phew. I capped the bottle and turned off the light. The faint odor of black licorice hung in the air as I stood by the window and watched Scarlet, still prostrate, in front of the glowing Yardsaver shed. Nothing had changed down there. I didn't know if that was good or bad.

At least Frieda's roommates hadn't come up from the Beast Feast. Pirate would certainly be one of the last to leave the party. This room was closest to the storage shed. It was the least I could do, to watch over Grandma after I nearly messed her up tonight. And being with Frieda, even if she had fallen asleep, her lashes twinkling in the moonlight, was better than being by myself.

I don't know when I fell asleep. I certainly hadn't meant to. But somewhere in the early morning, as I sat below the open window, my night caught up with me. And that was a big mistake.

A heavy scratching grated me awake. My hands found the rough wood wall behind me and the musty carpet underneath. "Grandma?" I asked, right before a heavy hand clamped over my mouth.

What the—? Oh my God. Vald? Smoke swirled in the air around me. I felt suffocated, cut off.

Strong hands whipped me around, and I saw his face in the moonlight. Dimitri!

"Quiet," he commanded, his Greek accent more pronounced than before. Boy, did he look ticked. He wore black from head to toe and looked more like a Navy SEAL than the *GQ* businessman I'd met. His eyes flicked over my revealing shirt and leather pants, and I felt myself flush.

I hadn't been in my room to meet him. Had he searched the whole bar? Or had he sensed me? "How did you find me?"

He clamped his hand over my mouth. "I said— quiet."

Frieda was gone.

*What happened to Frieda?*

Something was very, very wrong. I yanked his hand from my mouth. He let me do it, a steely warning in his eyes. "What happened? Where's Frieda?"

"I don't know and I don't care." He wrapped an arm around me and guided me to the open window.

He couldn't possibly think . . .

Oh no. This is not how it was supposed to work. So much for my fantasies of a romantic tryst in the moonlight.

"I'm not going anywhere with you." I fought his grip. Anxiety churned in my stomach. I might not be a part of this coven, but I could feel something was utterly, terribly wrong. And where was Pirate? I had to get downstairs. Anywhere. I had to see what was going on.

Dimitri picked me up and started down the ladder propped against the outside of the building. I kicked at the empty air. Eep. I hated heights and I hated having to cling to his shirt for dear life. Worst of all, I hated seeing the dark Yardsaver shed, its doors flung open.

As soon as my oxfords hit the rock-strewn ground, Dimitri pulled me toward the woods beyond the back of the property.

This was crazy.

"We need to go back!"

"I forbid it."

"You whaaa—" We zoomed through the forest like we'd hopped on Grandma's hog. I didn't know how he did it. My legs ached and my lungs burned like we were running full speed. But we weren't running. We practically flew. The moonlight flicked eerie patterns on the back of Dimitri's back as we raced through the trees.

Wind whipped through my hair. I wanted to scream. Of all the hacked-up, strange and downright disturbing things that had happened since I met Grandma, this had to be the worst. Not because I was in any imminent danger—and lord knew I probably was. But because those witches back there needed me. I knew it like I knew my last name. And I was doing the worst possible thing. I was running.

Dimitri had pushed me too far.

# Chapter Seven

I had no idea how long we sprinted before we lurched to a stop. The woods screamed with insects, animals and— *Please let it be just insects and animals*. After the zigzag path we'd cut through the countryside, it was impossible to tell where we'd come from or where Dimitri was headed. My heart sank. I didn't know how I'd ever find my way back to Grandma.

Dimitri pulled me behind a thick tree. The rough bark scraped against my back. Every one of my nerve endings erupted as his hard body pinned me. I clutched him, trying to gain a foothold in the fallen leaves and soft dirt underneath. Heat burned through his soft black T-shirt. I braced my fingers against his chest. At least he seemed as out of breath as I was. And dang, there wasn't an ounce of fat on the man.

Enough.

"What do you want?" I asked, letting go of his shirt, wishing I could shove past him. "Because it had better be frickin' amazing." And I couldn't think of anything worth Grandma's life.

Dimitri was going to lead me back, whether he liked it or not. I hoped I wouldn't be too late.

He planted his hands on each side of my head. "I'm saving you from what could turn out to be a very unpleasant evening." He bowed his head, breathing heavily. Whatever he thought we'd needed to escape, we'd run full out. He lifted his head, listening to the sounds of the night swiftly turning to morning. "You can start by thanking me."

He had to be kidding. "Don't hold your breath, buster." Something very bad had happened. My best guess? Grandma's mind meld with Vald the demon hadn't gone as planned. Frieda said Grandma had to draw herself closer than anyone else would dare. Grandma had rushed in without preparing and, after our night, she'd been bruised and tired. "Did it ever occur to you that I might have been able to help Grandma back there?"

He looked at me intently. "The Red Skulls can take care of themselves. They've been dealing with Vald for thirty years. You, on the other hand, could get yourself hurt . . . or killed."

*Killed.* The way he said it chilled me to the core. Worse, he was right. As it stood, I was no match for a fifth-level demon like Vald. And if the witches did have a plan, I was willing to bet it didn't include me. Or Pirate. *My poor dog.* Tears burned at the backs of my eyes. Pirate trusted me to keep him safe.

*Focus.*

I couldn't let this get to me, or I wouldn't be good for anyone. "Okay," I told Dimitri, easing him off me. The crisp night air crept between us, tugging at my nipples. "I might be more of a liability than a help at this point. I'll stay out of the way of anything big. But I need to get my dog."

Doubt touched the back of my mind. I wondered if I truly should have helped the witches in some way. Is that why they'd tried to give me the potion? Vald had been chasing Grandma and the coven for thirty years. It couldn't be a mistake that tonight, the night I arrived, he chose to attack. Well, if that was the case, they should have had the decency to let me in on it. As it stood, I had to make a difference where I could. And that meant protecting Pirate. From the way Dimitri was scowling, I could tell he didn't like my plan one bit.

Tough tootsies. I was half cold, half sweating and completely tired of standing around. "So are you going to help me get Pirate or what?" I ducked around Dimitri. The cold night seized me, gelling the sweat and making me wish I had a lot more on than Frieda's tank top. I took my best guess as to the direction of the coven and started walking.

Dimitri captured both my wrists in one hand. "Not on your life." Heat crept up my arms, and I had an acute awareness of the crushing power he held in check.

"Do not fight me on this." I bit at every word, locking down my frustration until I could barely stand it anymore. Dimitri's fingers bit into my wrists and that was all it took. I let out a shout to rival any battle cry. *I had to.* If I didn't let the frustration boil, I'd start crying. I couldn't afford to fall apart now or someone could get hurt—or killed—and it would be my fault.

He yanked me against his chest, infuriated. "Has it occurred to you I'm trying to save your life?" he asked, his face inches from mine. "The witches have a plan. You don't. If that really is Vald back there—and my guess is it is—he could suck out your soul before you could even begin to look for your little dog. There's no foreplay. No warning. It's gone. And so are you."

Fear clenched my gut. "But I'm a demon slayer." I was the only one who could—potentially—kill the jerk. That had to give me some kind of an edge.

He shook his head, a wry smile not quite reaching his eyes. "Not yet, you aren't. Have you ever tried to steal a demon's essence? Thrown a switch star?" His eyes narrowed at my obvious bewilderment. "Your grandma didn't even tell you about the Three Truths did she?"

I shook my head.

"Dammit!"

So he had a point. This was bad. Maybe I didn't have any business going back there and maybe Grandma and the Red Skulls could handle themselves. Lord knew it would have been easier to run, hide until I'd done my homework. But I didn't have the luxury to wait. I'd never forgive myself if something happened to Pirate while I stood around and did nothing.

I blew out a breath and faced the man, looming above me in the moonlight. At that moment, he reminded me of an enraged mountain lion, as cunning as he was dangerous, with a territorial streak a mile wide.

And he wasn't going away. "I understand where you're coming from," I told him. "Heck, under other circumstances, I'd agree with you. But in the last twelve hours, I've lost my home, my job, my friends, my clothes . . ." Did he really need me to go any farther? "Hell's bells, I've lost any sense of what is normal in the world. I'm not losing my dog!"

He didn't even have the courtesy to blink.

I shoved past him. "Fine. If you're not going to help, you can get the frick out of my way."

Endless trees loomed in every direction. I took my best guess at a direction and set off.

"Lizzie. Hold on. You can't."

On the contrary, I could and I would.

Besides, when Dimitri first took Grandma and me to the coven, he'd been worried about the troll hitmen after us. Maybe I'd get lucky and only find assassins. What would the old Lizzie have had to say about that?

He caught up with me, lingering a step behind, casting his long shadow over mine in the moonlight. "Don't go back there. It's . . . dangerous." He sounded worried.

"Déjà vu," I said. "We already had this conversation."

"There are things at work that you cannot understand."

Okay. That ticked me off. "If you're even thinking

about turning into mystery man again, you can forget it." I needed as much information as I could get right about now. If he couldn't be honest with me, then I didn't need him.

Of course I couldn't let it go. "And another thing," I said, pounding my way through a thick swash of fallen leaves. "I know you're not human. And you know what? I don't care. I don't. But if you're going to do a light show with your eyes and then practically fly through the woods with me, then you can drop the act, okay? It's not working." Lies, all lies.

I couldn't hear him behind me, which was creepy, but I knew he was there. Finally, he said, "It's complicated."

"Yeah, well so am I, buddy."

All things considered, I thought I was handling my new life pretty darn well. I may have had to put up with demons, imps and a crazy grandma, but I didn't have to put up with any b.s. from Dimitri. I tromped through the underbrush, kicking at it as I went. Maybe I'd sic Ant Eater on him.

*Just move.* And listen for the screams. Or barks. *Please be okay, Pirate.*

I had to find my way back, or this would all be for nothing. I forced my anger away, opened my mind. I had to start using some of the magic that had screwed up my life or I'd never be any use to anybody. I felt the cool breeze of the night on my face. My mind reached out in front of me like fingers through water. I could almost hear it. I shifted direction. This could be it.

*Calm down. Feel this. Let go.*

"Give it up, Lizzie."

Ignore him. *Feel.* I started to jog through the trees, their branches whipping against my arms and shoulders. My breathing fell into a steady rhythm. I saw the coven like a dot of light in my mind.

My feet dodged fallen tree limbs and roots. I didn't even need to look down anymore, I realized with a start. This felt right.

Dimitri might think he could keep me from Pirate, but there was one thing he hadn't counted on. I had an inner compass. I could sense it. I knew it like I knew my way home. Excitement, satisfaction, pure joy swelled inside of me. This is what I was meant to do.

"Stop!" Dimitri tore through the woods, hot on my heels.

No way.

*Hold on, little guy, here I come.*

So I didn't drink the protective potion. I made a mistake. Now I was about to make things right.

"Lizzie, no!" Dimitri yelled as I felt the earth give out beneath me.

I fell. It was like falling in a dream, until I hit the ground hard. My head rang with the impact. Pain shot through my ankle, my shoulder. I lay on the rocks and dirt for a moment. What happened? I stared up at the rock walls surrounding me, illuminated by the bright moon and stars above. I'd fallen into a crack in the earth. Grass and weeds clung to the top, about five feet up. I wiped the dirt from my forehead, tried to stand. "Crimeny!" Pain seared my ankle.

I could hear water trickling. I turned around and saw the entrance to a cave. I knew what this was, a cave fissure. It had been a passageway until part of the cave collapsed and formed a ravine of sorts. Thank you, Discovery Channel.

Dimitri appeared at the top of the hole. Oh goody.

"Make yourself useful and get me out of here."

"Don't move, Lizzie."

Yeah, right. I didn't have the luxury of slowing down. I tested my ankle. It hurt like heck, but I had to keep moving.

"Listen to me," he said, serious as death. "Look to your right. Turn slowly."

I didn't like that tone. I turned. The fissure ended about six or seven feet to my right, the rock forming a vee. And in that vee . . . Oh no. I saw movement. I squinted, my heart slamming in my throat. A big, black snake coiled in a nest of fallen leaves.

"Yaak!" I jerked back and it hissed, its white mouth illuminated in the moonlight. Cripes.

"Wait," Dimitri said. "Wait until it calms down."

That could take a while. I tried not to breathe too deeply.

"That's it," Dimitri said. "That's it. Now back away."

I gulped and took three steps back.

"Slow," Dimitri cautioned. "Easy. That's it. Easy. I'm lowering my shirt. Grab on to it and I'll pull you out."

I kept my eyes on the snake, its fangs jutting from its gaping mouth.

"That's it. Okay. Reach behind you."

My hand caught hold of the black T-shirt, still warm from his body.

The snake reared back, fangs out. Not good. "Fast! Fast! Fast!" I wound my fingers around the cotton of his shirt and scrambled up the rock wall, my injured ankle burning with the effort. Dimitri gripped my hand in his and pulled me to safety. I let him have his T-shirt back and stood there, catching my breath. Yikes. That was close.

Dimitri's gaze slammed into me. I'd ticked him off, or at least worried the snot out of him. Good.

I shook the dirt and leaves out of my hair. If I didn't know better, I'd think he enjoyed standing there shirtless. Of course he looked fabulous. His chest—well-muscled, but not overdone—gave him an air of understated sexiness. A swirl of black hair traced its way down his lower stomach and down toward his . . . oh my. I blame my overt interest at a time like this on either head trauma or years of reading Johanna Lindsey, probably both.

He saw me watching him and his lips quirked into a predatory grin. "We can do something about this attraction if you'd like."

"Yeah, let's make out. That'll solve everything." Besides, if he thought I wanted to touch him after what he'd pulled, he'd better think again.

I stared out at the trees surrounding us, trying to get my bearings. "I should have ducked into the cave," I said. Then I might not have needed him at all.

"Bad idea. There are bats in there." He pulled his shirt over his head. "Three of them have rabies. Guess which three you would have found?"

My ankle throbbed. I leaned against a tree for a second. I planted my hands on my knees and blew out a long breath. "Why?" I asked, not even expecting an answer anymore.

"Simple. You're a demon slayer. That means you're attracted to danger, problems, things that need to be fixed."

Oh, I had a problem all right. He was standing right in front of me.

"Think of it as a slayer skill," he said, "a very valuable one. You need to be able to sense evil. Your powers give you an understanding of the nature of whatever it is you need to face. Now, if you were trained properly, you would have been able to make your way back to the coven. And I would have let you go. But, sadly, you are untrained. Uneducated. Underdeveloped. When you tried to focus on finding your way back, instead you began sensing every potential danger and running right for it, with no distinction between the supernatural and a cottonmouth snake."

Boy, he sure knew how to make a girl feel good. "So you're saying my supernatural compass is broken?"

He considered the question. "Not broken. Untrained. Weak. Immature."

"Got it."

"Coarse. Unpolished."

"Zip it, Obi-Wan."

He raised a brow. "I can train you, strengthen your powers. With my help, you can use this ability to your advantage. So that you can sense evil, even before it closes in on you or those you care about."

Very tempting. I gritted my teeth. So if I'd known my magic from a hole in the ground, I might have even prevented whatever had happened tonight. Talk about a guilt trip.

Dimitri dangled one heck of a carrot. Maybe I would take him up on his offer to train me. But first I had to get back to the coven. Pirate was in trouble. I didn't need the powers of a demon slayer to know that. *Please don't do anything brave, doggy.* "Get me back there."

He cracked a smile. "Not until we're done here."

"Oh, we're done." He could play hide-and-seek in the woods all he wanted. I had more important things to do.

He was having none of it. "I'll tell you about Vald."

"Yes, you will. Later. Now we find my dog." He was stalling me. I knew it. I'd seen it at naptime at Happy Hands. I recognized the signs.

I planted my hands on my hips, wishing I had a clue which way to head. Which sparked an idea . . .

Dimitri needed me safe. I had no idea why he cared so much. At the moment, it didn't matter. That was my bargaining chip. And I'd use it on him like I used Goldfish crackers on my three-year-old preschoolers.

"Hey," I said, tugging at his black shirt, right above a bulging bicep. "If you don't take me back to the coven right now, I'm going to jump back in with the snake."

He seemed almost amused. "It left."

"What?" I reached out with my mind. Blast. He was right. Worse, I didn't even have a desire to jump into the hole, which meant even the rabid bats had wandered off. Just my luck.

I cleared my mind, focused my thoughts. I could feel danger to my left, fifty yards. I limped as fast as I could in that direction, hoping my ankle would loosen up. Or fall off.

His humor faded. "Where are you going?"

"Over here," I huffed, pain slicing through my foot. *Whatever I find, please don't let it be too horrible.* How far was I willing to go?

"What are you trying to pull?" Dimitri's voice betraying a hint of concern. "Okay. Hold it. Lizzie!"

But still, he let me hobble closer to . . . it. Arrogant jerk—why didn't he stop me? I didn't have time to be fighting everything in the woods. I struggled to see something, anything in the darkness ahead. It was no use. I couldn't see more than four or five feet in front of my face.

Still, I hurried as fast as my ankle would allow. I had no idea what I'd find. An angry bear? Axe murderer? Deer stampede? I supposed it didn't matter. Whatever it was, I headed right for it.

"Wait!" Dimitri blocked me. "Don't."

I lifted a brow.

He refused to back down.

"Take me back or I'm never speaking to you again." I practically spit venom myself. He looked as angry as I felt. "I don't even need to go in. You can go. But we need to head back now." I stared him down. "Do what I say or whatever it is you want from me, you won't get it. I promise you that."

He stood there, indignant.

"You wanna go again?" I asked. "I sense something nasty back behind that tree over there."

A muscle twitched in his neck. "Fine." He gripped my shoulders, too tightly. "I'll take you to the coven. But you're not going to like what you see."

# Chapter Eight

It looked like someone had detonated a bomb inside the Red Skull biker bar. Crimson smoke poured from the rickety two-story structure. I felt a wave of pain for the witches, for how scared they must have been when the coven had come under attack, for what they had undoubtedly lost.

I covered my mouth with my hand, as if I could somehow block the acrid sulfur burning down my throat with every breath. Dimitri squeezed my shoulder. It felt good to have him there. I wouldn't have wanted to be alone at that moment. The forest around the house had fallen silent—not a cricket dared to chirp. The air felt heavy, foreboding.

A strange vapor curled from the edges of the Employees Only door at the back. It hissed from every window frame and—I gasped—it billowed from the open window of Frieda's second-floor room. It was eerily similar to the mist I'd seen filtering out of the Yardsaver shed earlier tonight, when Grandma had communed with the demon Vald.

I checked out the storage shed and saw it had melted at the edges. A trail of charred grass and cooked asphalt led from the shed to the bar. My heart skipped a beat. "Holy Hoodoo."

Dimitri's shoulder brushed mine. "I wouldn't call it holy."

Pirate was nowhere in sight.

Every idiot demon slayer instinct I had ordered me—no, screamed at me—to race into the house and face whatever lurked inside. Dimitri had been right about one thing. I was enthralled with anything and everything that could snap my limbs or chop my head off.

As if he could sense my fear, Dimitri leaned closer. "Having second thoughts?" he asked, his voice edged with concern.

Um, yeah. I watched as shimmers of light danced in the upstairs windows. How about third, fourth and fifth thoughts? At least Dimitri was starting to treat me more like an ally than a ward to be protected.

Maybe I was getting through to him. I could use a partner right about now. A low moan sounded from somewhere inside the house, and I fought the urge to run far, far away. If I had this much trouble even looking at the house—imagine how Pirate must be feeling if he was still inside. *Hang on, little guy.*

Now that he wasn't trying to hold me back, Dimitri could turn out to be my ace in the hole. "Let's," I choked. Embarrassed, I cleared my throat to make it work right. "Let's circle around front to see if we can learn anything."

We ventured as far as the trees and shrubs would hide us. A violet haze enveloped the street out front. The precise line of bikes we'd seen on the way inside tonight lay scattered like matchbox toys. I took heart that about half were missing. At least some of the witches had gotten away. Dimitri's SUV lay on its side with the windows smashed in. It was impossible to know what hit it, but if I didn't know better, my first guess would have been Godzilla.

I didn't see the bike with the sidecar. I hoped Bob had made it out okay. I wished I knew whether Pirate had gone with him. One thing was certain. Grandma would not have left the bar with any of her coven members still inside. That meant two things. Number one, we had to check this place out whether we wanted to or not. And number two, I had a confession to make.

Dimitri stood beside me, dark and strong. This wasn't going to be easy. I blew out a breath and hoped I wasn't about to torpedo our fledgling truce. "I have to tell you," I said, practically wincing. "I was supposed to receive the coven's protection tonight, but it didn't happen."

Dimitri stiffened, anger pouring from him in waves. *Good going, Lizzie.*

"I thought they were smarter than this," he hissed. "If you were a member of our clan, we would have conducted a protection ceremony as the first order of business. They have no right to have a slayer in their ranks if they can't defend what's theirs."

*Theirs?* Hello, twenty-first century calling. Oh who was I kidding? I had bigger things to worry about. I'd set off his protection vibe. Big mistake. "It wasn't their fault," I said, thinking of the botched ceremony in the basement. "It was mine. When it came down to it, I just couldn't drink that nasty potion. Look, I'll explain it all later. The point is—"

"The point is we're closing in on a demon infestation and you don't have the proper knowledge, training or security." He loomed over me until I had to crane my neck to see his stormy expression. "You refused your own grandmother's protection. And now you've shunned my efforts to spirit you away from this hellhole until we pursue a *dog* that may or may not even be inside."

The way he said the word *dog* ticked me off. I opened

my mouth to tell him and winced as screeches echoed from the house, like metal rubbing glass.

"We gotta do this," I told him. I didn't know what was happening in there, but it wasn't good. The sooner we snuck in, the sooner we could run like heck.

He drew in a hard breath. "We'll go in there," he said, his gaze trickling through me, "if you accept my protection."

I didn't like the sound of that. Dimitri wanted something from me. He hadn't told me what, which in my mind meant it was probably something I didn't want to give. It made me nervous to think of him having power over me.

"No. Let's go." I was doing fine on my own, wasn't I? Eek. I didn't want to think about it.

"Lizzie," he prodded. "You know it's the right thing to do."

*Oh, I knew.* I sighed, torn between the urge to get this over with and the knowledge that he was right. I'd refused to drink the witches' protection potion. I didn't want to make the same mistake again. I clenched my jaw until it throbbed. Grandma said I shouldn't trust him. But I needed him. And without the protection of the witches, I was probably crazy to even think about being as close as we were to whatever lurked inside that house. There was bravery, there was independence . . . and then there was pure stupidity. I didn't need to go into this half-cocked. And if Dimitri could help me prepare, well, I had to accept that gift.

"Fine."

He tried to hide his pleasure, but I could tell he was as happy as if I'd told him he could keep me in a lockbox and throw away the key. I'd let him enjoy his little victory.

"For now," I added, wishing I could scrub the crooked smile off his face.

Warning bells sounded in the back of my mind. *He's too happy.* Of course those were the same warning bells that told me not to drink Grandma's protective potion. I buried my concerns. I had to, or we weren't going to get anything done here. "How long will it take?"

He reached into his pocket and withdrew a small, velvet pouch. He tipped it into his palm and out slid an emerald the size of a grape. I whistled despite myself. It was shaped like a teardrop and glowed from the inside out, like it had its own energy, which of course was impossible—like everything else that had happened.

"This is an ancient stone from the Helios clan. My clan. A proud and ancient order of griffins from the island Santorini. I will offer it," he said. "You will accept it."

No problem.

"And my protection."

He had to throw that in.

"With free will," Dimitri added.

Ah, so that was the key. Okay. I was willing. For now. "Let's get this over with," I told him, eyeing the blue and red orbs cascading from the bar's rooftop vents.

Dimitri held his hand under mine. His callous fingers sent a rough heat spiraling through my veins as he placed the gem in the center of my palm. It felt toasty, whether that was from his pocket or from something else. I felt its energy flow through me like a soft touch. "I offer you the protection of the Helios clan, freely given, freely taken."

A bronze-colored chain, as thin as a spider's thread, snaked from the tip of the teardrop. "Um," I began. The unexpected intimacy of the moment caught me off guard. I wasn't quite sure how to proceed.

"I accept." I paused for a heartbeat. "Freely," I added, fighting my reluctance.

It must have been good enough because the emerald glowed warm in my palm. My hand shook as the chain wrapped itself around my wrist. I resisted the urge to pull it away, to break the hair-thin band.

"Relax." Dimitri's touch reassured me as he pulled me farther into the cover of the woods. A breeze caressed my shoulders as I leaned back against the trunk of an old walnut tree. His emerald felt heavy on my wrist. It was strange, but I did feel closer to Dimitri, connected somehow. He narrowed the space between us. Was he going to seal the deal with a kiss? It occurred to me that I should keep my distance. He'd already bound me to him with the emerald. I didn't need any more complications, but I couldn't quite make myself walk away.

I should have been afraid of what would happen next. Instead, I found myself anticipating it. Dimitri was the kind of man who made women want to touch him. Too bad I wasn't immune. I knew Dimitri wasn't entirely human. And I wasn't sure I trusted him. But we did want a lot of the same things. And I had to admit he fascinated me.

Dimitri hitched one leg against the tree and drew a long bronze knife from a holster in his boot. The thing was ancient, with strange carvings and green gemstones wrapped around the hilt. The polished blade gleamed razor sharp. There'd better not be blood involved in this ceremony.

Dimitri ran his thumb along the blade of the knife. "Remember this favor, Lizzie."

Somehow, I didn't think he'd let me forget. Frieda was right. It seemed Dimitri's help did come with a price tag attached.

"Let's not forget you owe me too," I told him. If he hadn't kidnapped me, I would have been able to get

Pirate out on my own, before the house started smoking from every nook and cranny. I was about to get into that when I felt my wrist go disturbingly heavy.

"What the—?" I looked down. The wisp of a bracelet had thickened into a manacle. Of all the things I might have expected to happen tonight, I hadn't even dreamed of this.

Mother fudrucker!

I watched in horror as thick chains snaked from the cuff around my wrist. They slithered down my leg and captured my ankles. Fear slammed into me. "What is this?" I clutched at Dimitri. He stepped back, empty of emotion.

"What are you doing to me?" I cried. The chains wrapped around my waist and wrapped around the battered walnut tree. "Stop!" I struggled with everything I had, but the chains were relentless, twining around my body, trapping me like a fly in a spider's web.

That liar! Dimitri had betrayed me in the worst possibly way. My heart slammed in my chest. "What are you doing?" I demanded, my voice cracking with emotion.

Dimitri's gaze traveled the length of my body, sending a rush of hot anger through me. His mouth tugged into a smile, but there was no understanding or warmth. As he advanced on me like the predator he was, I struggled against the chains, dreaming what it would be like to slap the smile off his face. Dimitri leaned in close, his face inches from mine. He radiated heat and a raw power. "I'm doing what needs to be done."

His eyes burned with something that wasn't quite desire, although there was a lot of that too. He cradled my head in his hands. And curse my mutinous body, red-hot anticipation shot through me like wildfire.

"Don't even think about it," I told him, my voice not as steady as I would have liked.

"I'm protecting you," he said against my mouth.

He had to go there. As far as I could see, his protection was one of my main problems right now. "Yeah?" I thrust out my chin and ignored the heat spiraling through me. "Who's going to protect me from you?"

He pulled away, which was what I wanted. Still, it seemed like I'd missed out, which made me even angrier. I hated games.

Dimitri brushed my forehead with his lips, strong and confident. I felt his touch all the way down to my toes. Arrogant jerk. He seemed to enjoy taunting me. And I hated myself for buying into it. He'd be better off facing Vald than enduring one minute of what I'd do to that high-handed, good-for-nothing, two-faced brute. I never should have trusted him. Never. If I had to do it again, I'd take his teardrop emerald and shove it up his nose.

I struggled against the manacles at my feet. See, this is where trust got me. My whole life, I put my faith in people who paid me back with half-truths and downright lies. Now one of them had lashed me to a tree. He'd better hope he found Pirate, Grandma and the Hope Diamond in there. Maybe then, after a hundred years had passed, I'd consider speaking to him again.

I yanked at the chains. The teardrop emerald whipped against my wrist. Never. Never again.

Dimitri gave me a long, dark look before he headed into the house, alone.

He stayed inside the house too long, way too long. With every passing moment, it grew less and less likely I'd ever see him again. Blast it. I struggled until I felt like I'd run a marathon. The chains didn't budge. A trickle of sweat ran down my back. What if he didn't find Pirate? Or Grandma? What if he ran into a ticked-off Vald? He'd carried one ancient knife inside, and even though it was sharp as all get out, it didn't look very sturdy. What would I do out here, chained to a walnut tree, if Dimitri didn't come back?

Dawn approached, bathing the world in shades of gray. Still, not a bird chirped. Not one car drove down the road in front of the bar. It felt like we'd landed in purgatory. A drain pipe on the side of the house clattered as it began to shake.

Dimitri burst out the front door—*without Pirate*. His black T-shirt hung in bloody shreds, and he looked like he was running for his life. He leapt behind his overturned SUV as the house exploded. I would have given anything to duck. Windows shattered with the force. Smoke poured from the house as it sagged in on itself.

My chains coiled away from the tree. I lurched forward, catching my balance as they wound away from my ankles and up my legs. It was the worst feeling in the world, like something living had attached itself to me. But I had bigger things to worry about.

Dimitri bolted for the nearest motorcycle still standing, a silver Harley with red skulls painted on the side. "Get on!" he hollered to me. He slid onto the seat, rolled the throttle and hit the ignition. The engine roared to life. I ran straight for him, my oxfords crunching against glass and debris.

For a split second, I thought about grabbing my own bike and getting as far away from here as I could. But I didn't know how to ride. Worse, I had no idea where to go.

"Now!" he yelled.

The bike didn't even have helmets. Some protector. I caught a glimpse of a pink helmet, half buried under a collapsed bike. It was mine now. I grabbed it and nearly jumped out of my skin when I saw the chain

around my wrist had morphed into body armor that
stretched across my chest. Intricate carvings wound up
the armor, with the teardrop emerald centered above
my breasts.

Dimitri slammed his bike to a stop in front of me,
spitting rocks and dirt as I shoved the pink helmet on
my head and climbed behind him. I wanted to ask him
if he'd found any sign of Pirate, if he'd seen anything
else inside the house and if it was pure stupidity or a
death wish that had made him tie me up. Before I could
get a word out, he jumped on the gas. My back smacked
against the metal safety bar as we peeled out into the
dawn.

We drove for at least an hour on dusty, unpaved back
roads. Dimitri made sure to hit every pothole and anthill. I'd never realized what a smooth ride Grandma
delivered. I closed my eyes as we hit another
bone-rattling dip in the pavement. *Please be okay,
Grandma.* I didn't know where we were going, but
wherever it was, I hoped she'd be there. There were so
many things I needed to tell her.

Dimitri slowed in front of the first sign of civilization we came upon, an old broken-down Shoney's restaurant. Weeds crowded the parking lot, fighting for
space between the cracked concrete with its faded yellow lines. The Big Boy himself lurched to one side, in
bad need of a paint job and a can of Rust-Oleum. Dark-
ening shades draped the picture windows, their window boxes filled with faded plastic geraniums.

The bike swayed as we rounded our way to the back
parking lot. I could feel every muscle and tendon in
Dimitri's back as I gripped him tightly. The blood
on his T-shirt had dried, making the material crunchy.
The gashes on his back had already begun to heal.
Impossible, yes. But I'd been staring at the proof for

darned near an hour. Well, hadn't I known he wasn't quite human?

I eased away from Dimitri as the bike slowed. This place gave me the heebie-jeebies. A minicity of beaten-down trailers huddled at the edge of the lot. Near them stood a haphazard carport with a dozen bikes stashed inside. We pulled up to the end of the row.

As soon as Dimitri killed the engine, I poked him in the back. "Did you find any sign of Pirate?" If he saw my doggy in that awful house, if something *had* happened to Pirate, I needed to know.

"He wasn't in there," Dimitri said, shutting down the bike.

"Are you sure?" I asked. I had to know, because if I was going to hope . . .

"He's okay," he reassured me. "I looked everywhere." He took a deep breath. "I saw a lot of things, but no Pirate. And I didn't see your grandma either. Both of them must have made it out. I'll tell you more once we get inside. This is the safe house. It's run by some friends of mine. The Red Skulls were slated to meet here if something happened at the bar. Come on," he said, reaching for my hand. "Let's go on in."

I ditched his grasp and a flash of pain crossed his features. Well, tough. No way was I letting him near me.

Side-by-side, yet universes apart, we crunched through the gravel parking lot. My ankle throbbed and my legs felt woozy after that hour on the bike. In a lot of ways, stepping off a bike was like getting off a ride at an amusement park.

I tested the armor on my chest. Solid as steel and just as impossible to remove. I fought back a wave of claustrophobia. It was as if the bronze plates been welded onto me. "Mind telling me what you did to me?" I asked, almost angry I had to say anything to Dimitri at this point.

He walked beside me, his eyes straight ahead. "I gave you the gift of protection. Ancient magic, designed to defend you. Your *panos* will always be what you need it to be."

"Well, take it back. This is creeping me out." I didn't need body armor. *Please don't let me need body armor.* Lord, I couldn't do this. I didn't want this.

"It isn't my choice to make," he said, leading me to the front entrance.

"You are such a jack—" For the first time, I almost let something nasty slip. But then he opened the glass door and my mouth dropped open.

I hardly heard the tinkling of the bell as Dimitri ushered me inside. A woman leaned against the hostess's desk. She wore red button earrings and a matching bandana. Only it wasn't a woman. It was a werewolf.

# Chapter Nine

The werewolf's ears pricked as we entered the restaurant. She had a thick coat of streaky yellow hair and flashed claws that could tear your heart out. She growled, low in her throat.

I went on instant high alert. "Dimitri!" Some protector. He'd led me into the wolves' den.

"Steady." He placed a firm hand on my back. "She's just trying to scare you."

Yeah, well it was working. Never in a million years would I have expected to walk in on a werewolf, and at Shoney's, no less. This was supposed to be a family restaurant, one where people came to eat, not to be eaten.

The air around the werewolf shimmered and—cursed canines—she began to change. If I hadn't seen it with my own eyes, I wouldn't have believed it. Her body shifted and her hair receded until she was left with smooth tan skin, a sassy blonde pageboy haircut and cherry red fingernails to die for. Her body was sculpted, her breasts perky and she lounged against the hostess stand with the practice of a *Price Is Right* model. Unfricking-believable.

The formerly furry sex goddess dipped her chin toward Dimitri. "Hiya, babe. I knew I'd see you back here one way or another." From the way she said it, it was obvious these two had a history. And judging from how she undressed him with her baby blues, their relationship hadn't exactly been rated PG.

Lovely.

Dimitri ignored it, either oblivious or a good politician. "Andrea, this is Lizzie," he said. "Lizzie, this is my *friend* Andrea."

I didn't like how he said the word friend. Andrea didn't either. Her face twisted into the kind of snarl perceptible only to women. And I swear her fingernails grew half an inch.

*Don't worry, honey. I don't want him anyway.*

She sniffed at my borrowed clothes in disdain. "Nice pants."

Now I really wanted to be a demon slayer so I could fire some switch stars, or maybe a bolt of lightning, up her butt. As it stood, I simply nodded to the bitch (the word bitch being a technical term for her condition, of course).

The hostess area stood apart from the main restaurant by a wall of paneling that might have looked classy if it hadn't been cheap, faded and strewn with used ticky tack. An ancient M&M candy machine didn't quite camouflage the splintered hole behind it. The rest of the area was bare except for two bodyguards, who stood directly behind Andrea. They stared at me, heavy-lidded and suspicious. As if they had anything to fear from the non-demon-slaying demon slayer. They could rip my arms off without breaking a sweat.

Behind the wall, I could hear the murmur of conversation and the clinking of silverware. Sausage, potatoes, and eggs should have smelled heavenly, but after the night I'd had, the mere thought of food made my stomach sour.

"Don't tell me you're going out with this pop tart,"

Andrea sniggered, proving beyond a doubt she was no lady herself. "She wouldn't know what to do with a man like you."

*Oh puh-leeze.*

"Watch yourself, Andrea," Dimitri warned.

"Don't worry. I'd pick this one to be all bark, no bite," I commented, just to taunt her. Yes, it was shallow, but she deserved it. "Now are we done playing *Melrose Place*? Where is everyone?"

Andrea scowled at me. She hitched her head back and called to whoever was behind the paneling. "We got two more!"

A cascade of voices and a smattering of applause greeted her announcement. Frankly, I didn't know what we had to cheer about. The coven's hideout was destroyed, some of the witches were missing and a fifth-level demon could be popping by at any moment.

Pirate skittered around the corner and suddenly, nothing else mattered. *Thank you. Thank God he got out of there.* That moment was worth every second out there in those dark woods. I rushed to my doggy, scooped him up and hugged him tight. "How are you doing?" I asked, stroking him, inspecting his back, his paws, his tail, everything. His paws were black with mud and— phew—he could use a bath, but otherwise he seemed to be all right. "You okay?"

He licked my arms, my elbows, everywhere he could reach. "Damn, Lizzie. Don't you ever scare me like that again. I mean I was scared. I was more scared than when you went to Florida and left me at that doggy day spa with the shaking pet pillows."

I buried my nose in his hair, so glad to see my little dog. Someone had even made sure he had fresh bandages for his back.

"Aye-eee!" I heard Frieda approaching before I ever saw her. I could smell her too—cigarettes with a hint of cinnamon gum.

She hugged me from behind. "You disappear again and I'm going to kick your butt into next Sunday." She emphasized her threat with a pop of her gum. "So now," she said, chewing as she talked, "you feeling all right?"

I nodded. Talk about a loaded question. I couldn't go home, the coven was destroyed. I had no idea what to do with my utterly cool yet completely frightening demon slayer mojo and now I'd given Dimitri enough power over me to make me very, very uncomfortable. "Where's Grandma?" I asked. I couldn't wait to see her. She'd tell me what to do.

Frieda locked her elbow in mine. "Well, I'll say one thing. It was a hell of a fight. Come on back to the dining room and we'll tell you all about it."

We followed Frieda around the divider and into the main restaurant. Immediately, I could see there were two different groups of people occupying the space. The werewolves dominated the center of the dining room and had set up the Rootin' Tootin' Breakfast Buffet. At least that's what the sign declared in big block letters. That morning, they'd opted to stick with the basics— sausage links, breakfast potatoes and scrambled eggs. A pimply teenager nodded at me as we passed. His gangly arms led down to massive, hairy wolf claws. Built-in pot holders, it seemed as he clutched a steaming platter of undercooked bacon.

Pirate wriggled in my arms. "Oh lookie there. Bacon! I couldn't eat any before. I didn't have any appetite before, but now I think I'm over it."

I stroked the wiry fur on his head. "Later, Pirate. Right now, we have to find Grandma."

"Oh now, Lizzie," he began reluctantly. "She never liked me much and besides I don't think you need to be hearing about the deal them witches made with those werewolves. You won't be in the mood for no bacon after that."

*Deal? What deal?*

"Pirate," Frieda growled.

"All I'm saying is if Lizzie's the one who's got to schlep everywhere, getting rid of those black souls for a bunch of smelly werewolves, then she should at least get some breakfast first."

*Black souls?* Pirate was right. My stomach had begun churning enough at that point to make breakfast impossible. I glanced back at Dimitri, hoping this deal wasn't another one of his tricks. From the murder in his eyes, I guessed not.

"Frieda, care to enlighten me?" I was suddenly feeling quite murderous myself.

Frieda cast a worried glance over her shoulder. "Come on back, honey. I think Ant Eater would like to have a word with you."

"Oh, well if Ant Eater is behind it, I'm sure I'll love it." The last time I'd seen Ant Eater, she'd been holding me by the throat. It made sense she'd want to throw me to the werewolves. Grandma would straighten this out. She had to. It worried me that I hadn't seen her yet. *Don't get ahead of yourself, Lizzie.*

As we weaved through the tables, I could feel the eyes of the werewolves on us. One in particular struck me hard. He stood with his back to the wall and a rifle on his shoulder. I did a double take. He was built lean and menacing, like a bad-boy drummer in a rock band. Tattoos wound up his arms and neck, past the blond hair that hung in over-stylized hunks almost all the way down to his shoulders. The only thing that gave away his species was the way he sniffed the air. That and he seemed more than comfortable in the middle of a Shoney's full of werewolves.

Dimitri, walking behind me, touched me on the arm, his fingertips almost brushing the edge of the armor that curved around my side. "That's Rex," he said, giving me a light squeeze. "Stay away from him."

I could feel Rex's eyes on us. He reminded me of a predator, watching, waiting to discover a weakness. I glanced back and picked up the pace when I saw his fierce smirk. He looked like he'd won the lottery.

The werewolves were the only ones eating. The witches stuck to the booths along the right wall, injured and shell-shocked. Sidecar Bob had set up a haphazard triage station on a few tables he'd pushed together at the end of the row of booths, out of sight yet close enough. It didn't look like anyone was in the mood to venture far.

Frieda led me to the last booth, the one closest to the restrooms. Dimitri walked behind me, as if I wanted him around after what he'd pulled. Maybe Ant Eater would do me a favor and pound him into next Tuesday.

"What happened back there, Frieda? It was Vald, wasn't it?"

She wrapped a comforting arm around my shoulder. "Oh honey, let's hold off for now, okay?"

Hold off? What could possibly be more important? "Do you think he'll try to follow us here?" I asked. "And where is here?"

Frieda shook her head as we passed two booths of witches. I saw the tall, red-haired one, Scarlet. But no Grandma. "Come on now, hon."

"Actually, Vald could have followed us quite easily," Dimitri said, making sure any of the witches we passed could hear him. Nice, considering these people were probably scared out of their wits as it was.

Dimitri didn't seem to care. "Nowhere is safe," he said, anger and accusation seeping into his voice. "That's why you need to be trained. And protected."

"Okay, Mr. Agenda. Point taken." I didn't care if he was mad. I touched the bronze armor molded to my chest. Dimitri had gotten what he wanted.

Ant Eater wore the expression of a soldier who had just returned from battle. Her eyes were hollow, her features taut. She pounded a skinny red coffee stirrer against the restaurant table with the *rat, tat, tat* of a machine gun. Green soot dusted her curly gray hair.

I slid into the booth across from her, wanting her to speak, but wary all the same. I knew it would be bad news.

And I was right.

"Your grandma has been taken," she said with about as much emotion as if she were telling me my car was wrecked or my condo needed a new air-conditioning system. It seemed Ant Eater was nothing if not practical.

I knew Grandma wouldn't have left the coven until every last witch made it out, but it hurt to hear she hadn't escaped. "What do you mean *taken*? By who? And why aren't you trying to get her back?" Grandma had been a member of the Red Skulls for decades. These people were her family. What were they doing sitting around Shoney's?

Ant Eater slammed her hand on the table and the coffee stirrer went flying. "Don't you even start on me, hotshot. You're the reason we lost her."

I willed myself to stay calm. "Pirate, why don't you go see if Sidecar Bob needs any help."

"Oh, but Lizzie, I missed you." His large, black eyes pleaded with me. "And now I have you and you're right here and I don't want to leave you."

"Pirate." I hated to be stern with him, and I wanted

nothing more than to hold my doggy tight, but I had a feeling this was about to get ugly. Reluctantly, Pirate obeyed.

I squared my shoulders and faced Ant Eater. From her accusation, you would have thought I'd trussed up my grandmother myself. No getting around it, though. *I was supposed to be there.* A wave of guilt crashed over me. They'd offered me their protection because they knew this was coming. I'd let them down. If I'd found a way to stay, I might have been able to prevent this. "I had no idea . . ." I began.

"Save it," she snapped. "Vald approached like a stale wind from the north. We're Southern witches. It's harder for us to detect a northern presence. But your Grandma Gertie, she knew. By the time she found us, every one of us was facedown in our possum stew." She planted her elbows on the booth table between us. "See, demons like Vald aren't all fire and brimstone. They're sneaky. Sure they enjoy the stark terror on your face before they steal your soul, but they'd just as soon swipe it from you when you're not looking."

Incredible. "Is that what he wanted? Your souls?"

"If he'd cared enough, he'd have had 'em." She paused, no doubt enjoying the stark terror on my face. "No." She shook her head. "He wanted you."

"Me?" I practically stammered. I didn't know anything. Even if I was supposed to be some almighty demon slayer.

"Don't play stupid." She banged her hand on the table and sent the salt and pepper shakers flying. "Vald is stronger than we thought. Our protection spell—that potion you drank—should have bound us all together. We would have known he was coming for you. You would have felt it too. We should have been able to beat him off, or at least stall him enough to escape. I don't know what happened," she said, eyeing me accusingly.

Oh no. Dread swelled inside of me. It was my fault. Grandma had shown me nothing but respect and honesty since I'd met her, and this is how I paid her back. If it weren't for me, she'd be at the Red Skull bar with her friends, doing what she'd been doing for the last fifty years. Instead, I'd hopped on her bike and screwed up her life worse than she could have ever done to mine. And it happened because I was a coward, because I couldn't accept her or her potion. I was the worst kind of hypocrite, and I really hated that. "I didn't mean . . ."

Ant Eater yanked a sawed-off shotgun from the seat behind her and leveled it at me. I lost my breath as I gaped down the enormous barrels of the gun. She jabbed it forward, and it nudged my left breast. A chill seeped from the cold metal and crept right through me.

"You fucked up," she said, low and deadly.

Off to my left, I heard Dimitri cock a gun. I stole a glance. He aimed a pistol at Ant Eater's head. The restaurant had gone silent as a graveyard. She'd shoot me. I knew she would.

"You aren't fit to be family," she said. "I'd like nothing better than to put a cap in your ass right now."

Frieda slipped into the booth next to me, shaking. That made two of us. "Put the gun down," she ordered, her voice steadier than her body. "You know Lizzie is the one person who can save Gertie. I don't care what you think about Lizzie. Shoot her now and you'll never see Gertie again."

Tears welled in Ant Eater's eyes. She gritted her teeth, her gold cap gleaming with spittle.

In one fluid motion, she launched herself out of the booth and stormed for the bathrooms. The ladies' door slammed behind her and every one of us breathed a sigh of relief.

"Oh, Frieda," I said, wanting to hug her. Every bone

in my body had turned to mush. "Thank you." I really hadn't wanted to test that armor.

She slid into the seat across from mine, more serious than I'd ever seen her. "Save it for someone who gives a damn. I wasn't kidding when I said you were the only one who can help your grandma. I hoped Ant Eater would be able to put it a little better, but the truth is Vald has Gertie. He's taken her back with him—to hell."

Frieda raised an eyebrow as my jaw fell open. "Oh yes, buttercup. Hell is real. And there is no escaping without a slayer. You."

I blanched. No way was I ready for this. I didn't think I'd ever be ready.

Frieda didn't seem to care. "Now Vald hasn't been able to get Gertie all the way into the second layer of hell. She's weak, but she's fighting like a double blast of dynamite. She's clinging to the first layer," she said, battling tears. "No question about it, your grandma is a fighter. But she can't hold out forever. No one can."

Tears burned the back of my eyes. Poor Grandma! I felt so helpless. She was suffering horribly and it was my fault and I didn't know how we were going to get her out of there. And to twist the knife further, I still couldn't understand why she ended up there in the first place. "What does that demon want if he doesn't want her soul?" I asked, trying to hitch my voice above a whisper.

"He wants you to go after her. And you can! You can defeat him, Lizzie. You have the power. You just need to learn how to use it."

Frieda burst into tears. There was something she wasn't telling me. And if it was even more mortifying than Grandma being tortured in hell, I couldn't imagine what it could be. "We need you trained yesterday. You're the only one who can enter the second layer of hell and defeat Vald."

"Me?" Holy Hades. "Grandma was supposed to be the one to teach me," I said, rapidly losing all hope. "Who else is there?" *Please don't let it be Ant Eater.* She'd shoot me in the kneecaps every time I made a mistake. And I knew I'd make plenty.

Frieda took a deep breath, not liking her answer any more than I probably would. "That's the thing. No one else is qualified to train you. Except him."

We both cast a glance at Dimitri. He towered over the booth, his arms crossed over his chest. "I said I'd do it. Lizzie is safe in my hands. As long as we do it my way." He shifted his stance. "Now what is this I hear about Lizzie working for the werewolves?"

Oh no. This was no time to bargain. I couldn't help resenting him for trying to be practical at a time like this.

Frieda frowned, clearly uncomfortable in her role as the coven spokesperson. "We worked out a deal with the werewolves in exchange for their help this morning. Think of it as a training run, Lizzie. It'll be good practice for you."

I nodded, my head bobbing while my brain spun furiously. I had to train to be a demon slayer and work a job for a mercenary group of werewolves, all the while my grandmother fought Vald as he tried to suck her into the second layer of hell. Oh geez. I couldn't do this. I'd never had this much responsibility in my life, not to mention this many people counting on me.

I had to ask the question burning the back of my brain. Maybe if I asked it out loud, it wouldn't be as scary.

"What if I screw up?"

Frieda eyed me, as serious as death. "You can't, Lizzie. You just can't."

I was afraid of that.

# Chapter Ten

I jogged after my new trainer—the only man who could help me save Grandma—as his boots crunched across the parking lot. One hushed conversation with the red-headed witch and instead of training me, Dimitri made a beeline for the bike we rode in on.

"Where in Narnia do you think you're going?"

He slammed to a halt, and I nearly ran into the back of him. "Back to hell," he growled. "Or at least as close as we've got to it around here."

What had Scarlet said to get him riled up like this? I didn't know and, frankly, I didn't care. Well boo frickin' hoo. "You're not going anywhere."

"You don't own me, Lizzie." He stalked toward the bike, yanking on his black leather gloves. "Besides, we're not going to get too much training done without your switch stars. They're back in my wreck of an SUV, along with something else I have to retrieve." His eyes bored into mine. "Now."

"Don't you give me that," I said, keeping pace with him. If anyone had a right to be annoyed, it was me. Everyone was counting on me, on us. "You're a selfish jerk, you know that?" A muscle in his jaw twitched. "Um-hum. And you know what? That's fine. When you're finished training me, you can build a tent and camp out there for all I care. But right now, your job is to help me get Grandma back. So get your buns back here and teach me, damn it."

He appeared to think about it for a nanosecond. "No," he said, checking the knife at his hip. And the knife in his boot. And the dagger in his back pocket. Holy Hades.

"Dimitri!" We didn't have time for this. Grandma was in the first layer of hell—and sinking. Ant Eater lent me out to the werewolves on what sounded suspiciously like a demon hit job and now Dimitri—my protector, my trainer—was about to ride off.

"This Harley's not leaving until I say so." I dashed around him and climbed up on the bike, my tiger-striped pants catching on the leather seat, my feet not quite reaching the running boards.

Yeah, yeah, he could have lifted me off like an afterthought. But I had a feeling he was a closet gentleman. Or at least not the type of guy to toss me Jerry Springer style off the bike.

I was right.

"You don't get it, princess." He glowered at me. "This isn't about us."

"Then what's it about?" This was not the time for Dimitri to be holding out on me. Again.

"Look," he snapped. "We had a deal, remember? I train you. You do as I say."

In his dreams. "Our deal is simple. You train me. Now."

He dug a hand through his thick dark hair. "Fine," he said. "I'll get you started. But then I'm out of here." He brought up a finger. "Now, listen. If you want to help your grandma, you need to master the Three Truths." He counted them off on his fingers like he was the preschool teacher. "Look to the outside. Accept the universe. Sacrifice yourself."

Oh, help me Rhonda. I knew this drill. Give the demon slayer a bunch of busywork while Grandma suffered and he raided the Red Skull for some hoo-ha bit of dangerous magic Ant Eater probably had brewing in the men's toilet.

"I'm not trying to pull anything over on you," he said, the corner of his mouth twisting into a wry smile. "Trust me."

"Like I did right before you chained me to a tree?"

"Hey," he barked. "I was out of options." His eyes softened and he gripped my wrist, sliding his thumb over the sensitive skin underneath. He leaned close enough to kiss. "Besides, it wasn't all bad, was it?"

He'd held me against that tree and done delicious things. I fought back a blush just thinking about it.

"In your dreams." Dang, he was 100 percent male and he was going to be a pain in my rump if I didn't watch it. For some girls, it would be the ultimate fantasy to receive a huge, honking emerald from a man like Dimitri. But I knew all too well about the strings attached.

I'd felt his kiss right down to my toes. Right before he chained me to a walnut tree.

Well he wasn't going to schnooker me this time. I ducked out of his embrace. "You are not getting on this bike."

He threw one leg over the Harley and slid in front of me before I knew it. He tossed a wicked grin over his shoulder before he slowly, intentionally used his firm backside to nudge me into the passenger's seat. I could feel the heat rolling off him. He held me there, against the back bar of the bike, the stitching of his Levi's practically burning a brand into my leather pants.

Sweet switch stars.

"Are you two done?" asked Scarlet. I felt the color rise to my cheeks. I hadn't even seen her walk up. "We don't have much time before there's nothing left to save." She frowned. "And Lizzie, you need to go get your dog."

Pirate had the worst timing. "What's he doing?" I fought back visions of a ruined Rootin' Tootin' Breakfast Bar.

She looked at me like I'd sprouted wings. "How should I know? Frieda took him to the trailer where you'll be staying."

New visions of a trailer full of shredded toilet paper. "Did he eat first?" Pirate liked to shred things when he was hungry, or bored, or excited or really whenever he felt like it.

"I don't even want to know what you're talking about," she said. "Just get over there. Your roommate can't stand dogs."

Roommate? Well, it made sense. The werewolves did have to take in a whole coven. "I would have thought a werewolf would like dogs, you know, due to the whole species thing."

Dimitri blanched.

Scarlet rushed to explain. "We'd never put you with a werewolf. Do yourself a favor right now, Lizzie, and don't trust a single one of them. Especially Rex. He's gunning for the alpha slot and you do not want to be within ten miles when that happens." She glanced at Dimitri. "Hopefully, we'll be out of here before the shit hits the fan. Just remember, coven stays with coven. You're in the second trailer behind the Dumpster. You can't miss Ant Eater's bra rack out front."

"What?" It was my turn to blanch. "You put me with that crazy woman?"

She seemed unaffected by my naked distress. "Ant Eater is in charge now, and that's the way she ordered it."

"She pulled a gun on me in a crowded restaurant!

What's she going to do when we're alone? No. I won't do it." Come on. Dimitri had to back me on this.

Scarlet shook her head. "It's a done deal, Lizzie. Do what Gertie would have done," she suggested. "Buck up."

"Oh, no you don't. Don't start preaching my grandma back to me." If she thought for a minute she'd sway me with a low-down, dirty tactic like that, she was crazier than Ant Eater.

"Consider it your first test," Dimitri said, eerily confident in my questionable abilities.

He ran a familiar hand down my leg as I climbed off the bike. He only got away with it because I was in shock. Then he settled on a meaningless demon slayer Truth that wouldn't help me rescue Grandma and certainly wouldn't do me any good now. "Accept the universe, Lizzie."

"Oh yeah. That's exactly what I wanted to hear."

He fired up the engine and peeled off down the road.

"What am I supposed to do with that?" I asked Scarlet as she buckled her helmet. She shrugged, gunned her engine and took off after him.

I couldn't believe it. Dimitri insisted he was my protector, demanded to train me and as soon as I actually wanted him around, he took off.

As for his demon slayer Truths, he might as well have handed me a cross-stitched doily with *Don't worry. Be happy!* for all the good three lousy sayings would do me right now. I'd never save Grandma with him as my mentor. Heck, I might not even survive ten minutes in a trailer with Ant Eater. *Accept the universe.*

"Screw the universe." I needed some switch stars.

Dimitri had better get back quick because there was no way I would wait a second longer to start training and no way I'd live long anyway in a rusted-out trailer with Ant Eater. Clouds rolled across the sky and the air felt like it was going to rain any minute. I stomped over tufts of weeds and various other lawn junk as I zeroed in on the trailer with a front porch full of bras. No telling why Ant Eater had fled with her motorcycle bags full of bras rather than her über-rare herbs. No telling why Ant Eater did anything.

The magical do-it-all breastplate began to hum. Even Dimitri's emerald knew I was in trouble. I kicked an empty Budweiser can across the field. "Frickin' Dimitri and his two-ton emerald. If I could do it again, I'd tell him to stick it in his ear." The metal warmed against my skin. I held my breath. It was doing it again.

The hum turned into a steady vibration. Creepy, creepy, creepy. *Think of something else.* Yeah, right.

I stood motionless as the bronze metal slid over my skin, reforming into—what? I cringed to think what I needed now. I closed my eyes and wished for a full suit of medieval armor. That could come in handy against Ant Eater.

Alas, my mystic emerald had a mind of its own and I soon found myself the proud owner of a metal helmet that refused to come off. Goody. I couldn't keep my hands off my head as I walked the rest of the way to the trailer. It felt like a baseball cap without the brim. It wasn't uncomfortable, just unnerving.

Ant Eater better not try to whack me in the grape with a baseball bat. My fingers probed the intricate designs of the helmet and skittered over the teardrop emerald embedded front and center.

"Okay, stop fiddling with the hat and face the music," I told myself as I stood in front of the trailer I was going to share with Ant Eater.

The wood of the front porch had cracked and grayed with age. The entire thing rocked slightly as I hoisted myself up the stairs. Along with Ant Eater's enormous red bras, as well as a leopard-print teddy I refused to

think about, the porch sagged under the weight of a
rusted washtub full of discarded beer cans, the front
bumper of a car and too many petrified hand towels to
even count.

I paused, blew out a breath as I contemplated the holes
in the front screened door. Shotgun blasts? No question about it, this was the worst roommate situation I'd
ever faced. Ant Eater scared the beeswax out of me.
Part of it was the fact she'd tackle you first and ask
questions later. But most of it stemmed from the sheer
rage I'd seen in her eyes this morning. We'd have to
find a way to make peace or it would be a lot harder to
help Grandma.

I smoothed a few stray hairs out of my eyes and
pulled them behind my ears. Well, she hadn't thrown
me off the front porch yet. I supposed that was something to celebrate. The sun peeked out from the clouds
and I caught a glitter out of the corner of my eye. Tiny
rhinestones clung to each red bra, forming little skulls
at the center of each cup. I swallowed hard and opened
the front door.

"Lizzie!" Pirate popped up from where he'd been
curled up, watching the front door. "Am I glad to see
you. I've been dying for some company and this lady is
no company at all." Pirate's collar jingled as he skittered toward me. I scooped him up in my arms, revel-
ing in his warm little body.

Ant Eater tossed me an acidic glare and went back
to stacking glass jars in a small pyramid next to a beat-
up brown couch. She'd tied a black leather skullcap
over her short silver curls. Chocolate brown furniture
cluttered the narrow front room. Ant Eater had shoved
most of it toward the back hallway in order to make
room for stacks and stacks of pickle jars. Roadkill
magic. Well, I'd seen Grandma's jars. They shouldn't

surprise me by now. Except—my heart hiccupped—the goo in Ant Eater's jars seemed to be alive.

"Hi there," I said to her. I was not going to let this woman intimidate me. I picked my way across a yellow-brown rug that probably hadn't started off that color. Lamps decorated with belching frogs topped white plastic end tables. Somehow, I'd expected these mercenary werewolves to live better. Perhaps this was simply an outpost where they stashed fugitives like us. I shuddered to think what kind of mission they had in store for me.

She hunkered over the jars, her wallet chain swinging from her back pocket. "Go to your room. It's in the back. And stay the hell away from me."

My stomach clenched. If there was one thing I couldn't stand, it was bullies. And she was one of the worst I'd ever met. I had to stand up for myself now, or she'd only get worse. "No," I said, a little more breathless than I'd intended. "Let's get one thing straight. You are not going to treat me that way."

She paused, her back to me. And that was another thing. The woman had to have at least two dozen jars stacked along the walls. How had she fled the coven with all of them? Perhaps Ant Eater had more notice of the attack than she'd let on. The thought made me very, very uncomfortable.

Slowly, deliberately she reached for a jar with—ohmygosh—a preserved human ear inside. I braced myself, ready to duck if she tried to throw it at me.

She held it up, her wide face flushed with anger. "Know what this is? This came from another smart-ass." Her bushy brows plummeted downward as she sneered. "I warned him. Said if he touched my motorcycle again, I'd bite his ear off and keep it in a pickle jar." The distended ear bobbed in the grayish liquid.

Ant Eater seemed to relish the fear tingling up my spine.

A nudge at my leg nearly sent me jumping out of my skin. But it was only Pirate. He danced in place on his two front paws. "Now I think this might be one of those situations where we let the old lady have her way," Pirate said. He turned tail and hurried back through the trailer. "I'm all for fighting and all," he called from somewhere down the hall, "but that is just wrong. Ohh, water bed!"

I wanted to follow him. I really did. There was no reason to provoke a crazy bully who would like nothing better than to whack me in two with the samurai sword in the corner, or the very large machete under the coffee table or the—geez, there had to be at least twenty shotguns stacked in there. Not to mention the pistols lining the counter by the sink.

"Yeah, that's right, Lizzie," she said, daring me to push it. "Back away."

I wanted to. But, "No."

"What?" she spat.

I could feel my blood pounding in my skull, but this was no time to roll over. "If you want to share a trailer with me, there's no reason why I can't sit here on the couch and read a magazine." I eased onto the squishy sofa and practically sank down to the floor. The thing was worse than a beanbag chair. And there were no magazines. Fine. I'd relax and contemplate the Three Truths of the demon slayer. *Look to the outside. Accept the universe. Sacrifice yourself.*

*Sacrifice myself? Please don't let it be today.*

Ant Eater charged me and slammed the couch over backward. Pain exploded in my head as it smacked against the linoleum floor. "You're the only one who can kill Vald, and you want to read a magazine?" She stood over me, fuming. "You worthless sugar-tit! You can't even spit, and you're the one who has to save Gertie. Time to feel some pain, princess. You'd better get used to it."

She seized the toad lamp and yanked the cord from the wall. I scurried past the breakfast bar into the arsenal of a kitchen as the lamp crashed into the mugs above me and sent a whole rickety shelf tumbling down. The rack pounded into me and the cups sliced at my back as they shattered. I reached for one of the guns. My fingers touched the cool metal, and I stopped. I didn't need to make this worse.

There had to be another way.

*Look to the outside.*

What outside? Outside myself? Okay. I'd stop worrying about myself and focus on the problem. Every red jowled, overblown, lethal inch of her.

I faced the crazy woman. Rage boiled in her eyes. "Stop!" I ordered. "Let's talk—" She reached under the coffee table, grabbed the machete.

"Yeeee!" Pirate launched himself at her ankle.

Oh my word. Where had he come from? "Pirate, no!" He chomped his teeth into her leather chaps.

"Son of a bitch!" She whipped her leg around and launched him into the hallway.

"Pirate!" *Please don't be hurt!*

Ant Eater hurled the machete at my head. I hit the floor as the heavy blade shattered the kitchen window behind me.

This time, I did grab a gun, a Glock. It was like the one Cliff and Hillary kept in their bedroom in case burglars invaded the minimansion. I double, triple checked to make sure the safety was on and shoved the hulking pistol under the waistband of my too-tight leather pants. Pirate and I had to get out of here. But to do that, we'd have to get past Ant Eater.

Sarsaparilla!

I'd have to take her down.

"Pirate, you stay put!" I called to him, but when I stuck my head around the corner of the breakfast bar, I saw him crumpled in the dirty hallway. "Baby dog!"

Rage boiled inside me. She could hate me all she wanted, but if she hurt Pirate, I'd never forgive her. "You bitch!"

She snarled like the predator she was.

And holy Hades. A dark *thing* hovered over Pirate. A cloud of jagged black creatures—more than I could begin to count—swarmed, writhed to form a single, horrible monster. How dare she cast a spell on an innocent animal?

I glared at Ant Eater. "What kind of sick, twisted freak are you?" I had to get Pirate out of here.

My eyes flew to the samurai sword by the door. She saw where I was going and raced me for it.

She beat me.

I slid the last few feet like a ball player sliding into home and spiked her ankle with my oxford. She let out a howl of pain, but held tight to the sword. She ripped it from its sheath and drove the razor-sharp blade down on me. It clanged against my helmet and ricocheted to the floor. Panic screamed through me. I scrambled backward, into the corner between the front door and the breakfast bar.

My back knocked against stacks and stacks of pickle jars. I grabbed the nearest one and threw it at her head. It smacked her in the chest with a dull thud.

"Get your hands off those!"

"Drop the sword!"

Her face twisted in hate and she charged right for me, sword raised. My hand dove for a red swirling jar at the bottom of the stack. I had to have that one. I aimed it straight for her sneering nose. It exploded at her feet with a deafening crash. Red smoke shot through the room, suffocating every surface. Ant Eater dropped the sword. It clattered to the floor as she fell to her knees, her hands clutching her throat.

I ran past her and found Pirate. He lay on his side, half curled in a ball. I pushed through the hot, stinging magic. It bit like a thousand fire ants, but I didn't care. Pirate was alive. Relief poured through me. Blood oozed from the back of his head, and he was wheezing as bad as Ant Eater. I gathered him up in my arms and hurried him outside while I could still see the light from the doorway.

A crowd of witches and werewolves had gathered in the yard. They stood in shocked silence as I lowered Pirate to the ground outside the trailer. His breathing had grown even more labored. I didn't know what to do.

# Chapter Eleven

"Ant Eater?" Frieda called as she struggled across the lumpy yard in three-inch heels, watching in horror as smoke poured from our trailer. "What'd you do to her, Lizzie?"

*To her?* "I don't know. She's back in the trailer. Something's wrong with Pirate."

Betty Two Sticks lumbered up, her Woody Allen glasses fogging with the wet heat escaping from the trailer. *Heat?* "I think she threw a death spell," she told Frieda.

"What'd the jar look like?" Frieda demanded.

"How'd you know—" I hadn't said anything about a jar.

"We don't have time! What'd it look like?"

"Red," I said. "Swirly. A pickle jar with a gold lid." I'd wanted that one. I knew I had to throw it. I took a deep breath. My go-for-the-most-dangerous demon slayer mojo had gotten us in some serious trouble this time.

"Anaconda spell." Frieda's voice dripped with fear and contempt.

"How'd she beat it?" Betty challenged, pointing at me.

"Don't matter," Frieda said, trying to yank me away from my dog. "You gotta go back in there."

Pirate had curled on his back, fighting for every breath. I never should have brought him here.

"Listen to me!" Frieda demanded. "You let loose one of the death spells. You're going to kill Ant Eater and your little dog, if you don't reverse this now. Find the white jar. Betty, you get the matches. Go!"

I dashed back inside. The air felt wet with smoke. It reminded me of the way Hillary used to make me steam my pores. But it wasn't hard to breathe. If anything, it was easier. Seeing was another matter. I stumbled over Ant Eater's body. I found her arms and struggled to drag her out of the trailer. I had her head onto the front porch when Frieda started screaming again. "Get the jar. Now!"

A cloud of red smoke churned inside the trailer. I couldn't see a foot in front of my face. I felt my way along the wall next to the door, nudging the floorboards with my feet until I knocked up against a pyramid of jars. I grabbed as many as I could carry and headed for the front porch. I lined them up on the weathered gray wood. Two blues, a pink and the ear jar. No good.

Ant Eater's fingertips had turned blue. Her face wedged against the open screened door.

I ducked back inside. On the fourth trip, I found the white jar. While the contents of the other jars swirled and smoked, I could have mistaken this one for a jar of white paint. But then I noticed the tiny bubbles, like soda fizzies.

Frieda grabbed it from me. "You can't look at it too long." She'd pulled off her hair scarf and used it to shield her face from the smoke pouring from the front door.

We left Ant Eater on the front porch, half in and half out of the trailer. By this time, the crowd had swelled to a throng as every witch and werewolf within ten miles gathered to see what Frieda would do next.

Frieda dumped the white liquid out near the front

steps of the trailer. "Let death be broken. Let life surmount."

Her face took on a look of panic. She turned back to Betty and me. "Shit. We don't have a death. We need a death. Betty?"

"I'll get the roadkill."

"No, wait." I had a better idea. I dashed up the front steps of the trailer and found the ear.

She nodded. "Drop it in."

I twisted the jar open. Formaldehyde fumes burned my nose. Eyes watering, I dipped my fingers into the liquid and retrieved the ear. I threw it down onto Frieda's soup and tried not to wince as it flopped wetly into the white goo. She struck a match, dropped it and the whole thing went up like she threw lighter fluid onto a burning barbeque pit. Energy rushed past us in a soundless wave. I found myself holding my breath for no reason as I reached down for Pirate. He coughed.

"Baby dog!" I scooped him up in my arms as he hacked up a storm. Finally, he opened his eyes. "Are you all right?"

He blinked, his eyes watering. "Oh yeah, sure," he said, his voice hoarse. "I get whacked by crazy ladies all the time." He sneezed.

I hugged him to my chest.

"Now that's nice. I like that," he said, his cold nose finding my collarbone. "Anyone ever tell you how pretty you smell?"

Like roadkill and severed ears, I imagined, wiping my free hand on my ruined pants. The outfit Frieda had lent me was a total loss. Of course so was the outfit Frieda had on, I noticed, as she knelt over a coughing Ant Eater, who was still half in, half outside the trailer and holding the screened door open with her head.

Time to face the music.

"How are you?" I asked, careful to stay out of her reach.

Ant Eater hacked like a seasoned smoker and looked at me through bloodshot eyes. "They tell me you walked right through a death spell."

I hadn't really had time to think about it until right then. But I had. Several times if you wanted to count my trips in and out of the trailer, trying to track down the white jar to reverse the spell. "I guess it doesn't work on me," I said, in the understatement of the year.

Ant Eater nodded. She coughed several times, without covering her mouth. When she finished, she used the back of her hand to wipe away a clump of spit from her bottom lip. She eyed me like I'd grown four feet and gained two hundred pounds. "How about I don't try to kill you and you don't try to kill me?"

"Deal," I said.

"Now get me up," she said, struggling to sit. "And get some of the young ones in here to clean up the place. I want all my jars in my room. If I gotta live here with this pain in my ass, we might as well keep a tidy living room." She snapped my bra and chuckled when I jumped. No way I'd ever understand Ant Eater.

"You still want me to live with you after I nearly choked you to death?" If anything good had to come out of the afternoon, I hoped I could at least end the nightmare roommate situation.

She adjusted the American flag bandana around her neck. "I don't want your dirty undies hanging next to mine either, hot stuff. But I don't see anyone else around here who wants to live with you while Rex is out for blood."

"What?"

She seemed to enjoy my shock. "Yeah." She paused

for a long, hacking cough that brought tears to her eyes. "Assholes like that will zero in on a weak spot. You." She braced her hands on her knees. "I was getting to that in the diner before your boyfriend pulled a gun on me."

I wanted to remind her she had a shotgun pointed at my chest at the time, but I stopped myself.

She grinned and wiped her eyes on her bandana. "You might be useless, but after today, I got hope."

"Thanks."

"Rex won't come round here." She eyed her shotgun. "Mine's bigger than his."

I'd known we weren't completely safe here, or anywhere, but . . . I glanced back at the rapidly thinning crowd. "Don't we have a deal with the werewolves?"

Ant Eater succumbed to another coughing fit.

Frieda chewed at the corner of her unadorned lips. "For now. The fact is the alpha wants to use you to clean up around here. Rex is gunning for him hard. If you screw up, or if Rex kills you, the alpha looks weak."

Oh great. Kill me to get to some guy I've never even met before.

Frieda tugged at her soot-stained corset top. "You okay, babe?" she asked Ant Eater, who nodded, face red, as she hunkered over to catch her breath. "Come on inside. Both of you. You'll feel better after a shower and a change of clothes. Andrea and some of the wolves headed to the Goodwill in Monroe City."

While Ant Eater shuffled inside, I turned to Frieda. "I'm sorry about these," I said, rubbing at the leather pants she'd lent me. A hunk of gravel dislodged from the pants and clattered to the deck.

"Well," she said watching the gravel bounce under a petrified towel, "like the saying goes: it's not what you lose, it's what you do with what you have left."

"Who said that?" I asked, following her through the screened door. "Maya Angelou?"

"Oprah."

Amazingly, the red smoke had whooshed away as fast as it had appeared. But dang, we'd sure made a wreck out of the place. Frieda helped me hoist the saggy brown couch upright. We planted Ant Eater on it. Frieda and a few of the younger witches helped me clean up the broken glass, then headed out, leaving me with a sleeping Ant Eater. I was about ready to take a break myself when Andrea the Annoying banged on the screened door. I don't know why she bothered because she barged right in before I could invite her . . . or tell her to scram.

She stepped her high-heeled boots daintily around an overturned coffee table. "Heard about your accident." She tried to contain a snigger but couldn't. "Pity power struggles are always so messy. I wouldn't want to end up on the wrong side of one. Bloody, bloody, bloody messes if you ask me."

"Thanks for the sentiment. Now leave."

"I brought you some new clothes. Alpha's orders," she said, dumping a bag on the floor.

I wondered what was behind the personal delivery.

She flipped her platinum blonde pageboy hair. "Good thing you didn't kill Ant Eater," she said, breezing over to the couch with a paper shopping bag. "We had to make a special trip to Leather Up for her. My boss has a thing for the ladies."

Oh, this was getting old. "Pack up your fake boobs and your fake hair and your fake attitude and scram before I show you what I did to Ant Eater."

Andrea opened her mouth to respond, then closed it again.

"Now," I said.

"Enjoy your new clothes," she grumbled, the trailer door banging on its hinges behind her.

I picked my way past broken glass to retrieve the bag. All things being equal, I would have rather collapsed in a chair and slept for a week. But I did need to get cleaned up, and we had a lot bigger problems than my lack of sleep. I had to learn everything I could once Dimitri hauled his butt back here. I'd given him power over me. It was as real as the teardrop emerald I wore. Now it was time for him to do something in return. He knew more about my powers than I did. It seemed like everybody did given the afternoon I'd had. And we'd need every power we possessed to get Grandma back.

At least I'd gotten something out of Ant Eater's rampage. When I stopped worrying about myself and focused on the problem, I did get better at fighting her. *Look to the outside.*

An uncomfortable thought struck me. Perhaps Dimitri had been right to leave me on my own this afternoon. He'd given me a powerful instructor—me. I'd learned to trust my instincts. It was an unspoken kind of learning, a feeling that can't be taught from the outside.

*Accept the universe.* I toyed with the plastic handles of the bag. I did get help in the form of a power I didn't even know I had. And even though I still couldn't pry it off, the helmet had come in handy against Ant Eater's sword. While I was feeling brave, I looked inside the bag. Eek.

Inside, I found a pair of chewing-tobacco-stained men's cleats and what could best be described as a mumu.

"What am I, Mrs. Roeper?" I griped to myself. Nobody else was listening. I held the nylon day dress out in front of me. Yellow birds paraded, beaks open, over a loud green-and-blue checkered background. It would have made an ugly tablecloth. As a sack-shaped dress? It was the most hideous thing I'd ever seen. Andrea had gotten the last word.

The last item in the bag—much to my relief—was a pair of granny panties. Those I could wear.

But I had bigger things to worry about than fashion. I took a shower and donned the mumu. It fit like a Hefty bag and was almost as attractive. I paired it with the scarf Frieda had used as a face mask. Lovely. At least the scarf around my waist gave me a hint of a figure, even if it was eerily reminiscent of a twist tie. I swung my arms. At least I could move in it.

I tugged on the cleats, along with the men's gym socks I'd found rolled up inside. They were certainly more comfortable than my ruined oxfords and besides, they might help with my training. Athletes wore cleats when they threw baseballs. I'd wear them to hurl switch stars. Andrea, the tarnished angel of mercy, had actually given me a pretty good demon slayer outfit.

Pirate lifted his head. "Dimitri's back."

"Now how could you possibly know that?" I asked, moving toward the window.

"Doggy intuition," he said, following me.

Darned if he wasn't right. I pulled the dusty curtain aside and saw Dimitri and Scarlet pulling up in the Shoney's parking lot. Well thank goodness. We had work to do.

I caught up with Dimitri—yummy in a clean black T-shirt and a pair of Levi's 501s, having coffee at Shoney's with a man who could have been Mr. T's evil twin. The guy wore stacks of jewelry, and his foul temper made me want to take three steps back.

Dimitri raised a brow at my outfit. "Lizzie, this is Fang. He's the alpha of the Blue Moon Pack." He shook a packet of sugar into his coffee and stirred it, as non-chalant as if he were catching up with an old friend. I didn't buy it for a second.

Fang, huh? So this was the wolf Rex needed to beat. Yikes. I hoped Fang held on to power long enough for us to rescue Grandma and get the heck out of Dodge. The large werewolf looked me over like I'd escaped from the loony bin. I hoped it was the outfit. "This is the slayer, huh? Not what I expected." His eyes narrowed.

"I get that a lot," I told him.

Dimitri patted the seat next to him, and I slid into the booth. This had disaster written all over it. If the Red Skulls didn't need this guy's protection, I would have been out of there faster than you could say "dead demon slayer."

Fang leaned his meaty arms on the table. "The black souls hovering around here are a threat to my pack. Get rid of them by midnight tomorrow, or all bets are off." He glared at us, clearly expecting a challenge.

Dimitri merely raised a brow. "Fair enough," he said. His hand found mine and gave it a squeeze. "You ready, Lizzie?" I nodded, eerily unsure of what I'd just agreed to do.

# Chapter Twelve

Well thank God and hallelujah. I slipped two fingers into the delicately carved holes of the switch star. *Think of it as a tricked-out Frisbee.* The switch star was flat and round, about the shape of a small dinner plate. Five blades curled around the edge. They'd been dull in Dimitri's hands. When I touched them, they glowed.

Dimitri guided my shoulders into position, his grip firm. "Remember your stance."

The evening breeze whipped a few loose tendrils of hair into my face, tickling my nose. I resisted the urge to scratch and instead studied the target, a fifty-gallon plastic drum that had once held Grade A Lard, or so it said in industrial block letters on the side. Cliff and Hillary's tip-top arteries would have clogged at the sight of it.

We stood far back from the village of trailers that dotted the grassland behind Shoney's. In theory, we were at least a football field away from prying eyes. In reality, several of the werewolves had followed us to the training grounds. They'd pulled up a few ramshackle sofas and chairs and, of course, Andrea perched on the end of the shabby gold divan closest to Dimitri. She wore a leather bustier overflowing with cleavage and had kept busy painting her nails and flirting loudly with every werewolf within a half mile.

Like I cared. She was small potatoes compared to

what Grandma was going through. Scarlet had spent the afternoon in the nearest thing she could find to a Yard-saver shed, an empty Dumpster back behind the restaurant. She'd reported Grandma was still trapped in the first layer of hell, holding on with everything she had, fighting Vald as he tried to suck her down into the second level with him. I had to get Grandma out of there.

The witches had gathered in the nearby woods for a purification and strengthening ceremony. Seems I wasn't invited to that one.

"Give me some space," I told Dimitri.

I eyed Pirate, sitting obediently on Sidecar Bob's lap. Pirate liked to holler out words of encouragement right as I was throwing. "And you hush now, Pirate," I said, drawing back to throw. He wouldn't last a minute on a golf course.

"Me? I didn't say a word. Except to wish you good luck. What's the matter with good luck? You could use some luck right now."

I brought my throwing arm down, refocused. A little bit of magic wouldn't hurt either. *Look to the outside. Accept the universe. Sacrifice yourself.* As much as I wanted to save Grandma, I wasn't too crazy about that last one.

The star felt weightless in my hand. *I can do this.* I had to. I was the only one who could kill a demon. Once I figured out my switch stars. I whipped the star back and fired it toward the target.

"Incoming!" Pirate hollered. The witches scattered as my switch star hurtled toward their sacred circle. Blast! I cringed as it crashed right through one oak tree, then another, and another, cleaving the tops right off.

"Watch it!" I yelled as tree limbs rained down on the coven.

The switch star circled high in the air like a boomerang and plunged straight for my head, its razor-sharp blades a whirl of lightning. I ducked. I knew I shouldn't, but I couldn't help it. The star smacked into Dimitri with a dull thud. I glanced back. He didn't look happy.

Andrea's laughter rang out, clear and bright, above the guffaws of the other werewolves.

Dimitri towered above me, my star spinning like a record on his finger. The look on his face reminded me of the perpetual knitted eyebrows of my high school driver's ed teacher, Mr. Wickler.

Sidecar Bob's wheelchair crunched over the discarded plastic cups and empty beer cans littering the ground. "You got some distance on that last one." He shook his head. "They'll just have to remember, no matter how bad it looks, you are the fated slayer." He tugged on his gray goatee for a moment. "You are the slayer, right?"

"So they say," I told him. "You should have been there this afternoon." If that hadn't proved I was up to the job, nothing would. I'd shown I could live through a death spell. Of course in the last half hour, I'd also managed to decapitate the Shoney's Big Boy. No getting around it. Those switch stars were unpredictable. According to legend, I was supposed to be a natural at this. My Great-great, (however many Greats) Aunt Evie had practically popped out of the womb throwing switch stars.

I blew out a breath. *Focus.*

Dimitri pulled me aside, taking me several yards into the target range. He stood close, his face earnest. "Okay, tell me what you were thinking on that one."

No doubt, he expected a pithy answer. Well, I was too frustrated to wax poetic.

"Lizzie," he said intently, rubbing his palms up and down my arms, as if he could draw it out of me. "Reach deep down. You're hiding."

He didn't know the half of it.

Dimitri wrapped a finger around a section of my hair, half-mashed to my head from my exertions this afternoon. He rubbed it between his fingers like it, I, was something special. "You can do it, Lizzie. You just need to let go. Sacrifice yourself."

Despite myself, I felt his touch wind through my body.

I nodded. I had to get this by tomorrow night. We had to do the job for the werewolves in less than twenty-four hours. *Please let me be ready.*

Grandma was suffering, and it was my fault. If I'd done their ceremony right and let the witches bind themselves to me and my out-of-control powers, they might have felt Vald creeping up on them. I don't know how much help I would have been against a fifth-level demon, but they would have had a better shot of getting out of there. As it stood, three witches had been killed and—I shuddered to think—drained of their souls. Grandma could be next. I had to figure this out.

Dimitri, despite his deliciousness, had refused to tell me what else he'd found back at the Red Skull. Or, for that matter, why he'd been so prepared to swoop in and save me from Vald. I pulled another switch star from the hanging plant hook I'd jammed onto my scarf-belt. The switch star's blades radiated and spun. I clutched my fingers until I felt them dig into the metal holes. I drew back, fired. The star flashed through the air and dropped to the ground like a dead weight. It sprayed a shower of dirt and grass about ten feet in front of me.

I held my breath as a wave of dust blew over us. In the moment's calm, I distinctly heard one werewolf say to another, "I think she's getting worse." I would have been insulted if I hadn't feared they were right.

*Let go. Sacrifice yourself.*

I didn't know how.

"Again," Dimitri said.

I nodded, and reached for another star.

Scarlet climbed out of the Dumpster after another session with Grandma. Behind her, the sun cast purple shadows over the horizon. Her red hair stuck together, stringy and greasy. Her T-shirt, wet with sweat, clung to her curves and hitched under her bra straps. And, phew, she no doubt smelled like the Deluxe Sanitation Master she'd been calling home lately.

I'd hidden behind a moldy refrigerator, the largest piece of junk I could find among the discarded tires and sinks and other debris crowding the grounds. Scarlet had been channeling the first layer of hell for a good chunk of the day. The witches had been tight-lipped about what she'd discovered. With Ant Eater in charge, I was firmly out of the loop.

I watched Scarlet walk inside the Shoney's and meet Frieda at one of the back booths, within view of the Dumpster. Blast it. I stretched my cramped legs as far as I could without standing up. The witches' chicken fingers baskets arrived right away. Frieda must have ordered early.

This was it. I'd have to make do with the time I had.

Back at the Red Skull, I'd never made it into the Yard-saver to confess to Grandma that I didn't take the potion. Now, I had even bigger problems and no Grandma. I was dying to know what Scarlet had been doing in there. Not that I expected to conjure up whatever these witches did in the Cave of Visions. But if there was a tiny bit of my grandma in there . . .

I clambered up on a stack of wooden produce flats and slipped inside the rotting Dumpster. If I thought the acrid smell of garbage burned my nose from the outside—jiminey Christmas—try standing on the stuff.

I cringed as I sank down to my ankles in the remains of this morning's Rootin' Tootin' Breakfast Buffet. The back of my mouth watered. *Don't heave.* I didn't know how Scarlet did it.

A cockroach landed on my shoulder. "Off! Off! Off!" I leapt and flung it away. The thing shot to the other side of the Dumpster. I hoped.

However bad it was in here, it had to be a million times worse for Grandma.

I swallowed hard. "Grandma?" I focused on her ten-ton diesel voice, the way she cocked a grin. "I don't know if I had to come in here to tell you this, but, well, I'm here now." The garbage shifted under me, and I had to adjust my stance.

"I want to let you know I'm working on things, getting better." I rubbed my arms. I felt so alone. "I miss you like crazy." I paused as tears welled behind my eyes. "Then again, I'll bet your butt is nothing like Dimitri's when he throws a switch star." I smiled and let the tears fall. "Even so, I would have really liked to have you as my teacher."

I scanned the darkness for something, anything to show she heard me. "I'm doing pretty well with the Truths. They sure helped me pitch Ant Eater on her rear this afternoon." I couldn't help but smile. "Thought you'd enjoy hearing that." I sighed. "But the whole idea of sacrifice is so hard for me. *Sacrifice myself.* I don't know. I like myself. I don't want to change. Maybe I don't know how." I wiped my eyes on my sleeve. "But I'm working on it. I am."

Muffled voices sounded outside the Dumpster. No, I needed more time. "Grandma, while I'm here, I need to tell you something else."

*Why did this have to be so hard?*

"I'm sorry," I said. "I'm sorry I thought you were crazy when you showed up at my house. I'm sorry I made you drag Pirate into this. I'm sorry I got grossed out by the raccoon liver and the animal pelts, and I'm sorry I didn't drink the protection potion you worked so hard to give me. I should have told you. I tried to tell you. But when that didn't happen, I should have told somebody else. If I hadn't messed things up, you might still be here instead of—" I couldn't even say it. I didn't want to think about Grandma being taken by Vald. She must have been so scared.

"I'll bet you tried to kick him in the balls." My voice hitched with tears. "You probably got him a few times. Knowing you." I wiped at my face. "Well hang in there. I'm coming." I laughed despite myself, and self-consciously smoothed my hair behind my ears. My fingers touched the edges of the bronze helmet. "I'm sorry I let Dimitri do this to me. It's, he's . . . complicated." The emerald glowed warm against my fingers. "Still, you might end up liking him. I do. I just wish I knew what he wants out of all this." I couldn't shake the idea that he might not have my best interests at heart.

"But don't you worry about that. You be strong. You fight. I'll come for you soon." Or die trying.

I'd promised her I could do this. I launched another switch star into the dirt. I squinted my eyes closed as the cool night breeze blew back a wave of dust. Hells bells. For the last five hours, I'd blamed the were-wolves and their loud partying for my lack of aim. At three A.M., they'd finally settled down and I'd run out of excuses.

A pair of boots crunched behind me, and I could sense a trace of sandalwood in the air. Dimitri.

*Keep your distance.*

Repeat as necessary.

*And uncurl those toes immediately.*

It had become my personal mantra, except for the toe-curling part. That was simply an annoying side effect—one I'd conquer soon enough. I stared out at the trees at the edge of the practice field, willing myself to stay strong until I could look at Dimitri without wanting to wrap myself around him like Pirate on a pork chop.

"What are the Three Truths?" he asked, smooth as silk on naked skin.

I gritted my teeth. "Look to the outside. Accept the universe. Sacrifice yourself." I threw another switch star. This one skipped over the field in front of us like a flat stone on a pond.

He moved in close behind me. "Focus, Lizzie. Lives depend on this."

Like I didn't know that. "Thanks for the pressure."

I could feel him like a solid wall behind me. Sexy, powerful and completely *not* helping. He snorted. "You don't understand the Three Truths or you'd have released more of your powers."

I knew that. I knew all of it. *Except how to put everything together.* And here he was trying to tear down my walls when I needed everything I had just to keep myself together.

"Look, hot stuff," I said, turning to look him straight in the eye. Darn it. He did look concerned. If anything, though, it made me even more frustrated. "I'm doing the best I can. And I think it's darned good considering last week I had a home, a job and a bunch of friends waiting to celebrate my thirtieth birthday. Now I'm supposed to automatically understand three mysterious Truths while doing a hit job for a bunch of werewolves before my grandma gets slaughtered by a demon."

The lines around his eyes crinkled as he grinned. "Hot stuff?"

Oh no. We did not want to explore that right now.

I planted my hands on my hips. "How are you helping me?"

He flashed a crooked smile. "I tossed you in with
Ant Eater."

I gaped at him. He left me alone with that psycho *on
purpose*? I couldn't believe it. "Then as protectors go,
you stink." Damn the man. "And stop grinning at me."

"You looked outside yourself," he pointed out.

At the risk of life, limb and dog.

He took me by the shoulders and I felt everything,
down to the night breeze on my cheeks and his warm
fingers through my lumpy dress sleeves. The raw, almost exposed part of me wanted to cover up and run
for the hills. The part of me that wanted to jump his
bones turned a few cartwheels. So much for my iron
control.

He drew me closer. "I'm willing to bet you reached
for the death spell only when you looked to the outside. You stopped worrying about yourself and focused
on the problem."

Easy for him to say. "I almost killed Pirate and Ant
Eater."

"You wouldn't let that happen," he said, his lips
inches from mine.

Oh lordy. Why was I getting turned on during a discussion of my particularly horrible afternoon?

"You accepted the universe." He brushed his lips
against my forehead until my toes curled like the traitors they were. "You did," he insisted heartily. "Nothing happens by chance. The tools and the people to aid
you will appear. You found what you needed this afternoon. And I am the person you need. You found me
on the road," he said, eyes twinkling.

That was a nice way of putting it.

"Accept help, Lizzie," he said, too earnest to resist.
"You need to be open to the universe if you expect to

rescue your grandma. And you'll definitely need it if you want to defeat Vald."

Fear tickled my stomach. "I don't know if I can do it."

His eyes searched mine. "You have to kill him, Lizzie." It felt like he was on the verge of saying more when he abruptly let me go.

Dimitri shoved a hand through his thick, dark hair. "You can do it when you sacrifice yourself. Look beyond what you think you know," he said earnestly. "I've seen you, Lizzie. You've spent your whole life burying your instincts. Step back from that. Search for who you really are. Trust yourself."

"Okay," I nodded. Trust myself. I bent over and stretched my hands to my toes, wrapping my fingers around the ends of my second-hand cleats. He might as well have told me to fly.

"Take this," he said.

I straightened and found him holding a blue Gap bag out for me. "This is from the universe."

Inside, I found khaki pants and a white button-down shirt. "Dimitri!" I couldn't believe it. "This is perfect."

It truly was. I pulled the pants and shirt from the bag, holding them up one at a time. They were just like the ones I'd ruined. And he even got the sizes right. It didn't surprise me that Dimitri had taken in every detail of my former self. It was uncanny at times how precise he could be. But never in a million years would I have expected this.

"Thanks," I whispered.

"Are you all right?" he asked, clearly unsure what to make of my reaction.

I nodded, afraid I'd tear up if I said more. I didn't know what to say. No one had ever done anything like that for me before. Growing up, when Cliff and Hilary had bought me gifts, they gave me what they liked, not what I liked.

Even for my thirtieth birthday, I planned the dinner, maybe a little afraid someone wouldn't. And I specified no gifts. I didn't want to expect them.

"I'm almost afraid to tell you, but there are shoes in there too." He eyed me uncomfortably. "Those oxfords you like. Size eight." It had to be the closest Dimitri would ever come to rambling.

My head stopped up and my giggle came out more like a snarf.

"Are you okay?" Dimitri frowned. The man would run headlong into a demon-infested biker bar, but he seemed terrified I'd break down in tears. So much for wanting me to get in touch with my feelings.

Screw it.

I pulled him down and kissed him thoroughly. Yeah, it was probably a mistake. That was the last rational thought I had for awhile as he devoured my mouth, to my complete and utter delight. His fingers traced my shoulders, trailed down my spine, up my sides, all the way . . . oh my.

Embarrassed, I pulled away. I could feel my face burning. It grew even redder when I saw the intense, exuberant expression on his face. "This doesn't mean anything," I told him.

"Of course not," he replied blithely.

So much for my iron control.

He pulled me into the crook of his arm and gave a squeeze. "Anything to make you happy."

"You did," I said, enjoying the feel of him. Let him have his fun. No one had ever done anything like this for me.

I knew whatever was going on with Dimitri and I couldn't be permanent. Once I learned to control my powers and rescued Grandma, I'd go back to teaching at Happy Hands. He'd race off to live his exotic Greek demon slayer trainer life. I snuggled closer, taking in his rich sandalwood scent, knowing I didn't need to tease myself with any possibilities. But I could wish.

Back at the trailer, I grabbed a quick shower and changed into my new clothes. They felt right. I wondered if Dimitri knew how much he'd given me.

Pirate padded into the front room where I sat on the edge of the brown couch, tying my shoes. He'd been sleeping. "You coming to bed?" he asked, ending the question with a humongous doggy yawn.

I tugged on the laces. "Too much on my mind."

Pirate nudged my leg with his nose. "You want to talk about it? You know how I like talking about things with you."

I sighed. "Sorry, guy." I needed to learn how to sacrifice myself and while I had no idea where to start, I knew it wasn't here. Pirate was the least introspective creature on the planet.

"Oh, I see. It's important enough to keep you out all night with Dimitri, but as soon as I want to talk, it's 'never mind.'"

I sunk back into the couch, trying to ignore him.

Dog tags jingled at my feet. "You know what your problem is? You never let anybody help you."

"You're a dog!"

"Now that hurt. Fine. If you want to think about your problems all by yourself, then you do that. I know when I'm not wanted." He turned to walk back into the bedroom.

"Pirate . . ." I said, looking away, trying to think of a way to reason with a twelve-pound terrier.

He spun back around. "What? You want to talk? Let's talk."

"No." I caught a faint glow outside. I heaved myself off the couch and pressed my nose to the window. "Stay right here."

Light poured from the Dumpster. Scarlet must be channeling something big. I banged out through the screened door and jogged across the field. The hulking remains of refrigerators, washing machines and cars cast dark shadows over the ground.

Grandma staggered out from behind the Dumpster and my heart stopped. Whole sections of her long gray hair hung in shreds. Blood clotted her head. Her arms twisted at painful and unnatural angles.

*Was it really her?*

I approached slowly. The scent of garbage and—was that a tang of ozone?—grew stronger. Sidecar Bob had said it himself—a demon can take on many forms.

The figure perked up when she saw me. *Grandma?*

"Shit, Lizzie. This isn't the goddamned Easter parade. Get over here!"

I wanted to skip. It was her! My mind reeled. "Oh my word. Grandma!" Her back hunched at an odd angle and she looked ready to collapse at any moment. "You look terrible!"

"Thanks for reminding me," she huffed. "No. Don't touch me," she said as I came close. "I'm on borrowed power. It'd be like jamming your finger in a light switch." She struggled to stand as straight as she could. "Now, when are you going to stop throwing switch stars at the dirt and get me the hell out of here?"

My throat had all but closed up. I swallowed. "I'm trying, but I'm not there yet." My excuse sounded lame, even to me. "I'm so close. I know I have the power. I just can't seem to find it."

She rolled her eyes. "You know what your problem is?" She threw her arms out like an Italian grandmother. "You're so busy worrying, you're not doing. You're going through the motions. And frightening a lot of people from the sounds of it." So she'd heard about Ant Eater. "Your mind is too crowded. 'I didn't take the potion. I don't want to feel all exposed and girly in front of Dimitri. Ant Eater is a big bully.' "

"What?" I couldn't believe it. "How did you know about the potion?"

"You told me."

No, I didn't. I never had a chance to tell her.

"Shut your mouth, Lizzie. You're catching flies." She eyed me, hands on her hips. "Did you come to the Cave of Visions to keep a secret? Honestly, Lizzie, sometimes I don't understand you at all."

She'd heard me in the Dumpster. She'd actually heard me!

"And what the hell is with that emerald skullcap? You look like a rapper."

My hand flew to my head. "It's Dimitri's. I gave him power over me. I had to do it."

"I don't like the sound of that. You have enough going on in your life right now, and you don't need to be wasting time with a man who doesn't know how to stay in one place."

I blinked once, twice. "Are you lecturing me?" At a time like this?

"What? You don't think you need it?" She huffed and tossed the remnants of her long gray hair over her shoulders. "It's like when Frieda gave herself seven fingers on each hand. The whole time Ant Eater brewed the Erasure herbs, I made Frieda talk to me about that man of hers. Kept her mind off it. I told her she'd better take the chance and yap away because that was the one and only time I wanted to hear about Eddie's smelly socks."

I'd bet anything Dimitri had his socks dry cleaned. But, okay, if she wanted to know, "We started off bumpy, but I really like Dimitri." More than I wanted to admit. "He's driven and determined," I told her. That sounded better than mysterious and studly. "He wants to help me." And take care of me. It was a new feeling for me and I didn't quite know what to make of it.

Grandma's image flickered. "I never thought I'd say this, but I'm glad we have him on our side. Just be careful. And watch the werewolves too. The mean one's about to make a power play and our coven is a perfect excuse to cause trouble. Even if you get out of here before it all goes down, those wolves will get their pound of flesh. They don't do anything without getting double back."

Yikes. Maybe she could tell me what to do. "Ant Eater wants me to get rid of black souls for them. What are they?"

"Suicide for most of us. Training for you. If you decide to do it, bring Dimitri. You might just learn something." Her image flickered again. This time she yelped in pain and held her side as an invisible energy seared through her.

"Grandma!" It took everything I had not to touch her.

She clutched her abdomen. "Because, Lizzie, I don't want you to come after me if you don't think you can do it. I'm an old cuss. I've had my time. Don't let Vald take you, you hear?"

"No. I have to get you. I mean, look at your hands." Large holes sliced through her palms, as if an invisible blade cut her open right before my eyes.

"Oh yeah. Let's talk about how much my life sucks right now. Why can't you stay on track?"

Unbelievable.

I fought to look her in the face. Her skin had taken on an unearthly pallor and the wounds in her head began to bleed fresh. I had to get her out of there. "Tell me how to sacrifice myself. Just tell me, and I'll do it right now."

She shook her head. "You have to figure it out yourself.

But dammit, Lizzie. Think about it." An invisible blade sliced her neck. Blood flowed freely from the bubbling wound. "Shit," she gurgled. "You weren't supposed to see this."

Grandma clapped a hand over her neck. "If you cry, I'm going to beat the shit out of you. Now think about it. What does it mean to sacrifice yourself? Who are you really?"

I started to reply.

"Hup! I'll tell you who you are, Lizzie. You're a brilliant little snit who types out her grocery list on the computer, never had a library late fee and won't take a dump without planning it on your calendar. I'm willing to bet Pirate was the only half-ass thing you had to deal with before I showed up at your door."

"I'm not—"

She threw a hand up. "The night we met, you had timed directions to a restaurant you said yourself you'd already been to!"

As if I'd wanted to be late to my birthday party. "I'm organized."

"You're wound tighter than a gnat's ass! Let go! Trust your instincts. Stop thinking of every negative thing that could happen five miles down the road."

Well shoot. I didn't know what to think. It felt safe to know exactly how my life would turn out. That's why I planned everything so precisely. And why I'd stayed in my job for so long. And I didn't date unpredictable men.

I'd worked my whole life to be normal, accepted. Now Grandma wanted me to blow the whole thing out of the water. Slowly it began to come together. "That's what Dimitri meant when he said to sacrifice myself," I said for my own benefit, as much as hers.

"Exactly." She made a show of swooning. Oh geez. I hoped it was a show.

Grandma popped back up, a little more spry than I

would have expected. Her energy surged and her wounds disappeared. She almost looked like herself again.

Sacrifice myself. Okay. I could let go. A week ago, the mere thought would have given me hives. Now I felt giddy. I could do this. "Dimitri wants me to let go of myself." I couldn't help smiling. "I don't know why I didn't see it before, Grandma. Dimitri said as much to me. But then again, since when do men make any sense, right?"

"Oh yeah, I'm in hell and now you're grinning and making jokes." She waggled a finger, only half kidding. "Now do what you have to do to get me out of here. Besides," she added, "we've got some catching up to do. We missed out on a lot of years."

I planted my back against the outside of the Dumpster. The night sky shone rich with stars. "I'm sorry it took me so long, Grandma."

"Zip it. If there's one thing I can't stand it's whining. Besides, I heard it all in the Cave of Visions. You're forgiven. Unless you keep apologizing. Then I'm going to be pissed all over again."

I nodded. "Can you at least tell me why?" I asked her. "Why did Vald come after me that night? You must have known something could happen, or you wouldn't have tried to protect me. What does this thing want from me?"

She huffed so hard her nostrils flared. "Well, cupcake, it's like this. You probably keep hearing about your Great-great, Great—whatever—Aunt Evie. Lord knows I have. Aunt Evie locked Vald away in the second layer of hell. Aunt Evie was the most powerful slayer in the last thousand years. Aunt Evie made the world's best potato salad. But what you won't hear is that Aunt Evie had nothing on you. She never learned how to seize a demon's vox like you did that day in your bathroom."

"You mean the green light thingies?"

"If you want to call them that, then yeah. She had the power to lock Vald away." Grandma brought up a finger. "You have the power to destroy him. Capiche?"

I nodded. *Destroy Vald.* Yow.

"He's unhatching a particularly nasty plan, worse than anything I'm going to face down here, I'll tell you that. We're not sure what he's up to, but you play a big part. Now I think—aw, shit." Her image flickered.

"What?" Are you in pain?" I couldn't stand to see her like this.

"Thanks for reminding me, but it's not that." She stared over my shoulder.

Voices called from the field behind me. I turned. Ant Eater headed our way, trailed by at least a half a dozen werewolves.

"Tell them to stay the hell away from me," Grandma ordered. "I can't keep my energy with this many auras cluttering the air. Dammit! This is important."

"Stay back!" I called to the mob, waving my hands in the air.

"Lizzie, pay attention!" she demanded, as Ant Eater and the wolves surged forward. Grandma's image flickered and she let off a load of cuss words that would have made my adopted mother reach for her rosary.

She spoke quickly. "Vald wants you. He wants your power. In my vision, I saw the best time to strike. You have to—flisbit." She faded out, then flickered in again. "You have to prepare. Let go of yourself. Look to the outside. Accept the universe. Sacrifice yourself. And remember—"

Ant Eater stormed up in a rage. "Get your ass over here right now."

"What about Grandma?" I hollered. "Wait! Grandma! When is the best time to strike?" I demanded as her image crackled one last time and disappeared.

Ant Eater planted her hands on her hips. "What the hell are you talking about?"

She couldn't see her. None of them could, I realized.

Ant Eater seized my shoulder and forced me to face her. "We need you now. Rex made his move. The wolves have got the whole goddamned coven backed into a corner. Time to earn your keep." She cocked her gun.

"Okay," I said. I didn't even bother to question my new role. I knew it had changed this afternoon. Here was the test. Deep down, I ached to spend a few more minutes with Grandma, but she would have been the first person to tell me I needed to let it go. Our conversation was now in the past. I had to look to the future. And for once, I was ready.

# *Chapter Thirteen*

I followed Ant Eater to a rusty trailer near the woods. Werewolves jammed the entrance.

Rex stood at the door, a rifle slung over his shoulder. "Your asses are mine," he told us, way too pleased with himself.

"Stuff it." Grandma needed me. We didn't have time to get sucked into werewolf politics.

"Well that was brave," Ant Eater commented. "Stupid. But brave."

We pushed our way into the mishmash, the air hot with bodies and alive with voices. I found myself face-to-chest with most of the werewolves. Danger rolled off them in palpable waves. Every step we took, they jostled us back, as if they couldn't wait to take it further.

Dimitri's emerald hummed, which wasn't the best sign. The bronze metal of my helmet snaked down and wound around my neck. At least it earned me a little respect. The werewolves parted like I was tossing firecrackers. The ones nearest to me caught their breath and muttered their surprise. Something told me these men, these *creatures*, didn't gasp like girls every day. I drew my hand up, instinctively.

A rough-looking fellow with a nose ring winced as the metal around my neck churned and pulsed, like a liquid noose. *You got it, buddy.*

The metal locked into place and cooled to the touch. It felt like a metal collar, the kind gladiators wore to the arena. *Please don't let me be a gladiator*, I thought as the emerald bounced against the front of my throat.

"Nice trick." Fang stood in the center of the room, his Mr. T mohawk unmistakable. I stepped forward before Ant Eater could shove me, which no doubt she would have enjoyed, if only because it took the edge off. I could hear her behind me; *rap, tap, tapping* her nails against a stack of what had to be six or seven cases of Jack.

"Cut it out," I told her. We needed to show strength right now. The Red Skull witches were safe (relatively) and alive (for now) thanks to the good graces of these werewolves. Sure, Rex had been gunning for us from the start, but for the most part, the werewolves had earned our respect, if not our trust. They'd stuck their necks out and taken us in after Vald demolished the Red Skull. From his stance in the middle of the room, it was clear Fang still held power. And now he needed to discuss something. Well, fine. But we didn't need to look nervous about it.

*No need to borrow trouble.*

The Red Skulls stood behind Fang, cut off from the werewolves and from any means of escape. I caught a glimpse of Frieda near the kitchenette. Sidecar Bob was nowhere in sight—probably pushed to the back of the crowd. Not a bad place to be right now, I mused, as Rex glared a hole through me. I wondered what we did to warrant this showdown. Fang had what he wanted— my promise to get rid of the black souls. Maybe that wasn't enough anymore. Heaven help us.

"Bring the wolf forward," Fang commanded. The werewolves behind me hollered a litany of curses.

Just my luck. We'd ticked them off.

Nose Ring brushed past me, carrying a young woman. She couldn't have been more than eighteen. The girl's wide frame and sleek muscles sagged. Her long, dark hair was tangled in knots. He placed her in front of Fang. She floundered pitifully as she tried to stand.

If I didn't know better, I would have thought she was drunk. She pitched sideways. Oh my word, she was going over. "Grab her!" I rushed for her and managed to catch her under the armpits.

The rest of her body fell to the floor hard, taking me with it. I whacked my tailbone, but managed to keep her head from hitting the floor. Her eyes rolled back and she gurgled. "Are you all right?" My butt throbbed. She had to be hurting too. "What's your name?" I tried to pull her into a sitting position. She didn't seem to notice. Her breathing was labored and shallow.

"Hold on," I told her. "Excuse me, folks." I looked up to the three dozen or so people who *could* have shown a little concern. "Can we get a little help here?"

Fang stood over us, scowling. "Fine time to worry about her now, demon slayer."

Oh, let's not be catty. "What's that supposed to mean?"

"Who cast this spell?" he thundered, speaking to me but clearly making this a group discussion. "Was it you, demon slayer? Or the devil witches?"

"Try neither." I hoped.

*Don't piss off the werewolf, Lizzie.*

He grew angrier by the second, and it didn't help that he had about twenty friends ready and quite eager to tear us apart.

In an instant, he seized me by the throat and lifted me off the floor. I fought a wave of panic and clutched at his hands as my feet kicked at nothing but air. Unbelievable. The man could have strangled me with one large, meaty hand. Except he gripped the bronze choker at my throat. I smothered a yelp. Score one for Dimitri and his emerald.

The crowd hushed as Fang drew his face inches

from mine. "Your witches say they don't understand what's wrong with my daughter." He jerked me back and forth until my teeth rattled, as if he could shake the answer out of me. "Why, demon slayer? Why is this happening to our women and children? They can't move. They can't speak. They're the walking dead." I could see the fear in his eyes. Despite his bravado, he cared about these people. "Tell me what you did to them."

"I swear I don't know what happened," I whispered, dizzy from the onslaught. I looked past him to the witches. They huddled at the far end of the trailer, stripped of their roadkill magic. Frieda shook her head, sad, confused. Afraid. The werewolves had the Red Skulls backed into a corner. Literally. It wouldn't take much for the night to erupt into violence, and none of us had any illusions of victory.

Fang dropped me roughly to my feet, and I pretended it didn't scare the bejesus out of me. Just like that, the game had changed.

"How many women and children have been affected?" I asked him.

"Nine total. Six in the last hour alone."

Holy moley.

"This is an insult," he declared, as if the girl were nothing more than a rug on the floor.

I didn't know how or why the witches could possibly be involved. The Red Skulls wouldn't attack innocent people. Besides, we needed the wolves.

Ant Eater cleared her throat. Thank goodness. As Grandma's second-in-command, she had to talk some sense into these animals. "Fuck you," she said.

So much for diplomacy.

Rex's lips curved into snarl. "I told you it was a bad decision to take in the witches. Look at what they've done to our pups. We can't trust them, we can't trust their magic, and their demon slayer can't even throw a rock and hit something with it. How is such a gamma supposed to get rid of the black souls? Fang is feeble and weak to trust them."

Andrea curled behind Rex and planted a sloppy kiss on his neck. Oh ick. Now was not the time. "The witches need to pay," she said.

"We have paid," Ant Eater said, clearly annoyed. "None of you poseurs can axe a black soul. Lizzie made two disappear this afternoon."

I did? Did that mean those dark clouds hovering over Pirate and Ant Eater had been black souls? Phew. Clueless could be a perk sometimes.

Rex looked as surprised as I felt.

Ant Eater took full advantage. "Oh, that's right, you didn't see that because she did it while waltzing through a death spell that would have killed any one of you. So shut the fuck up and leave us alone. We'll honor our end of the deal."

The crowd murmured.

She scanned the multitude of faces, hands on her hips. "And another thing. We're not the reason your wolves are sick."

"Bullshit," hollered a wolf in the back.

"Oh yeah?" Ant Eater countered. "Get up here and I'll show you a spell that'll rot your balls off!"

Voices erupted into chaos. Rex slammed his rifle butt down on the dirty linoleum until he had everyone's attention again. "I say we kill them all," Rex said, with obvious pleasure. "The Red Skulls have broken their contract. And now their leader mocks us."

Way to go, Ant Eater.

"They promised," he said, gesturing with the rifle like a TV evangelist. "They promised they would not cast mortal magic without provocation. She said it herself: the slayer cast a death spell. We can't trust them. We have to kill them before they do any more damage."

Oh, now he had no idea . . .

The crowd hollered until the trailer shook and I could no longer hear what anybody said.

Curse it all. We didn't need this. The hospitality of the pack was the one thing standing between us and Vald. And now Rex just had to use my little run-in with Ant Eater to stir up trouble. I'd bet my last switch star he was behind the sick werewolves. It would be the perfect way to cast doubt on Fang's leadership and seize control of the pack. And what would happen to us then?

"The spell caused gagging, weakness, shortness of breath . . ." Rex bellowed. Testosterone hung thick in the air. Fang looked ready to snap.

Ant Eater gripped the sick girl's hands and dragged her up.

"Let go of her!" Fang ordered.

I watched in horror as Rex's hands split into massive, furry, skeletal *things*. He drew his razor-sharp claws back, ready to rip Ant Eater open.

"Hold it!" Fang commanded.

Rex wasn't going to listen. Oh my God. He was going to kill her. And challenge Fang's authority. And start a bloodbath.

Rex sliced his hand through the air in frustration.

For a split second, nobody moved.

Ant Eater blinked twice before hauling the sick girl over her shoulder. Call it bravery or sheer cussed stubbornness. She bent under the weight, keeping an eye on Fang the whole time. "No more using your people like party props," she said. "She needs a doctor. Not this shit."

Oh yeah, way to piss them both off. Problem was, Ant Eater was right.

Frieda moved forward, scared silly but prepared to take the girl. The werewolf with the nose ring stepped in and, more gently than I would have thought, he lifted her into his arms. They passed her back through the crowd, hopefully to someone who would actually take care of her.

Andrea shook with anger, her blonde hair falling into her eyes, her boobs practically popping out of her corset top. "You live and breathe by our good graces and you gutter rats have the nerve to insult us. Our leader"—she said the word with distaste—"might not be willing to hold you to the fire, but the rest of us are."

Fang looked ready to rip her a new one. He dragged her backward by her neck and threw her to the floor. She yelped in pain and scurried behind Rex. Fang's face twisted into a mask of rage. "Our pack had none of these problems before we took in you witches and your corrupt spells."

Ant Eater rested her hand on her revolver. "Hold up, asshole. That was a personal thing between the brat and me. We ended it this afternoon. None of you were invited as far as I can tell. And the anaconda spell doesn't make you sick. It makes you dead."

Right on, sister.

Rex seethed. "Of course the witch will claim this isn't her fault. We should eliminate them now before they can cast any more of their death spells. I know a demon who is willing to pay big."

*Vald? He wanted to hand the whole coven over to a fifth-level demon?*

So much for rescuing Grandma. I'd be joining her if Rex had his way.

The werewolves erupted, pelting the witches with beer cans and bottles. A window shattered.

"Halt!" Fang ordered. "What I say goes, and I haven't made my decision yet." While the crowd quieted down, he kept an eye on Rex and said, "The debt I owed to Dimitri is paid and then some. You witches are a menace."

Andrea curled herself around Rex like a python. She snarled at Fang, showing as much disrespect as she dared. "For all you know, these witches killed your son," she spat. Then to the group, she announced, "JR is missing. There is no second-in-command."

Fang launched himself at her, ready to tear her throat out. Rex met him halfway, luring the pack master into a face-off.

Ant Eater let out a string of curses that would make your hair curl. "Why does everything have to be a god-damned pissing match?"

Like she was one to talk.

Violence could erupt at any second. The werewolves held the whole coven hostage. Any show of weakness could tip the balance.

I held my head high. *Fake it 'til you make it.*

Sidecar Bob rolled haphazardly in the melee. He covered his head with his hands as pack members surged around him. Rex descended on Bob like a pit bull on a pork chop. He grabbed Bob by the ponytail and lifted him until his neck arched forward, open and exposed. The crowd jeered their approval.

Did I tell you I can't stand bullies?

I started in for Rex, but before I could make it, the bulldozing took a deadly turn. I caught a glimpse of a dagger in Rex's right hand.

*Oh, no, no, no, no, no.*

I plucked a switch star from my belt and let it fly. It whistled through the air and sliced clear through Bob's hair. Rex leapt backward holding a shaking dagger and the remains of Bob's ponytail.

The crowd hushed and dropped back. Rex didn't know what to do.

"Well that sure shut 'em up," Ant Eater said behind me.

The switch star flew back to me and I let it spin on my finger for an extra second or two, enjoying the reaction. I figured the universe could grant me a moment of indulgence.

"We'll get your son back," I told Fang. "And I'll do what I promised about the black souls."

Rex stood defiantly in the corner. He recovered from his defeat a little too quickly for my taste. I strolled deliberately toward him. I had a pretty strong hunch he was behind the poisonings. I stopped in front of him, tilting my chin up as I addressed the room. "I'll get to the bottom of this, too."

Rex snarled at me.

Fang, the ungrateful beast, was beyond ticked. He glowered at both of us, growling low in his throat. "I'd hate to have to kill you, Lizzie."

I'll bet.

# Chapter Fourteen

"What in blazes is going on?" I struggled to keep up with Ant Eater as she banged out of the trailer and practically sprinted across the field. Not smart with all the—"Ouch!"—holes littering the ground. I rubbed at the ankle I'd nearly twisted, but gave it up almost as soon as I'd started. We didn't have time and, frankly, nobody cared but me.

Still, I couldn't resist asking her, "Did you see me throw that switch star? Whammo! I think I finally got it. I let go of myself and—urgle!" Ant Eater dragged me into a VW bus, abandoned near the edge of the woods. Even in the dark, I found the brightly painted peace signs and stars obnoxious. And, phew, the thing smelled like weed and Big Macs.

"Rex has to be behind the sick wolves," I said, crouching to fit as she slammed the back door behind us. I sat back and felt the beaded seat covers dig into my rear. It was a simple process of elimination. We didn't do it. Fang had no reason to upset his power base. "Rex will benefit most." And he sure didn't waste any time making a run for the alpha position.

"Nice job, Nancy Drew." Ant Eater stumbled over an aluminum ice chest and the whole bus lurched. "Shut up and listen," she said, pulling me close. "Fang's son was the original second-in-command here. He was no daisy ass, but he was a lot better than Rex. Now that he's gone, Rex is going to make our lives hell."

Ant Eater's WWE style of diplomacy didn't help any either. I'd met four-year-olds with more finesse. But now was not the time to discuss it.

"How do we even know JR is gone?" I asked her. I didn't trust a word that came out of Andrea's mouth. "Rex just wants to blame everything on us."

"Yes and no."

She knew more than she was telling me. Naturally. "Answer me straight or you don't want to know where my next switch star is going." I held her gaze, daring her to test me. "Are we behind any of this?"

"Yes."

"Jumping jehosefets."

"Can it, candy ass. We didn't make any werewolves sick if that's what you're asking. I'd bet anything Rex is poisoning his own people. Makes for a hell of a power play."

It was the only thing that made sense. Rex wanted power and with JR out of the way, Fang was vulnerable. If Fang looked like he'd put the pack in danger by taking in the Red Skulls, he could be left open for a challenge. And who knew what Vald was willing to pay for us. But that still didn't answer my question. "So what did we do?"

"You know you're supposed to collect black souls for the werewolves, right?"

Ah yes, the lovely assignment Ant Eater thrust on me. "What about it?"

"They're gone."

That should be a good thing, but from the look on her face, I could tell it wasn't.

"Remember those shadows that used to lurk everywhere?" She studied me. "Come on, slick. I know you saw two in our trailer."

The shadows I saw above Pirate and Ant Eater. "You said back there I got rid of them."

"I lied."

Wonderful. "Then where'd they go?" I asked, knowing I probably didn't want to hear the answer.

"Into JR. He's been compromised." She clicked her teeth together. "Bound to happen sooner on later, the way he's been on your tail."

"I never met JR." *Right?*

"He's been following you for some time now."

"Of course." I threw my hands up. One whacked against a wind chime hanging from the low ceiling. "Why not?" I was so sick of being the last to know—everything.

"Stop playing dumb. You know Dimitri was out there guarding you, long before you met your grandma."

I'd figured as much when Pirate had found his Phantom Menace. Sure all dogs bark at shadows in the backyard. Leave it to Pirate to find something real. But I didn't know Dimitri had brought friends. "Wait. Grandma Gertie only felt me when I was about to change. How could Dimitri know?"

"Now how the hell am I supposed to know that?" She blew out a breath. "First we'd have to get him to admit he was actually skulking around in your rose bushes. Slippery cuss. Dimitri's played kissy face with the pack over the past couple of years. You can ask him about that your damned self. Now, here's where we're screwed. JR, heir to the werewolf pack, was Dimitri's backup. Like any asshole spy, he searched the house after you left, probably trying to guess where we were hiding out."

"And Xerxes the demon came back." My heart sank when I thought of that creature in my house again. Poor JR. I didn't even know him and, yes, he was a dirty fink for spying on me, but nobody deserved to have a shrunken, razor-clawed demon on their tail, especially after I'd sent a few green glowy things through Xerxes's skull.

"JR was attacked by black souls. A search party found him, strung out of his mind on your sofa."

I knew my home had been invaded, but my stomach churned to think of JR attacked in my living room. "What are black souls?" I asked. Frieda had said something about black souls when she first told me about this suicidal quest.

"They're trapped souls—too bad for heaven, too good for hell. If they don't find their way to purgatory, the demons capture them and use them. These are nasty-ass spirits. JR fought them off when they invaded your house." She shook her head. "Gives me the willies."

I couldn't imagine what it would take to fight off a black soul, but if it made Ant Eater squeamish, it had to be bad.

"They didn't possess him," she said matter-of-factly. "At first. But they followed him. They'll wear you down after a while, especially when you've got dozens of 'em after you, like he did. Then he got caught up in the mess on the night the Red Skull imploded. A real fucked-up situation. Nobody knew he was Dimitri's second. And it seemed Dimitri was busy with you. He didn't know his buddy was trapped until the next morning."

*So that's why he'd raced off on the morning he was supposed to train me.*

Oh my God. I'd been ready to drag him off his hog when all he wanted to do was go rescue his friend.

"This time, JR wasn't as lucky. Scarlet and Dimitri found him facedown behind the bar, possessed by black souls."

Dimitri must not have seen him the night before, when he'd rushed inside, looking for my dog. *A dog.* I loved Pirate with everything I had, but guilt stabbed me in the gut when I thought of how I'd worried about an animal when there'd been a real person trapped in there.

"They'll possess any body they can, make the person stark raving mad before they drain his energy and turn him into one of them."

"Where is he?"

She shook her head. "Dimitri has him stashed in the woods somewhere. Fang found out right before he dragged us into the trailer. Dimitri thought he could trust Fang. Just goes to show you werewolves are animals. Doesn't matter that JR is a big boy, or that he worked with Dimitri all the time. No telling what Fang's gonna do if you don't handle it."

We had to fix this. Wait. I had to fix this. "How much time does he have?"

"A day, maybe less," she replied, the glow from the van's overhead light glittering off her gold tooth.

Why did everything have to be a frickin' emergency? "Why didn't you tell me?" I could have at least tried to prevent this. I was the slayer.

"Ha! As I recall, you happened to be cursing me with the anaconda spell. When I came to, the black souls had fled the trailer. Means they'd found an open body to possess. I didn't know who until Scarlet told me."

"Dimitri, then." The jerk. "Why didn't he find me before *this* had to happen?"

"Probably because you were off skulking around the garbage dump."

Talking to Grandma. I would have done anything to have her with me right now. This was such a mess.

I shook off the self-pity. I had to try to save JR. He was Dimitri's friend, and besides, he'd been out there helping us. Those sounded like much more noble reasons than the sheer fact that they were going to kill us if I failed.

"Tell me," I said, "I have the power to pull these black souls out of JR and help them find their way."

"No," Ant Eater practically shouted. A tentative knock sounded at the door. "Go away!" she hollered. "Now you listen to me, missy. Your job ends when you pull the souls out of JR. Let them find their own way."

It didn't seem right.

"You've got a job to do. You do it. And only it. Don't try to channel Mother fucking Theresa."

How could she say that? "But I could save those people."

"They aren't people anymore!" Her gold tooth glistened with spittle. "They're things."

"You said yourself they're lost souls. You don't want the complication."

"Damned straight. Look, Lizzie—that ain't our problem." She planted her hands on her hips, right above the Glock stuffed into her pants.

"Get your hand off the gun." She was making me nervous.

Her eyes bored into me. "JR is possessed. Fang wants to kill us and Rex is gonna sell us straight to Vald if you fuck this up."

Heavens, I hoped I could handle this. "Why didn't Dimitri tell me any of this?"

*Why was I always the last to know?*

"*He* didn't want to freak you out. *I* don't care."

"Fine," I snapped. I'd defeated Xerxes. I could walk through death spells. I had to believe I could maybe, possibly, *hopefully* do this too. And I absolutely refused to give anybody the satisfaction of seeing how afraid I was. "So now I'm up to speed."

"That's it?" She looked at me like I'd sprouted horns.

Score a point for the demon slayer. "What do you mean, that's it? What else can go wrong?" Unless they'd found another possessed werewolf on my yellow flowered throw rug and imps in my underwear drawer.

I slid past her and threw open the door. Frieda practically fell inside. She'd chipped all the cotton-candy pink nail polish off one hand and had started in on the other.

"Horse feathers, Frieda!" We'd told the Red Skulls to run. I appreciated the support, but at the same time, we were trying to get her and the Red Skulls out of danger. "You should have left when you had the chance."

She twisted her plastic beaded necklace between her fingers. "You think I don't know that?" she snapped. "Heavens to Betsy, I was scared out of my skivvies for you in that trailer." She eyed my switch stars, glowing pink. "What happened? What are we going to do?"

There was no "we" about it. The Red Skulls had to get out of there. From what I'd seen in that trailer, I had the distinct feeling we'd already sprung the trap. The Red Skulls were caught up in a dangerous game of werewolf politics. Whoever won, I knew it wouldn't be us.

Ant Eater poked her head out of the rusting car and scowled at Frieda. "Holy hell, blondie, if I didn't know any better, I'd think you had a death wish." She hitched up her leather pants. "Tell the coven I meant it when I said to bail out."

Frieda hesitated, clearly worried about us.

"Lizzie and I will go after JR. We owe him. Besides, it'll give you guys enough lead time to escape. We'll meet up at the *Dixie Queen*."

Frieda nodded, twisting her necklace into new knots. Ant Eater glanced at me. We'd take the fallout if we failed—and if we succeeded. It was the best way for the rest of the witches to escape.

I was ready. Still, I couldn't help thinking about

Pirate. "Take good care of my dog, will you?" Tears burned the backs of my eyes. I didn't know what he'd do without me. Or what I'd do without him if . . .

Frieda gave me a little hug. "Bob has him. We'll take good care of him." To Ant Eater she said, "We'll be packed and out in ten minutes."

Ant Eater slapped her on the butt as she left. Together we watched Frieda dash across the uneven field in platform sandals.

"So what's the *Dixie Queen*?" I asked her.

"Hideout number four hundred and twenty-six. A mothballed Mississippi cruise and casino boat. The beds suck, but the roulette wheel still works. Least it did in '88."

"You know, you should go with them," I told her.

She puffed out her cheeks, still watching Frieda. "Yeah? Who's gonna watch your pansy ass?"

I had to think I could do this. If I couldn't, Ant Eater probably wouldn't be able to save me anyway. At the Dumpster, Grandma had told me what it meant to sacrifice myself.

It amazed me how well Grandma knew me after our short time together. She'd been dead accurate when we talked out by the Dumpster. I always did type out my grocery list on the computer. I never had a library late fee and I never did anything crazy until she showed up at my door. "Grandma said I needed to be more half-ass."

"Oh and now you're going to listen?" Ant Eater snorted.

"Yeah," I said, enjoying the moment.

Grandma said it herself. The last slayer had the power to lock Vald away. I had the power to destroy him.

"Vald wants you," Ant Eater said.

I knew it.

"If he finds you before you're ready," she said, "he could kill you. Or worse."

"Thanks for the pep talk."

"Candy ass."

"Road bitch."

She took a deep breath, then blew it out, watching the bobbing lights in and around the far trailers as the Red Skulls prepared to flee. "I'd slit my wrists if anything happened to the coven."

"Go."

She shoved herself away from the rusting hippie van. Before she could get far, I reached out and snapped her bra. She didn't turn around, but I heard her chuckling as she jogged out into the night.

Fang and about a dozen werewolves led me down a narrow path into the woods. Dozens of flashlights bounced off the darkened trees. I didn't miss the two large bodyguards who slipped behind me, cutting off any hope of escape. I kept my focus on the trail.

*Show no fear.*

It would have been nice to have some warning, especially since Dimitri knew about JR. Then again, what could I have done?

*Gee, Lizzie. I hope you get this demon slayer thing down soon because my friend JR is possessed and his dad, the alpha wolf, is going to kill you if you don't fix it. Oh, and Rex might kill you anyway. If he doesn't sell you out to Vald, the fifth-level demon, instead.*

And where was Dimitri? With JR, I hoped. We'd been walking for about a half hour, deeper and deeper into the woods. I knew we were getting close. I could touch the fear sizzling in the air like an angry mob clamoring for release. I chewed at my lip, every nerve on high alert. It felt like we were walking into an ambush.

The path opened up on an isolated cemetery. These were old graves, or at least they'd seen better days.

Mausoleums scattered across the wide open ground, topped with crosses, angels and crescent moons. Many of the wolves bowed their heads as they passed through the iron gates.

Rex did not.

A stream must have run nearby. I could smell dampness. The crickets and other creatures of the night seemed to have abandoned this place. The air felt heavy and foreboding.

I didn't like it one bit.

A hollow pounding tore through the night, like a cannon firing on sheet metal. I swallowed my fear and jogged past a series of low graves, toward the source of the noise. Past an altar to the full moon, I saw it—a shadow deep in the cemetery.

On high alert, I traveled around a cluster of silo-shaped mausoleums beyond the altar. These graves held the remains of several alphas and their families. Crowned half moons carved in stone topped each tomb. I ran my fingers along the inscription, common to each round mausoleum. *Never backed into a corner.* Glad they didn't have that problem. I sure did.

At least a dozen werewolves massed behind me. As I came closer to the source of the noise, I could see a dented horse trailer chained to a thick tree. It shook on its hinges like the Tasmanian Devil himself whirled around inside.

Now what was I supposed to do with that?

A hairy, clawed hand tore at the tiny window at the top. A snout followed—pulsing as it sucked air.

I turned to a scowling werewolf behind me. "Don't tell me that's—"

We heard a high-pitched whir, like eighty blenders grinding ice.

The ground shook. Dimitri shot out from behind the trailer, waving his hands as he made a mad dash for us.

"Back! Back! Back!" He grabbed me and we tumbled behind the closest alpha tomb.

Red-hot air shot past us and the sickening smell of sulfur assaulted my nose. I was smushed between Dimitri's warm body and a slightly wet patch of grass, but frankly, I didn't care about the cold seeping through my khakis. His weight on top of me, though slightly suffocating, was at the same time solidly comforting. He didn't know how glad I was to see him. I clutched him tight, closed my eyes and focused on his deep, heavy breaths and clean scent. It felt good to have an ally.

Before I knew it, Dimitri stood. He reached a hand down to help me to my feet as he squinted against the dust in the air. Every single werewolf, in front of us and behind, lay scattered in the grass.

"They're stunned." Dimitri blew out a breath. "I hope. Anyhow, we have to focus on JR. It'll take him a few minutes to build up his strength again."

We made a beeline for the trailer. His fingers danced over the locks as he yanked them open, one by one.

Um. Perhaps that wasn't such a good idea.

Dimitri tilted his head back at the crippled wolves. "Same thing happened to me when we found JR at the Red Skull. One second I had him cornered in the kitchen, and the next I was flat on my back with my friend ready to rip my head off."

I wished I'd been further along in my training that morning so I could have gone back with him. I hated to think what he'd risked for his friend. "Is there anything left of JR in there?"

"Right now? I don't know." He glanced at me. "I like to think something held him back before Scarlet threw her paralyzing spell." He shook his head, as if trying to rid himself of the memory. "It took four jars to pull him down. Even then, we hardly got the silver chains on him before he went crazy."

That might have been the last time I saw Dimitri alive. "Sorry I chased you across the parking lot."

"I'm not." The corner of his mouth almost twisted into a grin. "All things considered, that was the best part of my day." He yanked open the last lock. "You ready to see this?"

Ready as I'd ever be. *Trust yourself, Lizzie.*

Dimitri threw open the door. JR lurched for me like a feral animal. The man was built like a linebacker. He'd regained his human form, but there was no humanity left in his red eyes. JR's midnight black hair shone with sweat as he yanked against his chains, his meaty hands and feet, his wide chest bloody from the struggle. It didn't even seem like he felt the pain. What would we do if he changed back into a wolf? Would the chains hold him?

I felt the familiar urge to run like hell. Call it self-preservation.

*Sacrifice yourself.*

I *soooo* hated that last demon slayer Truth.

JR panted like he'd just eaten an entire village. Every time he exhaled, a thousand tiny needles pricked my skin. In his chest, I could feel them swirling. Dozens upon dozens. I couldn't get my head around how many black souls churned inside him. They were so angry. They needed a place to be; they missed their bodies. And they wanted him, bad.

"Lizzie?" Dimitri touched my shoulder.

"I don't know what to do," I whispered.

When I'd faced Xerxes in my bathroom, I had no choice but to fight him. It was self-defense, pure and simple. But now, I could feel JR slipping away. He shouldn't have lasted this long. Dimitri's friend was a fighter. I wanted to help him, but I didn't know if what I was about to do would save him or kill him.

*Sacrifice yourself.*

"Down, boy," I said, easing myself into the trailer. His chains rattled as he whipped his head from side to side—fighting to control his raging body. "Work with me, JR."

I reached out to touch his heaving chest and his hands flew to my wrists, trapping them. He could snap my bones without thinking. "Easy," I told him, feeling anything but. "Easy," I repeated. I inched his hands and mine toward his chest. "See, JR? We can do this."

*As long as you don't eat me.*

The moment my hand touched the hot, flushed skin over JR's heart, I felt a jolt, like I'd wrapped my hand around a live wire. His hands flew back, freeing my wrists. *Look to the outside.* I let the hum of his body wash over me as I inched my fingernails into his chest. The skin crumpled back like wet newspapers and I could smell his coppery blood. I dug farther, pushing past muscle. I dug through bone. The cracking of his ribs sounded like a batch of popcorn on the stove.

At last, my fingers whispered over his beating heart. *Please, don't let me hurt him.*

I stared down at my wrist, embedded in his chest. *Please don't let me hurt him worse.*

I could tear his heart out of his chest like an Aztec nightmare. It would be over before any of us could stop it. My fingers slipped over the pulsing muscle.

JR stared at me, eyes as wide as the full moon. I caught a glimmer of recognition.

*Help me.*

"Oh God, JR. I'm trying."

He groaned in pain as tiny knots bubbled in his heart. They felt like marbles. I coaxed the largest one to the surface and pulled it free. It almost slipped from my hand. "Shit!"

I almost lost it. And if I couldn't even keep hold of one . . . I fought back a wave of panic. *Sacrifice yourself.*

I took a deep breath, opened my mind, forced myself to relax and release whatever power I had. The thing wobbled in my palm.

Holy Hades. It sucked me down. As if in a dream, I watched a pretty brunette swimming in a lake at sunset. No. Not swimming—drowning. Do something! I clutched the edge of the boat.

*I didn't push her. She fell!*

But we didn't do anything to save her. Save her! She choked on the water, her eyes pleading.

*No! She's a whore. Let her get what's coming to her. I loved her! Can't anyone understand that? I loved her. But I won't have my children growing up with a slut for a mother. She deserves to die.*

It was in the past, a memory of the black soul I held in my hand. I felt its agony and its pleasure as the woman fought the water, gasped for her life. We ached and we laughed, as we watched the woman slip under the waves.

Holy moley. I gripped the black soul in my palm. There were more. I heard their faint screams, watched them bubble in JR's heart. I didn't know how either of us was going to survive this one.

"Heaven help us, JR."

I inched my other hand inside his chest—past flesh, muscle, ribs. Slowly, deliberately, I eased the lumps up from his heart and plucked them like weeds. Every one I touched wanted to penetrate me. *Wanted me.*

*They deserved to die.*

*I was following orders.*

*No one will ever know.*

They screamed for release.

I gripped them hard as they surged through me.

"Lizzie!" Dimitri's voice came from another universe.

Swallowing, I tried to answer. I felt like I was moving through water as I pulled my hands from JR's body.

JR panted hard, his eyes unfocused. There should have been enough blood on the floor to fill a bathtub, but when I pulled free, the wound closed as if it had never been there.

My mind swam. They'd left him. They were mine now. And I wanted them.

"Let them go," Dimitri was saying.

My head felt like it was stuffed with cotton.

"Lizzie!" he demanded.

I was weak. All my life I'd been weak. I'd been a sucker, always doing what people expected. Good Lizzie. Perfect Lizzie. Now, with these souls at my command, I felt powerful. And I didn't need Dimitri or anybody else telling me what to do.

"Back off." I shoved Dimitri as hard as I could. He crashed against the wall of the trailer. Good.

I had to get the souls inside me. I brought them to my chest, willing them. *Please.* I felt their power.

"Damn it, Lizzie!" Dimitri yanked my hands from my chest.

He was turning into a real pain in the ass. I wondered how hard it would be to kill him. He pulled me against him and the souls surged.

*Another body!*

*He's mine! Mine!*

*Get away!*

I felt myself sway. The negativity, the greed—it wasn't me. This wasn't me! I fought for control. I'd opened myself too far. I started slamming the doors in my mind as Dimitri's power poured into me. I didn't care what he was doing or how he was doing it.

Dimitri's hands warmed mine and through the clamor of the black souls, I felt . . . peace. I remembered flying. Flying? Not in an airplane, but like I had wings. High above cornfields and cotton, soaring with the wind in my face. Happy. I saw a family with twin girls. Dimitri's sisters. I didn't know how I knew, I just did. They laughed together, their noses almost touching. I felt the love. It reminded me of how I always hoped my real family would be, if I ever found them.

Pirate, think of Pirate. He was my family—Grandma too. I couldn't lose her—or myself. Not now.

Dimitri gripped my hands tighter. Once again, I was flying. A mix of feelings slammed into me. I felt his red-hot desire, his churning doubt. And deception? I couldn't go there. Not now.

I took those feelings and swallowed them deep down inside. Then together, we pushed them up, up, as I opened my palms and let the souls rise up like fireflies, through the ceiling of the rusty trailer and out into the universe.

The sudden emptiness overwhelmed me. Worse, I knew what had almost happened. Dimitri pulled me against his chest, and I wrapped my arms as far as they would go around his broad back. I clung to him for a few long moments, terrified of what I'd come close to becoming. Those black souls wanted me, and I wanted to go with them. I'd learned how to open myself, to sacrifice myself, but I knew nothing about limits. It scared me to think about how good it felt to be with them. I felt powerful, alive.

What had JR felt? The werewolf's breathing had steadied, but he was still horribly pale.

Dimitri checked on him while I leaned my back against the wall of the trailer and fought the urge to close my eyes. The black souls had exhausted me. No wonder JR could barely move. He'd been possessed for days. I'd held the souls for minutes and I wanted to sleep for a year.

Just then my mind pricked. I felt a strange stirring outside. When I peered out of the trailer, an army of ghosts swirled past the tombs. People, werewolves, and—holy smokes—creatures I didn't even know the names for. "I see—"

*What did I see?*

Dimitri moved behind me. "They're called mnemonics," he said against my ear.

"Can you see them?"

"Sometimes," he said, simply. "Your experience with death opened you to new worlds."

They glided through the cemetery, unaware of each other, or of us.

Dimitri's voice ground near my ear, flooding my body with warmth. "Mnemonics are memories, nothing more. Their souls have moved on."

I leaned back against him and wrapped his arms around me. He felt solid. Good. I didn't know what I would have done without him tonight, or any other night for that matter. He caught his breath as I nuzzled against him.

"Okay, coach," I said, turning toward him, "how do you know so much?"

I about melted at the intensity in his dark eyes.

"I've spent my life looking for a slayer. You. Then I met you and—" He lowered his lips to mine and I sank into his kiss.

What started out gentle turned into a heady, powerful rush of pleasure as his mouth ravaged mine. Sweet switch stars. I needed this. I needed him. His hands moved up my sides, caressed the undersides of my breasts, and I nearly combusted.

This is what it felt like to be alive.

My whole body tightened. The man was darned lucky we were smack-dab in the middle of a werewolf cemetery or I might have lost all control. Then again, something told me he wouldn't mind.

I pulled back and he nuzzled at my neck, sending a whole new wave of sensations barreling through me.

"You do have a way of welcoming a girl back from the almost-dead."

"Promise you'll never do that again," he said against my collarbone.

I kissed him on the nose, trying to hide my worry. "Promise." I hoped. I still didn't know how I'd lost control of the black souls. Dimitri, through his sheer goodness, had pulled me back. I held on to him, savoring his warmth. "Who were the girls I saw in your memories?"

"My twin sisters." He lifted his head, grief written all over his face. "Taken by Vald. He wiped out my entire family."

I couldn't imagine his pain. "I'm so sorry," I said, knowing words could never be enough.

Dimitri reached into his pocket and withdrew a small, velvet bag. He tipped it and slid an intricately woven hairpin into his palm. At its tip, a gold griffin snarled, its orange eyes flashing in the moonlight. "This was my sister Diana's."

My fingers hovered above the griffin.

"Touch it," he said, his voice husky.

"Does it hold any kind of power?" I asked, remembering his teardrop emerald.

"For me." He turned it over in his hands. "Take it," he said, his fingers caressing as he wove it into my hair. "Diana would want you to have it."

I touched the jewel in my hair.

Smiling, I pulled him back to me. The kiss was warm, demanding, almost a promise. I could save what remained of my family, try to ease Dimitri's pain too. With his arms wrapped around me, at that moment, it seemed like there was nothing I couldn't do.

A cold wind blasted us apart. Fang crashed down on us. He lashed at us with clawlike hands. His anguished roar tore through the trailer. With a start, I realized it wasn't Fang. It was his spirit. He hunkered briefly over his son. With a wail, he launched up through the roof of the trailer and into the night.

I felt like the breath had been knocked out of me. "Who killed Fang?" I asked, already knowing.

Dimitri scrambled out of the trailer and I followed a breath behind. The werewolves sprawled over the grass. Save one.

Rex stood over Fang's bloody body, knife in hand. "You did."

# Chapter Fifteen

Rex dropped the knife and drew his shotgun, the double barrel aimed at my chest. I hurled a switch star without even thinking about it. It fired through the air like a rocket and cleaved Rex's skull down the middle. The murderous werewolf didn't even know what hit him.

The two halves of Rex's head smoked as his body fell to the ground. His blood pooled in dark circles on the grass. There wasn't much. The switch star had cauterized the wounds, leaving his head neatly sliced.

My stomach squinched. Yick. The smell of scorched flesh and hair made me want to gag. I rested my hands on my knees while I caught up with the adrenaline surging through me. I'd killed him.

I had to kill him. He would have shot us. But how I'd done it—clean through the skull—was awful. I clutched the switch star in my right hand. It had boomeranged back to me, not a drop of blood on it.

Dimitri took a deep breath, his gun cocked and ready. "We have to go."

"Urgle." I couldn't take my eyes off the filet of wolf.

Dimitri checked on JR, then grabbed his backpack from the rear of the trailer.

Poor JR. How on earth were we going to take him with us? He was built like a water buffalo. His black T-shirt, wet with gore, was the only indication I'd reached

my hand into his chest. The muscles and bone underneath pushed firmly against the wet cloth as he took
short, deep breaths. Even asleep, he was a force to be
reckoned with. I could feel the strength and power rolling off him.

I brushed the dirt from his black hair and noticed
he'd begun to gray at the temples. I don't know why I
had to touch him again. Maybe I just needed to do
something that didn't involve gripping his heart in my
hands.

What would JR be like when he woke up?

Dimitri threw his shoulder holster on. "Here." He
tossed me a set of keys. "Unlock him."

I pulled my hand back. Sure, we had to take him with
us, but I preferred my new friend chained. JR's eyes
clenched shut and he panted hard, like he was fighting
something.

The black souls had flown the coop, but that didn't
mean JR wasn't about to turn into a crazed werewolf.

Dimitri dumped a small arsenal out of his backpack,
along with some first-aid equipment—the basic tool
kit for taking someone apart or putting them back together. He glanced my way. "Sorry. I can't guarantee
he won't turn furry. That's what you're worried about,
isn't it?"

"I've had enough of rampaging werewolves for one
night."

"Touché. But JR's my friend and he's going to need
all the help he can get," Dimitri said, clicking an ammo
clip into one of the pistols. "He could be in trouble when
the pack recovers from that paralyzing spell. No telling which side is going to wake up first." He stuffed
the gun into his shoulder holster. "With any luck, we'll
be on the road by then."

"You mean we're not taking him with us?" At least
a dozen werewolves littered the ground around the

trailer. It was impossible to know who was friend or foe until they woke up. And then it would be too late.

I didn't want to know what would happen if Rex's people got to JR first. Would they execute him like Rex did to their former alpha, Fang? Or would it be something even more horrible?

"We can't just leave him here." Call it selfish, but my conscience wouldn't allow it. In my book, you didn't leave your friends to get stabbed, slaughtered or eaten. "We have to save him."

"We did," Dimitri said, regret plain on his face as he placed two loaded pistols and a knife next to the fitful werewolf.

Dimitri located a beat-up Yankees cap in the corner of the trailer. JR's, I assumed. He brushed the dirt off the brim and placed it on his friend's head. "If he's found with us, they'll execute him on sight."

He stood up to his full height, all business. He'd never looked more large or deadly. "You killed pack, Lizzie. You're their enemy now—and JR's."

In what universe did that make sense? "Do the words 'self-defense' mean anything to these people?"

He shook his head ruefully. "I'm afraid not."

I fumbled with the keys, shoving them into tiny locks and working the layers of cuffs away from JR's thick wrists and ankles. In another life I would have been nervous. Lord knew we had reason. We still didn't know if Pirate and the Red Skulls had escaped. I might be unchaining a crazy werewolf. And any time now, an army of hostile werewolves would wake up and find their alpha's jugular slashed and their second-in-command with a large switch-star hole through his forehead.

No way around it. I should have been scared as a hamster at a rattlesnake convention. But I wasn't. I was pissed. It wasn't my fault Rex died. He'd been gunning for me from the start. He saw me as a weak link the minute we set foot in Shoney's. Frankly, he might have been right. But I'd grown into my powers, and it was Rex's own friggin' fault he'd been too busy scheming to notice.

Rex had no right to mess with me or the pack. I yanked the chains from JR's chest and his eyes flew open for a moment. "Eep!" I pitched backward and landed hard on my rear.

I might have had the demon slayer bit down, but I had a lot to learn about hard-ass.

Dimitri leaned past me. "JR." He shook him. "Hey, buddy."

JR squinted up at us through bloodshot eyes. Thank goodness they were brown instead of the sickly red they'd been before.

The wolf shuddered.

Dimitri squeezed my arm. "Good job, Lizzie."

JR broke into a coughing fit. He gulped several breaths. "Talk about a hangover. I feel like the worm in the tequila bottle."

"Don't try to talk," Dimitri told him.

JR waved him off, winked at me and nearly passed out again. "Oh good. You found her," he said. His eyes focused on the chains hanging from the trailer ceiling. "This isn't the bar."

He still thought we were at the Red Skull. Good. He didn't need to remember what had happened to him after that.

"You had an accident, but you're okay. Your pack will explain." Dimitri shook his head. "I hate to do this to you, buddy, but Lizzie and I have to split."

JR coughed, catching his breath. "Something I should know about?"

"While you were out cold, the pack had a problem," Dimitri said, diplomatically.

JR knew without us telling him. "Rex."

"He's dead." Dimitri said.

"Good," JR said, grunting as he pulled himself up.

"But, listen, we think Rex poisoned half the pack. And," Dimitri said, clearly dreading what he had to say next, "Rex killed Fang."

JR nodded, unable or perhaps unwilling to speak.

"I got Rex with a switch star," I said to fill the silence. He needed to know someone tried to do something. "It was too late."

JR kept nodding.

"Take this." Dimitri gave JR a silver dagger. "These too," he added, handing him the pistols he'd taken from his backpack.

JR's eyes locked on something past my shoulder. "Go," he grunted.

I followed his gaze out into the cemetery. Lights bobbed up the path.

With any luck, it meant the witches had safely fled. A bubble of satisfaction welled in my chest. If those wolves were looking for reinforcements, they were out of luck.

But I also knew there'd be no way to explain the wolves crumpled among the graves, or the executed alpha. Or Rex with his head cleaved in half. We had to get out of there.

Dimitri tossed the backpack over his shoulder and jumped from the trailer. I was about to follow when JR's heavy hand gripped my arm. He squeezed once, twice. "Thank you," he said thickly. I had a feeling he didn't say it too often.

"Glad to help," I told him. And I was.

Dimitri and I dashed through the dark cemetery. The werewolves could see a lot better and move faster, but if we had enough of a jump on them, we could make it out of there with our hides intact.

We raced past the lonely graves scattered over the

far side of the cemetery. They were much older and—I stumbled through a thicket of weeds—untended. The families had probably died out.

Dimitri came to an abrupt stop before a blue granite structure. "Here."

The name said *Flier*. A black Harley leaned against the back of the grave.

I climbed on behind Dimitri, pressing myself flush against his back and holding on for dear life as the bike pitched forward. My handsome protector introduced me to a whole new kind of terror, zigzagging between trees, over logs and past the few graves that reached beyond the confines of the cemetery.

My brain rattled over every rock and hole we hit. Dimitri wasn't the best driver under ideal conditions. Now? I did everything I could to stay on.

Dimitri pitched the bike up a steep embankment and onto the road, a narrow strip of asphalt winding into the forest. He gunned the motor, and the wind whipped at our faces as we sped off into the night.

*We're coming to get you, Grandma.*

We'd done more than play pack politics tonight. I'd learned I could face off in a battle and win. I could live by the demon slayer Truths and trust myself, get outside myself enough to release my powers, even if I didn't fully understand them. It had to be enough.

Grandma had looked terrible when she appeared to me. She didn't have much time left. I couldn't afford to wait. We'd meet up with the witches at the *Dixie Queen*'s casino. Then I'd learn what I needed to do to find Vald. It probably wouldn't be too hard, I thought with a shiver. The demon wanted me.

Ant Eater told me I'd know it when the witches arrived at their new hideout. Somehow, I'd instinctively understand how to find them. I reached out with my feelings, searching for the comfort that everything was all right. Instead, I sensed dull emptiness and fear. No telling whether it came from the coven or from my own dark thoughts.

I gripped Dimitri tighter, feeling his warm skin through his black T-shirt. For a moment, just a moment, I allowed myself to take comfort in his closeness. I knew I shouldn't want him. He was nothing but trouble. But I couldn't help it. I needed a little good in my life after Rex, after the werewolves, after everything that had happened since Grandma pulled up to my front door on her pink-and-silver Harley.

I finally understood why Dimitri had sought me out and why he couldn't tell me the truth right away. The other day on the side of the road, I wasn't ready to hear about the fifth-level demon who'd taken his family. I didn't want to know I was destined to face that demon or that I'd lose someone too. I wasn't ready for my future or for Dimitri. But that had changed.

"I'm going to pass out." I sat on the side of the road with my head between my knees. The sunrise sent a tumble of red and orange streaks across the sky. I'd made Dimitri pull over in Tupelo, Mississippi. We had to keep moving. I knew that. But my arms felt so weak, my body so tired, I was afraid I'd fly off the bike like a tiddlywink if Dimitri hit one more pothole.

"When was the last time you ate?" he asked, rifling around in his backpack.

"Not a good idea," I said, my stomach threatening to riot. "I'm just . . . exhausted."

"Come on." Dimitri gathered me up in his arms. Yum. It felt too good. His warm, masculine scent nearly undid me. But as utterly content as I felt at the moment, I couldn't, I wouldn't go back to that bike.

"Oh no," I said, muffled in his shirt as he strode toward the Harley. "Let me die on the side of the road. I'm not cut out to be a biker babe."

"Hold on," he said, placing me back on the hog. "We gotta get you out of the open. I noticed a safe spot a few miles back. We'll go slow, okay?"

I nodded. "Where are you taking me?" Did he know of another hideout nearby? If werewolves ran Shoney's, perhaps a dragon BBQ joint would be just the spot—or maybe Dimitri knew of a Denny's run by leprechauns. I'd even be open to a mermaid water park. Anything to get me off this bike for an hour or two. "Where in the world of weird creatures are you taking me?"

"Motel 6."

I never would have thought of Motel 6 as a great place to take a break from werewolf fights and black soul possession, but we sure could have done worse. The bored teenager who checked us in was too busy chomping her gum to notice the switch stars I'd forgotten to take off my belt. She simply twirled a Kool Aid–red lock of hair and informed us we had a room at the back of the hotel, second floor.

This place was the Taj Mahal compared to the trailer I'd shared with Ant Eater. Much cuter company too, I mused, as Dimitri tossed his backpack onto the king-size bed.

Wait.

Dimitri was assuming a heck of a lot.

I eyed the humongous bed with its quilted seashell comforter. "Planning to sleep in the bathtub, are you?"

Dimitri flashed a smile that was pure sin. "If you'd been paying attention to the clerk instead of trying to hide your switch stars behind the gumball machine, you'd have heard for yourself. They only have kings left."

"Yeah, well don't get fresh."

Just my luck he listened.

Dimitri didn't try to peek when I took a shower, refused to look when I climbed under the covers and allowed me to sleep unmolested for the next fourteen hours.

Jerk.

My head felt hazy when I woke up to find him propped up in bed next to me. He held a small object in his hand, like a pocket watch. Inside glowed the image of two girls, asleep.

*His sisters.*

It hurt to think about everything he'd lost. All the same, I was glad he finally trusted me with the truth about why he'd hunted me down and why he wanted Vald dead.

I was about to ask him about his sisters when another thought hit me like a riptide. I sat up so fast I nearly knocked the thing out of his hand. "I know where the witches are," I gasped.

The *Dixie Queen* was moored in a deserted inlet of the Yazoo River, just south of the Tallahatchie. Before that moment, if anyone had asked me to find the Yazoo, I wouldn't have been able to point it out on a map. Now I knew exactly how to get there. I didn't know how I knew, I just did. Every one of the Red Skulls had made it. Thank goodness.

Dimitri shoved the object in his pocket. "Yeah, I know too," he said, somewhat annoyed. "Ant Eater got me on my cell."

Of course.

Speaking of slaying fifth-level demons, we had to get moving. "Why didn't you wake me up?"

"You need all the strength you can get." He gazed at me intently. "A window will open, Lizzie. Tomorrow. It's time to face Vald."

Holy schniekies. A little warning would have been nice. I didn't even like pop quizzes in school, much less a surprise ultimate face-off with an evil demon. "Why didn't you tell me before?"

"You were throwing switch stars in the dirt."

Yeah, yeah, and beheading the Shoney's Big Boy. I didn't need a reminder of how much I'd screwed up.

"Adding a deadline didn't seem like the best approach," Dimitri said matter-of-factly.

Truth be told, I was glad. Grandma needed help, the quicker the better.

"Vald has been drawing strength from your grandma, and from the remains of my family. But drawing energy is like sucking soda from a straw. Every once in a while, you have to take a breath. Tomorrow at midnight, Vald will take that breath. He'll be open, more vulnerable. It's the best time to strike."

"Okay," I said, nodding one too many times. "How do you know all this?"

"Everyone knows," he said, too matter-of-fact for my taste.

"Oh sure. Why not?" Everyone but me.

He shrugged. "Your grandma saw it in her vision before she was taken. Scarlet was there." So Scarlet knew and Dimitri and the coven. Heck, I'm sure Pirate had even heard of it by now.

"Fine," I said. We were going to deal with this. Later. In the meantime, "What's the plan?"

"We rest. Prepare. Tomorrow morning, we'll head out and meet the coven at the *Dixie Queen*. We're about four hours out." He checked his watch absently. "They're expecting us at noon. We'll discuss strategy. Then we face him and win."

Or lose. *No, don't think of what could happen if we fail.*

In less than twenty-four hours, I'd be facing off with

a fifth-level demon. My training had led me to this moment, to tomorrow's showdown. I hoped I was up to it. Grandma deserved more than to die in the second layer of hell. Dimitri's family deserved to be avenged. And afterward, I deserved to sleep for about a year. It blew my mind to realize that if I actually survived this, I'd be free to go home, to resume my life, to teach my preschool class. I wondered if I could ever go back. I hoped I could.

I dug my hand into the pocket of my khakis and found the jeweled griffin hairpin Dimitri had given me. I smoothed it into my hair.

Dimitri caught my hands and held them in his, palms up. My breath caught in my throat. Black marks singed my hands and fingers where I'd touched the black souls.

He brought my hands to his lips and kissed each black stain. "I thought I'd lost you back there," he said, lingering over my fingertips. "I would never have forgiven myself."

I nodded, fascinated as his lips and teeth grazed my skin. He was my protector. Yow. *Who was going to protect me from him?*

"You are so damned dangerous," he said, his mouth sinking into mine.

I responded with everything I had. Oh, yes. This was exactly how it should be. I wrapped my arms around him, threaded my fingers through his hair.

He eased his rough-and-tumble demon-butt-kicking body over me and I squirmed under his delicious weight. "Hot for teacher" didn't even begin to cover it. I was no slut puppy, but serve up a sexy protector, a couple of near-death experiences and—oh my word was that *him* on my thigh? A girl can only resist so much.

I tore my mouth from his. "Back off now," I said,

fighting the urge to wriggle against the hard ridge jutting from underneath his jeans, "or I'm not responsible for my actions."

"If you can still put a sentence together, I'm doing something wrong," he said, yanking off his black T-shirt with one hand. "Maybe this'll help."

If there's ever a time for a man to exceed all expectations, it's in bed.

I knew Dimitri was stacked, but—yee, hee lucky me—he had the chest of a Greek god. I ran my fingers over his olive skin. Mmm . . . his nipples were particularly dark, and rigid. I grazed them with the barest, teasing touch until they stood at attention. Hmm. And hello, abs. The man could have been an underwear model. I let my fingers curl into the black hair that ran down his lower stomach and disappeared under the waistband of his jeans.

He flicked his eyes up to mine, and his lips curled into a wicked smile. "Are you done fondling me?"

"Not by half." I scraped one of his nipples between my teeth and was rewarded when he gasped and about doubled over. Told him not to mess with me. He ran his fingers through my hair as I teased each nipple in turn, rolling them in my mouth.

"My turn," he gasped, gripping my head and plastering me with a hot, demanding kiss. He was all tongue and teeth. He stroked and demanded until my entire body threatened to implode. I squeezed my thighs together. If he could make me wet and aching without even touching down there, what would happen if . . . ?

He drew a sharp breath as I shifted my body to bring him in line with the part of me that screamed for his touch. Eureka! He felt rock hard, amazing. It had been way too long.

His mouth grazed the thin material over my breast.

God, who knew a white button-down could feel so good? I threw my head back, brimming with pure rapture.

"Watch me, Lizzie," he said, his lips hovering over me.

I stared at him, unable to speak, as he slowly started to unfasten each white button on my blouse. It felt like huge, honking bottle rockets were going off at the juncture between my thighs.

"Oh please," I croaked, wild with anticipation.

Dimitri chuckled. He drew back my bra with his thumbs. He caught his breath and his look of wonder brought hot tears to the backs of my eyes. He slowly lowered his mouth, his eyes fixed on mine as he took one screaming, begging nipple between his teeth. "Oh thank God!" I nearly exploded.

I wanted him. Now. Naked against me.

Which meant, oh geez, "Dimitri," I panted. I clutched his head, scooted that awful inch away from him. "We have to stop."

"Are you trying to kill me?" he gasped against my breasts.

"Of course not," I said, staring at the ceiling, trying to get a grip. "I may have wanted to maim you a few times, but that's in the past."

As far as our future together? Well, I didn't know. And there was the problem. As much as I liked to pretend I could have a night of blazing hot sex with no consequences, I wasn't the type. Damn, I hated being responsible.

"We don't need to stop," he murmured, "Stopping is bad." His lips found my other nipple. Another wave of pleasure seized me, sending spirals of heat through me until I was ready to surrender.

I knew he wasn't just talking about tonight. Somewhere along the line, he'd wound himself into my heart—for better or worse. There was no turning back now, no getting him out of my system. I wanted Dimitri with me. I wanted this.

*Think. Stop and think.*

I curled my fingers into the bedsheets to keep them from finding his beautiful butt. I was usually more rational. I decided how far to go before he, oh geez, his hands moved to my thighs and I nearly passed out from anticipation. I didn't plan this. But I could touch him a little, right? My hands wandered down his sides. It was like I hadn't had chocolate cake in a year and I couldn't stop with one bite. Only it had been more like two years and he tasted better than super-double-fudge icing and it would be so easy to slide my hand under the waistband of his Levi's 501s.

He ground his mouth against mine and I gave myself up to the sensation. Ribbons of electricity wound through me.

"Are we stopping?" he whispered against my lips. "I need to know. Now."

We both inhaled sharply as I slid my fingertips under the waistband of his jeans. His skin was superheated, his breath jerky. It wasn't fair. I had to decide once and for all. I touched the firm flesh of his lower stomach, felt the hair curl under my fingertips, knew if I moved a little more . . .

"No." I slid my fingers beneath his silk boxers. "We're not stopping tonight."

# Chapter Sixteen

"Hold still," I told him, as I explored rough hair and mmm velvety skin, practically thrumming with anticipation.

"Impossible. To do. When you—ahhhh!"

I slipped my fingers over his enormous length. His cock leaped against his jeans, begging for release. I ran a finger over his tip, already slick and ready.

He moved against my hand. "You want to play?" He yanked my shirt the rest of the way open, sending buttons flying.

"You bonehead! That was my only—"

"I'll buy you another one," he said, yanking down his Levi's.

I wriggled out of my khakis before Dimitri decided to shred them. They joined his jeans on the floor, and his boxers. Woo-hoo! He was hard, ready and giving me a standing ovation.

Nude, he was breathtaking . . . rock-solid legs, narrow hips and shoulders that could haul a truck. He wasted no time stradling me, his hands capturing my wrists above my head, his erection pressed firmly into my panties.

"Ahh, you and me, Lizzie," he said, blazing a slow trail of kisses across my collarbone, "we belong together."

"You sound like a Hallmark card," I said, wriggling against him. I didn't want to think. I just wanted to feel.

"We didn't plan it," he said, finding the sweet spot at the base of my neck, "but there's no sense denying it."

Oh, yes there is. I tried to tell him point-blank, but it came out more like, "Oh fargleee yeeees!" In my defense, he'd picked that moment to start rocking back and forth over my most sensitive parts.

I had no room for a handsome Greek protector in my life, once we killed Vald that is. I couldn't see Dimitri fitting into my old life back in Atlanta. He wasn't the type to argue politics with Cliff, or help run the Happy Hands Preschool picnic. This had to be a one-shot deal. Wham, bam, thank you mister "Zowww!" His tongue found the ultrasensitive nook behind my ear.

"You," he nipped lower. "Belong with me." Before I could answer, his fingers found the edge of my drenched panties. No fair.

"My people, we know these things," he whispered.

His people? Sure, his people. Whatever. Oh God, if only he'd move his fingers an inch to the left. A half inch. A centimeter. Anything. He ran his fingers up and down the edge of my panties, waiting. I tipped my hips up to meet his hand. "Less think-y. More kiss-y."

"You know you're mine."

"Whatever you say." I couldn't believe I was actually about to have sex with my studly protector. And his fingers, oh his fingers. He was so close! He hooked a thumb under the edge of my panties and kept it there, no matter what I did.

*Yes, yes. I get it. I'm yours.*

This was cruel and unusual punishment. "What am I going to have to do to get you to cut the chatter?"

He ripped off my panties and shimmied down my body.

He ran his hands up the insides of my thighs and

spread my legs wide. "Beautiful," he said before I felt his tongue dip inside me.

I nearly lurched off the bed. His tongue felt hot, branding me from the inside out. My hips—the traitors—thrust up on their own.

"Patience," he chastised me, before delivering a single, agonizingly slow lick.

"Bastard."

He chuckled and I felt his breath, warm against me, like its own caress. Holy moley, I didn't have a chance. His tongue flicked in and out of me. If he kept this up, I'd never let him go. My insides melted. Glimmering heat wound from between my legs and up . . . everywhere. I whimpered. I couldn't help it. He dipped a single finger inside of me and I wanted to scream. Fingers, tongue, mouth—he never stopped. My world revolved around the exquisite heat radiating through my body.

When I didn't think I could take any more, he'd pull back enough, just enough for me to settle down. Then he'd start again, licking, sucking, pushing, demanding. It was too much. I heard myself scream.

Finally, after I could sop up no more pleasure, he took mercy. He lifted his head, and cast me a wicked grin. "You know you belong with me."

I swallowed, desperately searching for my non-screaming, panting, whimpering voice.

"I think I've known for a while," he said absently, as if he wasn't hovering over my quivering girlie bits. "But it hit me like a sucker punch when I thought I'd lost you to the black souls."

It was hard to think with my whole body pulsing. But he seemed eager for an answer. Okay, so we were smitten. There was no way to know what would happen after tomorrow. I had to return to my normal life.

But I knew what I wanted right then and there. "Come here," I said, urging him into my arms. I wanted him, needed him inside me.

He snaked up my body, pure sin blazing in his eyes. He had to know what that did to me. He was all warm heat and hard muscle.

"I have to tell you something," he said.

Oh no. "Now?"

"Yes. Now." He frowned slightly, tipped my chin up and kissed me hard. His tongue found mine and pleasure rippled through every place he'd licked and then some. I could kiss him for weeks and still want more. I ground my naked body against his. Harder, faster, slower, I wanted him anywhere and everywhere I could get him. When we finally broke apart, we were both breathing hard.

"Once my people make love," he said, his lips inches from mine. "We have a hard time—agggguh!" My hips found him and pressed the tip of him inside me.

He was immense and I was drenched. My body gripped him, refused to let him go until he finished what he started.

"Ah," he said, trying to assemble a coherent thought. "I—" His breath jerked in his throat. Clearly, breathing was not a priority at the moment. He held me in a vise grip, fighting to keep me, and himself, from moving another inch. "My people," he gasped, holding me in place. "We have a difficult time letting go."

"Good to know," I managed to say on an exhale. I strained against him, hoping to end any conversation once and for all. But, dang, he was strong. And as far as him not letting go, well, his bad luck he fell for a demon slayer. "Don't forget. I'm going to hell tomorrow," I said, giving it one last wriggle.

He pulled out and my body screamed in protest.

"Well, sure you can go to hell," he said, his naked body pressed to mine. His cock hard against my thigh. "But I mean afterward."

"You know if you hadn't started talking, we'd be boffing our brains out right now."

"Soon. I'm not the kind of guy," he began. He reconsidered and simply said, "You need to know what you're getting into."

I'd already made my decision. Now my body screamed for him to finish what he'd started. "You want me. You need me. I'm yours." For tonight, for as long as I could have him. Or at least until we got back from hell. "Now will you pleeeeze—"

"What?" He asked, his mock innocence not fooling anybody.

"Do me," I demanded.

"With pleasure," he growled, his eyes hot with anticipation.

He opened my thighs and shouted as he slammed into me. I gripped his shoulders, his back, I matched him thrust for thrust. His muscles were tight with strain. Pure exhilaration spiraled through me and stretched taut. I stood on the edge. Heaven knew I'd been close, so close for so long. Dimitri pushed me harder, faster until I fell. Pleasure exploded from between my legs and radiated through me. It was almost too much.

"Stay with me," Dimitri whispered in my ear, as he continued to push me harder, deeper, faster than I'd ever been. I didn't care if the entire hotel came down around our ears. He ground his mouth over mine, nipping my lower lip, my neck, the tip of my ear. Our bodies grew slick with sweat. I wrapped my legs around him and felt myself coming again. Sweet pleasure washed over me until all I could do was clutch him and feel it in wave after luscious wave.

He tensed, thrust two times, hard. He clutched me so

tightly that he lifted us both off the bed as he pounded into me one last time. I came again and so did he.

We collapsed onto the bed, his head buried in the crook of my neck.

I woke to find Dimitri stroking my arm and sunlight creeping through the light-blocking curtains we'd failed to close the night before. Who knew hot love with Dimitri would be as exhausting as, say, battling a power-hungry werewolf or blasting a few dozen black souls? I snuggled closer, wishing we could spend the day in bed, knowing it was time to meet with the Red Skulls and make our final stand against the demon Vald.

I played with the springy dark hairs on his chest. "You don't have to go with me."

"Yes, I do."

I lifted my head to find him gazing intently at me. He flashed a cocky grin that made the skin around his eyes crinkle.

What do you say to a guy who'd go to hell and back, just to be with you?

I wrapped my arms around him. "Kiss me."

He devoured my mouth. It was like coming home. I ran my hands up his chest and to his shoulders, tight with tension. He kissed me like he was afraid to stop.

After a long, enjoyable while, he broke away. "Lizzie," he said, mouth brushing mine. "I need to tell you something."

"Oof." Then he'd better stop thumbing my nipples.

"Lizzie?" He pulled his hands away. My nipples whimpered in protest. "I've owed you the truth for a while now, but it never seemed to be the right time to tell you."

My brain swam back through a haze of desire. "And this is the right time?"

"No," he said ruefully. "But if I don't tell you now, I

might not get the chance before," he seemed reluctant to say it, "tonight."

"Okay. I'm listening," I said, praying it would be something simple, knowing it wasn't.

"I lied to you," he said, his mouth forming a grim line.

"About what?" I asked, getting that awful, sinking feeling in the pit of my stomach that our little love bubble was about to pop.

"I had to do it," he said quickly. "For my sisters."

Not helping. "What's the lie?" I asked.

*And why did this have to happen while we were buck naked at Motel 6?*

"I'm not your protector," he said simply.

I stared at him and managed a squeaky "What?"

"You don't have a protector," he said, as if every word pained him. "You don't need one. The truth is," he cringed as he said it, "I need a slayer."

The shock of it made my head swim. Dimitri needed me, not the other way around. A horrible thought slammed into my brain. *Had he been using me?*

I bolted upright in bed. He'd searched me out. He'd found me. He'd lied to stay close to me. Why? I yanked the sheet up over my breasts.

*What did he really want?*

"I had to do it," he said, reaching for me, fisting his hands when I ducked away from his embrace. "You're the only one who can save my sisters."

It didn't make any sense. I retreated to the corner of the bed, hauling the covers with me. "But your sisters, they're . . ."

"Dead?" He blew out a breath. "Not yet. I need your help. You have to understand—"

"I don't have to do anything. Of all the sick things to do, you lied about your dead sisters?" He'd planned this from the start. That's why he'd found me on the side of the road. That's why he'd trained me. Who knew if he cared about Grandma? Or me.

Sure, bang the demon slayer and get what you want. I understood. "You think this is what it takes to get my help?" He didn't have to do this. I would have helped him if I could—for nothing. His emerald glowed hot against my neck. I wished for the hundredth time I could chuck it at his head.

"You know it's not like that, Lizzie," he insisted. "I mean, it was." He drove a hand through his thick black hair. "Look, it took me years to find a slayer. You. And when I found you, I would have done anything to save my sisters, even seduce you."

"Not helping."

"But then I met you and you were different than I expected. Better. Amazing. I had to tell you I was your protector so you'd let me stay close. You can't think . . ." he began, reaching for me again, dropping his hand as I scuttled away.

"Dammit, Lizzie," he said, launching himself at me. He gripped my shoulders and forced me to look at him. "Where we are right now, this isn't a lie." I tried to squeeze out of his grasp, but his fingers dug in until it hurt. "I've been wanting to tell you the truth for days, but I was too scared." His familiar male scent, now tinged with a hint of sex, made me want to run for the hills.

I glared daggers at him.

"I'm sorry I didn't tell you sooner. But there was the real possibility that your reaction would be," he indicated my current rumpled, angry state, "less than positive."

"So you had to wait and sleep with me first?"

"Yes. No! I didn't want anything to come between us anymore. What we have here is incredible and I was sick of lying to you."

I hated him at that moment. I really hated him. He sure hadn't had trouble lying in the beginning. He'd fooled everybody. "You could have just asked me to help save your sisters."

"Would you have helped?" he asked.

I would have liked to think so. But when he met me, I'd never seen a switch star, let alone thrown one. All of a sudden, I wasn't too fond of myself, either.

"You didn't even know you were a slayer when I found you. My sisters need help now. Every female in my family falls into a coma after her twenty-eighth birthday. They're dead twenty-eight days later." He shook his head ruefully. "I met you with five days to spare. My sisters didn't have time for you to make up your mind."

"Well I'm glad you thought of everything." *Except me.*

I wound the sheet around myself. "About your sisters, they're not . . ."

He shook his head. "Tomorrow. He takes them tomorrow."

"And that's when you arranged for me to go in," I stated flatly.

He nodded. "That is why I sought you out. But that's not why I—" He drew back. "You've gotta believe me, Lizzie."

"Save it."

I didn't even want my brain to go there. I'd been ignored by men before, but never used. I couldn't believe the things he'd made me think and feel. I didn't want to think he'd lie to get me into bed. Then again, I hadn't suspected he'd lie to get me into hell.

Fighting to swallow the lump in my throat, I tried to be practical. At least we could help his sisters. He didn't deserve it, but they did. "Got any other big secrets?" I asked.

He looked guiltier, if that was even possible.

Un-frickin-believable. "This is about Grandma, isn't it? The night I met you, you tried to pawn off a murder rap on her. Was that a lie too?"

He looked as miserable as I felt. Good. "Tell me now or I'll never forgive you."

He sighed. "I'm sorry, Lizzie. But Gertie did kill your mom."

"You'd better know more than that. Spill it. Now."

Lord in heaven, he actually looked sorry for me. "Your mom, Phoenix, I don't know what she was, but supposedly, she was very powerful—a secret weapon against Vald. Unlike you," he said, forcing the words out, "she'd been training her whole life to face him. When the time came, she ran."

I couldn't believe it. I could understand, but I still couldn't quite think anyone would be that selfish. Then again, hadn't I felt like doing the same thing? "Where did she go?"

"I don't know. The point is, she left the Red Skulls to face Vald alone. The carnage was unbelievable. They lost everything. The survivors went on the run. Your grandma tracked Phoenix down to an occult shop they owned. There was a confrontation. Gertie made it out alive. Phoenix didn't."

Fine, so it looked bad.

I grabbed my underpants from the side table and saw they'd been ripped in half. Dimitri's story would explain why the Red Skulls hadn't wanted to answer any of my questions about my mom. But Grandma? It had to be an accident, or a mistake—anything but cold-blooded murder.

That had to be it. I leaped out of bed and started yanking my pants on. "It was a long time ago, Lizzie." Dimitri followed me, trying to get me to face him. I felt the hot tears coming and knew that if I looked at him I could lose it. Growing up, I'd had this picture in my mind of what my biological parents would be like. I never had much hope for ever meeting my dad. My birth certificate listed him as "unknown." But my mom? Call it a stupid gut feeling, but I always felt like I'd meet her someday.

Suspicion clawed at me. I wondered why Dimitri had decided to tell me now. Twenty minutes ago, I would have thought he was concerned. After the whopper he'd told about his sisters, "What do you want me to do now? Save your sisters instead of my murdering grandma?"

"No. Of course we'll get Gertie. Vald has them all."

I glared at him through a haze of tears. And why was a fifth-level demon following us around anyway? "It's your fault he got her, isn't it?"

"No, Lizzie. He's been holding out for you, wanting your powers. Sure, I followed you, but so did he. Remember the imps on the road? You may not like how I helped you, Lizzie, but you needed me to teach you as much as I need you to save my sisters tonight."

"Let's say it plain. You used me."

"Yes."

There. He admitted it. He'd used me for my powers, and my body.

He had the nerve to look exasperated. "We couldn't have a future with lies between us, and I want a future with you."

He stood there with a pained expression, waiting—for what I couldn't imagine.

"Forgive me," he said.

"When hell freezes over."

I tripped over a corner of the bed and he caught me. "Lizzie." He wrapped me in a bear hug.

"Don't touch me," I said, extricating myself. I found my bra wadded up next to the TV stand.

"Okay. Fine. Hate me. I hate myself right now too. But I was desperate to save Diana and Dyonne. It was the only way."

"Fuck you." There. I said it. And it didn't feel nearly as good as I'd imagined.

He stood, looking helpless and forlorn. "Despise me, Lizzie. But it ends as soon as we hit the *Dixie Queen*. We need you focused for tonight. Vald has your grandma, but what he really wants is you. You have more raw power than any slayer I've ever heard of, but you're still learning. Think about what happened with the black souls."

"Move." I had to find my scarf-belt.

"Vald thinks he can take your power. You can't let him, Lizzie."

"Oh, now you care about what happens to me?"

"I've always cared, Lizzie," he said softly.

I delivered a scalding look as I tried to button my white shirt. Hard to do when there were only two buttons left. I hurled the ruined shirt across the room.

"Okay. That's not true. I admit it. In the beginning, I only needed a slayer. I've been training my whole life to defeat this curse, to save my sisters. You have no idea how rare your skills—" He shot me a guilty look. "How rare *you* are," he corrected, a little too late. "When I sensed you, I went for you."

"How long did you follow me?"

"Lizzie, let's not get into this."

"How long?" I demanded.

"About a week. I sensed your powers through your grandma. She would have found you sooner, but her emotions blocked her. She cared about you. I only wanted to find you."

I'd asked for the truth. Too bad I never realized how bad it would hurt. But how could I have really prepared myself for him, or this?

"Vald wants you, Lizzie. Your grandma suspected. It's probably why he took her."

So now it really was my fault Grandma was burning in hell. "Well aren't you full of sunshine and donkey feathers."

"If a demon can harness power like yours, there's a good chance he can break out of hell."

"What? And walk the earth or something?"

"Yes," Dimitri said.

"So technically, we'd be better off forgetting the whole thing."

"What?"

I didn't mean it. I'd said it just to shock him. But after I said it, the truth of it stuck with me. If I did go down there and fail, the world would be in much worse shape than it was now.

And who was I kidding? I probably needed Dimitri down there with me. He'd certainly up my odds of succeeding.

If I didn't hate him.

I dunked his boxers in the soggy remains of last night's ice bucket.

"What the hell are you—?" He rushed to rescue his drowning underwear.

"Let's just assume I'm crazy enough to go and face Vald. How do I know you won't bolt and leave me down there as soon as we save your precious sisters?"

"You can't possibly think—"

"I don't know what to think," I said, ducking into the bathroom, finding his keys next to his wallet. I stuffed them both into my pants and yanked my hair into a ponytail. The griffin hairpin clattered to the floor and I left it there.

While he went to retrieve the hairpin, I threw his pants off the balcony. Since my shirt was ruined, I took his black T-shirt instead. I regretted it immediately. His musky scent overwhelmed my senses.

Damn the man.

But I wasn't about to walk out in nothing but my bra. And make no mistake, I was leaving.

I threw my oxfords into the saddlebag and fired up the hog. The motorcycle shook and groaned, as if it was trying to throw me off. I squeezed the handlebars until my knuckles went white. *Piece of cake.* If I could ice Rex, save JR and battle a demon in my bathroom, I could do this.

Dimitri yelled something as he came tearing out of the room in dripping wet—and hopefully ice-cold—boxers.

*Get out of my life.*

I kicked the bike into gear. It lurched forward like a drunken horse. Didn't matter. The only thing that counted was getting away, far away from him.

# Chapter Seventeen

According to Dimitri, the *Dixie Queen* was a four-hour ride. Hopping mad, it took me just under three.

He'd lied to me, and I fell for it.

*Was I that desperate for affection?*

Yes.

If he'd been honest earlier, we might have stood a chance. Now? He could rot back there for all I cared. At least it would be finished tonight—for better or for worse. And if I survived hell, I'd make sure Pirate and I never saw these people again. I wasn't stupid. There was probably more to Dimitri's story—which I didn't want to hear. And I knew there was a lot more to the story about my mom's death—which I did want explained. The witches had known all about my mom and my grandma. You'd think they could have been honest too.

Scarlet stood guard over the entrance to the long dirt driveway leading to the mothballed riverboat. I punched the bike and hurtled past her. Liars, all of them. Pond cypress and black gum branches reached out to snag my arms and swamp maples twined over the road. The marshlands radiated wet warmth and I could smell the river in the air.

If Dimitri had waited to give me any last-minute instructions, he was out of luck. I knew he'd slither his way to the *Dixie Queen* eventually. But I wasn't about to wait for him and I'd have a heck of a time listening to him now that I knew he was a two-faced lying jerk. Make that a using two-faced lying jerk. My stomach roiled at the mere thought of that man.

I swerved around a pothole and tried to think. Ant Eater could help set me up for tonight. I'd also duck into the Cave of Visions to try to contact Grandma. I didn't know how much she'd be able to help me while Vald held her prisoner.

Past a row of overgrown buckeye bushes, the *Dixie Queen* riverboat lurched on its moorings. The Yazoo River rolled upon itself as it rushed downstream, but not enough to cause that kind of rocking. The boat's rusted black smokestacks spewed a mustardy smoke and water poured out of the third floor in waves, like a wayward fountain. The clearing smelled like burned hair and dead animals. And—bad sign—the Red Skulls crowded the swampy ground out front. What had they done now?

The witches worked a crude assembly line in front of the boat. Frieda led a group as they scrubbed glass jars in several saddlebags filled with soapy water. Bob, with Pirate riding shotgun, transported the jars to Ant Eater and another group of witches, who seemed to be baiting them like traps.

"Lizzie! I'm here, Lizzie!" Pirate splashed through the puddles and leaped into my arms. I shut the hog off just in time to catch him and bury my face in the crook of his neck. Mmm . . . wet dog. *My* wet dog. I squeezed my puppy tight.

"You miss me? I missed you." Pirate wriggled in my arms.

"What's with the flooded boat?" I asked.

"Um, yeah. You might not want to mention that. Frieda is sensitive about that as it is. She tried to clear out some of the cobwebs with a wind spell and, well, you know how tricky that can be."

I had no idea, but I'd take his word for it.

"Lizzie." Ant Eater jogged over to me, as she un-wrapped a fun-sized Snickers bar with her teeth and plunked it into the jar under her arm. "Glad to see you're not dead."

"Me too."

She cocked a brow at my black T-shirt. Make that Dimitri's shirt. The thing felt itchy all the sudden.

"Don't ask," I said.

"Wasn't going to," she replied, smacking the black leather cell phone holder attached to her hip.

I should have thrown Dimitri's phone off the bal-cony along with his pants.

"Now stop farting around," she said, heading back to the stack of jars. "We got a problem."

"What do you mean you cursed the boat?" I asked as we stood at the edge of the *Dixie Queen*'s rusty gang-plank. The third-floor fountain splashed into the river on our right, tossing splatters of dull brown water that occasionally nipped at our legs and feet.

"Unscrew this." Ant Eater handed me an airline bot-tle of Jack Daniels. I watched as she poured the whis-key into the jar with the Snickers bars. "We weren't planning on coming back. So we booby-trapped the thing. Problem is, we were a little preoccupied."

"Drunk on dandelion wine," Bob added. I hadn't even heard him pull up behind us.

Ant Eater sniffed. "And hell, it's been twenty years."

"So we're not sure exactly what we booby-trapped." Bob navigated over the bumpy ground between Ant Eater and me. He reached into a bag slung over the back of his wheelchair and pulled out a ziplock bag of—ohmigosh—tails. Ant Eater offered him the jar, and he dropped two tails inside.

"What are you making? A counterspell?"

Ant Eater grunted out a throaty chuckle. "Oh no. That'd only make 'em mad. We lure the spells out, then, *whomp*," she clamped the lid shut, "back in the slammer."

"Why are you creating new magic?" Or simply a big mess. "What happens to the old magic?"

Ant Eater guffawed. "God, you are dense, Lizzie. This isn't magic," she said, shoving the Snickers-Jack Daniels rat tail mess under my nose. Ew. The pungent aroma of dead rat and whiskey stung my nostrils. "This," she said, screwing on the lid and shaking the thing up, "is a magical trap."

Pirate leaped into Bob's lap and I cringed when Bob scratched Pirate's head. I knew where that hand had been.

"Choking spells love Snickers," Bob said. "You can sometimes catch a Disintegration spell too. They go for most anything chocolate."

"You're talking like these are live things here."

Bob blinked. "They are. Our magic is most definitely alive." Bob thrust his chair backward toward the witch assembly line. He moved forward a few feet, then spun around to face me. "Forget that and you could wind up hurt." I followed him to the stack of jars already swirling with colored muck. "We've cleared out two dozen of the little boogers already."

"I helped with that one!" Pirate said, dancing in front of a Smucker's jar filled with a greenish haze. "I call him Larry." He spun twice. "See? Lizzie, Larry. Larry, Lizzie," he said, as if making an introduction.

Frieda dashed up to Ant Eater and thrust a jar into her hands. "I think I found it. This has to get rid of the, um," she eyed me, "issue on the main deck."

"What are you not telling me now?" Heck with magic

spells. I needed a good old-fashioned lie detector around these people.

"It's nothing," Frieda tittered about an octave too high and patted her canary yellow hair.

"Ant Eater?"

"None of your goddamned business." She held the jar to the light and studied the swirling contents. "Thing is, I hate to blast her out of here if we don't know where we're sending her."

"I programmed it for the Poconos," Frieda told her. "Phoenix likes the mountains."

"Phoenix?" I asked as Frieda practically jumped out of her platform sandals. How many Phoenixes did these people know . . . other than my mom?

Frieda gasped. Ant Eater's fingers tightened on the jar as she continued to swirl the liquid inside.

"Oh now, come on people," I said. "Aren't you going to say anything?"

"Frieda, Bob. Leave us alone," Ant Eater said, still focused on the jar.

Bob's wheelchair crunched across the leaves scattered on the ground. Frieda followed, reaching out to catch a ziplock full of mushed snake and stuffing it back into Bob's pack.

Ant Eater stared daggers at me. "Your mother is dead."

"Thanks for the sympathy." Couldn't these people be honest for five friggin' minutes? "Hey, I only want to know what's going on and nobody's answering my questions."

"Because, hotshot, what happened to your mom is for you and your grandma to talk about. I'm not getting involved."

Since when? "Funny, you don't seem to have any trouble involving me in *your* messes." As if it heard me, the riverboat groaned on its moorings. "Grandma could have told me the truth herself, but you know what? I didn't have much time with her until she was kidnapped and dragged to hell trying to save you." And me. "The least you can do is tell me the truth when I ask."

"That's where it gets hazy."

"No, it doesn't! Grandma is accused of killing my mom. There's no haze. There are the facts, and you owe me an explanation."

She tossed the jar at my head, and I struggled to catch it. "Seems to me you're pretty good at figuring things out on your own, lover girl."

"What? Did you know about Dimitri too?" Probably. Not like they'd tell me anyway. To them, I was just a walking, talking magical bag of tricks—to be used whenever they felt like it. They'd sold me out to the werewolves before I'd even begun my training. Sure, Lizzie will get rid you of a bunch of black souls, no problem! For them. How much worse was it going to be now? Well, I wouldn't be around to find out. As soon as I rescued Grandma, they could kiss my butt good-bye. A collar jingled, and I caught sight of Pirate out of the corner of my eye. He danced in circles, like he did every time his nerves got the best of him. "Pirate, take a walk."

"Oh, but Lizzie. This is just getting interesting."

"Pirate!"

He dispatched a sullen glance before he trotted for a patch of wild ivy.

"You done?" Ant Eater asked. "Because we gotta clear this place out, and you're not helping."

"Fine. You want me to help?" I stalked toward the rusted gangplank. If all I was good for was to clear out spells, face demons and basically do their dirty work, I didn't belong here any more than I belonged in Cliff and Hillary's big empty McMansion, or in my small boring house. I was sick of trying to be everything to everyone and coming up short every time.

"Lizzie, don't go in there!"

"Or what? I might inhale a few death spells? Maybe meet whoever you have hidden on the main deck?"

Ant Eater kicked the gangplank and nearly threw me in the water. I leaped the last two feet onto the boat and braced myself in the doorway as I caught my footing.

Her face crumpled with fury. "We never believed that about your grandma."

I turned to face her. "You didn't do anything about it, either." They were a bunch of observers. They ran, they hid. They couldn't even go on their own friggin' boat.

The dark spells churned in the musty ship behind me. They stomped and demanded my attention. I'd never been so attracted to danger in my life.

Whether it was anger or my demon slayer instinct to run for trouble, I used my foot to shove the gangplank the rest of the way into the water. If Ant Eater wanted to annoy me now, she'd have to chuck a jar at my head. I didn't put it past her.

A green-and-white flecked spell danced just inside the entryway. It zoomed for my neck and I swiped it out of the air. It buzzed in my hand like a fly. Choking spell. I crushed it in my hand. A second spell swooped from behind my left ear. I caught it. Giggle spell.

Too perfect. Yeah, it was wrong, but Ant Eater looked so furious down there on the lawn. I hurled the giggler at her and she exploded in a squeal of delight. Her rough-and-tumble body vibrated with titters, her trunk-like legs stomped as if fighting it before they relented and hopped daintily in time to her peals of laughter. Oh yeah. That was the first time I'd felt myself smile since

Dimitri and I . . . I didn't want to think about it. Ant Eater might try to kill me later, but it was worth it.

The rest of the witches backed up ten paces. Except Bob. "Try to save a few." Bob tossed me some jars.

"What? Can I put a bunch in one jar?"

"Depends on the species."

Yeah, well I wasn't about to stop for a lesson in Magic 101. I'd capture a few of the ornery ones and destroy the worst magic. I'd already seen what could happen when a death spell got out of hand.

"Just don't trip any Giggle Bombs yourself," Bob hollered as I ducked inside. "We need you coherent for tonight."

The ship rocked underneath my feet. Slot machines crowded the entryway, as if the *Dixie Queen*'s original patrons couldn't wait to get started. To my right, a roulette table stood abandoned, chips stacked on some of the numbers. If I didn't know better, I'd think I had interrupted a game. The white wood facade, rotting at the edges and chipped by age, extended back to a matching bar. Old-fashioned gaslight lamps lined the walls. As I watched, flames ignited in the glass bowls. It made me jump enough to rattle the glass jars I held, but I tried to look on the bright side. Nothing had tried to eat me or possess me—yet.

Beyond the large picture windows at the back, I could see the ship's balcony, flanked by a bright red railing. According to the emergency exit map, three floors rose above river level, one below. And of course, we had Ant Eater's mysterious visitor on the main deck, right above the massive, red water wheel.

A slot machine whirled and chimed, odd since the plug was nowhere near the electrical outlet. Instead it swished like a three-pronged tail. "Two in one day!" The machine's Lucky 7's spun around and landed on 7-7-7. "Tell me, young lady. You feelin' lucky?"

I hoped it was a pre-programmed voice. "Are you talking to me?" Please don't be possessed. I didn't have the time.

"Funny you should ask. Nobody's ever asked me that before. But I tell you, it's been lonely around here. Just the other day, or was it year? I was—"

Enough. I plucked a freeze spell from behind the roulette wheel and chucked it at Lucky 7. His voice, thank the heavens, groaned to a stop.

I couldn't believe I was wasting time on this boat when I should have been getting ready for my trip to hell. Or at the very least, I should have been in Dimitri's bed. If he hadn't been such a liar. Hell's bells, I was dumb. I heaved a fistful of betting chips. They clattered on the parquet floors. Everybody needed me for something. For as long as I could remember, Cliff and Hillary needed me to round out their perfect-looking family, like a wall prop with a manicure. Dimitri needed me to end the curse. The witches needed me to stuff a bunch of jars with magical wildlife. Why couldn't anybody just want *me*?

I stomped through the casino and toward the main deck, plucking magic from behind the round *Dixie Queen* life preservers and under poker tables. I learned to avoid itch spells, got caught up in a few transport spells. I had my suspicions about who planted those, since they always sent me to the men's john. And eyow— love spells tended to bite. None of it made me feel any better. If anything, by the time I made it to the back of the ship, I felt worse.

The main deck seemed empty. Leave it to Ant Eater to chase phantom strangers. She'd probably lied to keep me off the boat. Really, though—ever since I'd faced down the black souls, I felt pretty good about my odds with the average human. A gooey spell clung to the underside of the huge, red paddlewheel. I leaned under the railing to snag it with my fingers.

"Stop!" A pair of shiny red pumps clacked across the back deck of the ship.

I snapped upright. Oh my word. My voice dried up as I stared at a cheap imitation of my adoptive mother. The woman wore the same fashionable crimson glasses, as if she'd decided to be Hillary for Halloween. She'd styled her hair into blonde waves, like Hillary. Her gray pantsuit, although not as expensive as Hillary's (I hoped) accentuated her figure. Unlike my adoptive mom, it looked like this woman could put away a cheeseburger. Still, I noticed an unsettling resemblance, right down to her French-tipped fingernails. A green-and-white flecked choking spell zoomed for her neck.

"Watch out!"

She flicked it away and I watched it land with a plop in the river. "Oh don't worry," she said, misjudging my open-mouthed horror, "it can swim."

I felt my concentration falter. The gooey spell tried to sneak behind me. It'd be heck to catch if it made it under one of the tables. I lunged for it.

"Lizzie, no!"

Terror seized me as I watched my hands disintegrate. There was no pain, only a horrible numbness. Blood poured from my wrists. It too faded, along with my forearms, my elbows, my—oh my God!

"Elizabeth Gertrude Brown! Stop that immediately!"

The spell blew away on the breeze. Bit by bit, like a macabre puzzle, my hands came together again. I swallowed hard and flexed my fingers, trying to get a grip on what had happened.

I stood there for a long moment, stunned.

"I'm sorry I yelled, but you should be immune to

those spells. I don't know what's gotten into you," she scolded.

It couldn't be. "Mom?" I asked shakily, forcing myself to tear my eyes away from my arms and hands. How else would she know my middle name?

A single tear slid down the ruddy blush line on her cheek. "It's me, baby."

# Chapter Eighteen

This was so not the Oprah-style family reunion I'd dreamed of as a kid. I stood slowly, apprehension prickling my spine. "Are you dead?"

She wiped at her cheeks. "Not that I'm aware," she said, reaching into her pocket, then thinking the best of it. She withdrew her hand slowly.

I froze, every nerve on high alert. *The devil takes on many forms.*

"How do I know you're my mom?"

Her expression softened. "Do you still have that strawberry birthmark on the back of your left thigh?"

Cripes. After all these years—how did she get here? And why? "What do you want?" It came out harsher than I'd intended. Blame it on shock, or pure self-preservation.

"You're leaving with me. Come on," she said, heels clickety-clacking as she tried to lead me off the main deck.

Say what? I held my ground. "I don't think so." She couldn't just show up after thirty years, from the dead no less, and expect me to start following orders. And what about *I missed you, Lizzie. I love you, Lizzie.*

*I regret abandoning you, Lizzie.*

She turned, her hands thrust on her hips. "You have

no idea what kind of danger you're in," she said, desperation mixed with annoyance.

And she did? "Why are you in such a rush to save me?" I asked. After Xerxes the demon, imps, were-wolves, black souls, Harley witches and a lying ... whatever Dimitri was, "Why now?" I asked, reaching for my switch stars. I grasped the cool metal handles with my fingers.

"I thought I'd hidden you from this kind of life. These people. And those terrible switch stars. Please stop spinning that."

"What?" I glanced absently at the switch star on my finger. "Wait. You knew where I was all these years?" When Hillary put me in a fat camp for being five pounds overweight, when I wasn't allowed to wear jeans, even in the house, when I had to pose at those stupid society picnics when all I wanted to do was run around like a normal kid.

I'd dreamed about this moment—about meeting my birth mom. And it sucked.

"Lizzie," she said, and held up her hand. "We have to leave. Now." She made her way toward the pilot house, beckoning me to follow. What? Was she going to try and launch the ship? I could see us now, sailing down the Yazoo, mother and daughter on a bewitched boat.

I followed, mainly to bag a particularly nasty-looking lose your keys spell. I plunked it in the jar. If only we could rid the world of those things. I'd be willing to bet they reproduced like rabbits.

Oh, who was I kidding? I had a question I'd been wanting to ask for decades.

Mom said a few incantations over the door and the lock clicked open.

Now or never. The question burned in the pit of my stomach. "Why did you leave me?" I asked. *Please let it be because you loved me.*

She paused, doorknob in hand. "We don't have time for this."

"We do," I told her, my voice sounding steadier than I felt. "Because I'm not going anywhere until I get some answers." No matter how much it hurt. She owed me a heck of a lot more explanations than this one.

She shifted from one sky-high pump to the other, the thick, humid breeze blowing her overstylized hair up in wings around her head. "Lizzie, you have to understand. I gave you up precisely so I'd never find you again. And so these people wouldn't either. Do you know what they want you to do? Of course you do. You draw those switch stars like a gunfighter. But it's not fun and games. You could lose your soul."

The thought made me shiver despite myself. I didn't want to think about what I could lose. "They've got Grandma."

"I know," she said softly. "I felt it when they took her."

"We have to fix it." Together, we'd have a better chance at defeating Vald.

"No, Lizzie. We're getting out of here. End of story," she said, snagging the hotfoot spell that hovered at her ankle. "Gertie chose her path, and now she's living with the consequences. You can still have a normal life."

"Is this because Grandma tried to kill you?" I blurted. *Real smooth, Lizzie.* "I mean, everyone thinks she murdered you. I know you must have had a falling out, but she's your mom and—"

"Lizzie," she barked. Boy, it didn't take her long to find her "mom" voice. "Your grandma and I have had our issues, but we never came to blows. She helped me escape." Mom held on to the doorknob of the pilot's house, as if she didn't want me to see what lurked inside. "Just like I'm doing for you. You can still have a normal life."

I couldn't believe she wanted me to abandon Grandma. "Like you?"

"Yes. I write a small society column for a newspaper in Freeburg."

Where was a good choking spell when I needed it? "You can't just barge in here, scare the pants off me and try to get me to abandon the only real family I've ever had." Yeah, I knew it probably hurt her, but I wanted to at the moment.

"Drop the switch stars. Leave this place. Come live with me in my condo in Freeburg. I'll take you to the Lone Star Café and we'll talk about how you can have a new life without fifth-level demons, black souls or werewolves."

Poor Fang. "So you saw that too?" I asked, noticing a frozen underwear hovering near her left hip.

"I'm so sorry it ended badly."

"Me too." I caught a giggler and sent it to join the mustard-colored smoke drifting skyward.

"I had no idea they'd blame the poisonings on you."

Say what? If she wasn't my mother, I think I would have hurled a switch star. "You poisoned the wolves?"

"I had to get you out of there," she said, as if that was any kind of excuse. "You were too close to completing your training." She pursed her lips, then said, "Do you know it took your Great-great Aunt Evie a decade to master the Three Truths? Granted, she started at the age of nine, but still! She sat around for the next eleven years, waiting to turn thirty. And you, you zip right through and want to go face a fifth-level demon? For crying out loud, Lizzie, I wouldn't be surprised to see you go after the devil himself. And for what? You don't need this. It's a horrible, horrible life."

She'd sent me to join Cliff and Hillary in their perfect world, then she'd gone on to create a similar nirvana for herself. I couldn't have turned out any more different from each and every one of them. But it didn't matter now. We needed to focus on fixing this thing with Vald. "Help me save Grandma. You don't want to lose her. I know you don't."

A sad smile played across her features. "I'd rather lose her than lose both of you. I'm sure she'd say the same thing, Lizzie. She wouldn't want you going down there unprepared, and you'll never be good enough to face a fifth-level demon."

Okay, that stung. She looked at me like I was the most pitiful thing she'd ever seen.

"But I'm a demon slayer."

"So was I."

My brain buzzed as I tried to process that last thought. "You what?"

"That's beside the point."

"Oh no, no, no. Tell me right now what you're talking about, or I'm going to leave you and this conversation right now."

"I'm the chosen one," she said, as if she was about to tell me I needed to have a root canal. "I mean, count it out. Take it from your Great Aunt Evie, who was actually your Great-great, Great Aunt. Then her twin sister, Edna, but we don't count her because a demon stole her soul right after training. Skip three generations and you have me. And then, well, by accident—you."

Nobody had ever put it that way before.

"What do you mean I was an accident?"

"I was smarter than they were," she said, a little too deviously. "I studied everything they gave me, and I did more. I talked to everyone I could—visiting sorcerers, black magicians, warlocks. They thought I was a prodigy. And I learned things all right," she said with a wicked smile. "I learned how to beat it."

Jesus, Mary, Joseph and the mule. She foisted her destiny off—*on me?*

"It's the only way," she insisted, daring me to judge her.

I couldn't believe it.

"Let me get this straight," I said, rubbing my temples to keep my head from pounding out of my skull. "You were overwhelmed with your enormous powers, powers your loving family had trained you to use. So you dumped them on me, then scuttled me off to an adoptive family while you ran?"

She didn't even pretend to look guilty. "It was the only way."

"Bullshit." I needed to get off this boat. I stormed for the main staircase, nearly tripping over a stubbed toe spell. Mom chased me, setting off three frozen underwears. Served her right.

She ignored them as we clattered down the ornate iron staircase. "Stop being unreasonable, Lizzie. I thought if I hid you, you'd never know what I was or what you are. It didn't work. I admit that. We can still be a family and figure out a way to end the slayer line for good."

I came to a halt on a small landing, tears welling in my eyes. For the love of Laconia, I couldn't let her get to me. As a kid, I'd daydream about what it would be like to meet my real mom. She'd be beautiful and strong and not afraid of anybody. Instead, she was everything I feared I'd become.

I didn't know if I had the strength or the courage to defeat Vald. But unlike my mom, I knew I had to try.

"Run with me," she insisted. "We can find a way for you to reject your powers."

As much as I never wanted this, and as much as I'd always wanted my real mom, I couldn't have it this way. I needed her and she'd abandoned me. I wasn't about to leave Grandma in the same position.

"No, Mom," I said, wiping my runny nose on Dimitri's T-shirt. "I'm going to face Vald. You want to make a difference? Help me."

She fiddled around in her purse, her makeup cases clacking together while she rifled through lipsticks and who knew what else. "Here." She jabbed a lipstick-smeared hankie at me. "Wipe your nose."

Ew. These germ magnets should have been outlawed as soon as Kleenex was invented. But Mom seemed ready to wipe my nose for me if I let her. I found a clean-looking spot and dabbed to be polite. The hankie smelled like jasmine with a side of pickle relish. Strange. Mom drew a fragile breath as my world went black.

## Chapter Nineteen

Ant Eater thwacked me in the head. "Do I gotta watch you every goddamned second?"

I dragged my arms over my eyes, fighting the hangover of the century. My skull felt like an anchor on the hard, wooden deck. I was with my mom and she . . . son of a submariner, she drugged me. "Watch out for Phoenix," I muttered. "She has a hankie."

"Did you hit her with a Brain Stealer?" Frieda demanded.

"Oh, I'd like to hit her with a lot worse than that," Ant Eater countered, nudging me with her toe. I squinted my eyes open. The sunset cast low shadows over the deck of the *Dixie Queen*. Ant Eater, Frieda and about six other witches stood over me, forming a circle of curious faces. A white bandage tented Ant Eater's nose and gauze stuffed each swollen nostril. She must have beaten the giggle spell into submission. She glared at me from under two black eyes.

My heart thumped. I could feel my pulse throbbing through my body, against the moldy deck. Mom hadn't stolen me away. Thank God. I didn't know what I would have done if—"Where's Mom?"

Even Frieda managed to look annoyed at that. "She had a transport portal set up in the pilot's room. Lucky for us she decided to suck you down feetfirst. Sorry about your shoes. Ant Eater here hit her with a Hairy Ball."

"I was saving it," she grunted. "Lucky for you that bitch deserved it more. There'll be Bigfoot sightings in Fresco for sure."

"Don't call my mom a bitch," I said, struggling to sit up. Pain spiked through my head, making my mind swim for a moment. I'd lost my oxfords. Socks too. "Thanks for stopping her, though." I didn't know what I'd do if she'd kept me from Grandma.

Ant Eater sniffed, then winced. "Don't thank me, sugar lips. He's the one who got us up here."

Just when I didn't think my head could feel any worse, Dimitri stepped into my line of vision, his travel bag slung over his shoulder. Of course he hadn't taken the time to throw on a shirt. Damn the man. The hard plane of his abdomen disappeared into the dirty jeans slung low over his hips. Hurt, disappointment, heaven knew what else churned into a heavy black lump in my stomach. He looked contrite, sad, serious, all of the things I'd expect. And it pissed me off anyway.

"We were going to do a quick ceremony to polish up your aura," Frieda said, squatting down to brace me in a sitting position. "But we didn't see any possum on the way over."

I pinched the bridge of my nose between my fingers. It was a sad, sad day when this sort of stuff started making sense. "Don't worry about it, Frieda," I said. I'd hoped for whatever help they could give me tonight, wanted it. But in the end, it came down to one thing. I had to trust myself. I had to let go, accept my powers, trust the universe.

I also had to watch out for my mother, or a hairy

version thereof. Something told me I'd be seeing her again.

Scarlet popped a hard, red candy in my mouth. It tasted like strawberry cream soda and danged if it didn't work wonders on my magical hangover. As the throbbing eased and the cobwebs cleared, I lurched to my feet. "How much time do we have?" I asked, purposely avoiding Dimitri's gaze.

Ant Eater furrowed her thick eyebrows, suspicious—as she should have been—at my asking. "It's almost six o'clock now . . ." She added in her head. "Just over an hour."

That couldn't be right. "I thought our window of opportunity opens at midnight."

"That's hell central time," she said, winding her watch. "We're five hours behind."

Naturally. "Well, in that case, I have something to do."

Frieda knitted her brows. Ant Eater scowled. And Dimitri? I didn't give a flying fart what he thought as I sauntered barefoot off the *Dixie Queen* and made tracks for my Harley.


"You went shopping?" Pirate had chased my bike for the last quarter mile as I made my way back to the *Dixie Queen*. Pirate danced in place as I yanked off my helmet and climbed off the bike. Strings of lights illuminated the decks of the *Dixie Queen* as it bobbed in the ominously swelling current of the Yazoo River.

"Hey, I needed shoes." I was almost glad my mom's escape portal had sucked off my boring oxfords. My new black boots were comfy and kick-ass.

Pirate jumped up against one of my boots and slid right off the polished leather. "Those witches are going to bust a gut when they see you." He followed me as I strode toward the boat. "And did you know they have salami?"

"Look—sturdy heels. These are definitely me," I said, more to myself than my twelve-pound terrier. Pirate had moved on to chasing fireflies.

On the ride over this morning, I'd passed a shop in Greenville. A black awning with flames had invited The Inner Vixen to stop by for a look-see. I straightened my purple plaid miniskirt. I had to admit, it felt good.

Dimitri's emerald felt hard and heavy against the hollow of my neck. I didn't buy the skirt with him in mind. Okay. Maybe I did. He needed a reminder of what he'd lost. Besides, it had shorts underneath, kind of like the field hockey skirts I wore in high school. I'd be able to move a lot easier than I would in pants and, well, my legs are my best feature. Dimitri deserved to suffer. I topped off my kick-butt demon slayer outfit with a leather sports bra that looked more like a corset than anything. Still, it was comfortable, I could move, and I couldn't pass up the purple prairie clovers climbing up the sides. They were, after all, the sacred symbol of my demon-slayer line. I stopped believing in coincidences a long time ago.

Ant Eater's head popped out over the main deck. "Are you trying to piss me off?"

Pirate cocked his head to the side. "I think she wants us in there now."

I scooped him up and jogged over the rickety boards they'd found to replace the rusted gangplank. Let Ant Eater holler. For the first time, I felt like the demon slayer everyone said I would be. And while my nerves jangled at the idea of facing Vald tonight, another teeny, tiny part of me screamed to let me at him.

On the main deck, the witches worked in teams. Two groups had set up on the walkways to the deck, intercepting curious spells. Good thing I'd gotten rid of most of them, especially the Chokers. Another group had chalked off a large pentagram near the shuffleboard court. They sprinkled bits of gobbledygook and chanted. Ant Eater conferred with Scarlet. Dimitri was nowhere to be found. Probably lurking somewhere below deck. And if not? My heart sank. It would be easier without him.

"Nice skirt," Ant Eater sniggered.

"And here I thought you'd have something useful to say," I told her.

"You wish. Here." Ant Eater shoved a thick black belt into my hands. The leather had cracked with age. It looked like a utility belt of some kind, with small cases attached.

"What is this?"

"Just something I stole from Phoenix. It was your Great-great Aunt Evie's."

"She brought this with her today?" Maybe I could convince my mom to help.

"Nah. I took it after she fucked us over in '78. Phoenix don't want to be a demon slayer. She don't get the damned belt." Ant Eater focused on Scarlet again. She'd clearly had enough of me. "Now leave me alone."

I settled on one of the observation benches and studied the belt. It seemed to be a demon slayer tool belt of sorts. There was a slot for switch stars to the right of the crystal buckle. Inside the pouches, I found colored powders, stones, a cache of vibrating crystals. Maybe Mom was right. I didn't know what I was doing.

The belt felt about ten degrees cooler than everything around it. I popped another lid off one of the cases. "Stop!" a voice screeched and slammed the lid back down.

Pirate rushed to my side so fast he slid right past me and spun out behind the next bench. "What was that? You want me to eat it?"

"I'm not sure," I said, yanking at the clasp I'd opened. It wouldn't budge. I hoped I could handle this.

"Okay, people!" Ant Eater hollered. "Countdown is on. Five minutes. Move it or lose it!"

As the witches rushed to complete their tasks, I fastened the chilly leather belt around my waist.

"Ready, slick?" Ant Eater thumped me on the back. I nodded.

"Easy, Frieda," she called. Ant Eater leaned close enough for me to get a whiff of her garlic-tinged breath. "We're borrowing power from the portal your mom made. Makes for a stronger thread. We won't lose you as easy."

"Don't," I said. I knew she was baiting me, but she'd hit too close to the truth. I could feel Dimitri's eyes on me. He was here, no question about it. He rumbled in the background of everything I did, like an unstoppable freight train.

"I don't know whether to hitch a transport spell to his ass or get you guys another room."

The way he'd acted? "Transport."

She let out a grunting chuckle and dug into the pocket of her chaps.

"I was only kidding," I told her. "Really." I cringed as she shoved a purple noodle of a spell into the pocket of my brand-new skirt.

The witches moved in sober silence, a far cry from the laughter I'd witnessed in the basement of the Red Skull. They were worried. So was I.

I hugged my doggy tight. "You listen to Bob, okay? And don't eat too much salami."

He burrowed his head under my armpit. "Oh now, Lizzie. You know I can't stand it when you leave and you used to just leave for the grocery store and now you're leaving and I don't know if I'm ever going to see you again."

I kissed him on the head. "You will," I said, hoping I was right.

"I'm sorry, Lizzie," Bob said, "but we're going to have to chain him."

I did it myself. My doggy whimpered while I looped Bob's old ferret chain once, twice around a nearby bench and clipped the leash to Pirate's collar. Pirate watched me with big, sad eyes as I joined the witches in the semicircle.

Bob eased a Styrofoam cup from the brown paper bag in his lap. Ice ringed the top and steam bellowed from the wide opening.

"Liquid nitrogen," Ant Eater told me. "We have to get the portal cold enough. Bet this part was a bitch for Evie in 1883."

We watched as Frieda used a pool cue from the game room to draw a glowing, yellow orb from the pilot house. She carried it toward the center of the penta-gram. The five-pointed star cast faint glimmers of blue and silver magic. It offered protection, control. I needed every bit of it tonight.

"Any last words?" Ant Eater slapped me on the back. "Just kidding," she said. "Don't fuck up.

"Two minutes to midnight in hell!" she hollered to the group.

"Aw. Shit!" The orb bobbled on Frieda's stick before she lost her grip on it.

Oh no.

"Somebody catch it!" Bob hollered.

We scrambled for the orb as it zoomed low over the deck and hovered, out of her reach, over the back end of the boat.

"I'm sorry, I'm sorry, I'm sorry." Frieda dangled over the back rail in a vain attempt to capture the dancing ball of energy. I grabbed the pool cue from her and thrust it for the portal. It flitted out of my reach.

"What do we do now?" I shoved the cue at Dimitri,

who also failed. We had to get that thing into the center of the pentagram.

"Screw it. It stays there," Ant Eater announced, as if the portal wasn't hovering over the sharp paddlewheel and the churning river below. "Change of plans, people. Lizzie's gonna have to jump off the back of the boat," she announced. "New positions! We'll throw the stuff at her."

Ant Eater yanked me close. "You'll be gone before— you know—splat. Just don't miss."

So much for my protection.

"We're doing this, people," she called to the group. "Thirty seconds. Grab your possum teeth."

She positioned me at the center of the semicircle overlooking the dark waters below. "Possum lungs work better, but it takes forever to scoop 'em out."

"Thanks for the mental image."

If she was trying to take my mind off the portal to hell hovering in midair off the back of the boat, well, it wasn't working. *You can do this, Lizzie.*

The witches joined hands facing the back of the boat. I stood between Ant Eater and Scarlet. Dimitri leaned against a nearby bench. He had no right to be anywhere near us tonight.

The Red Skulls closed their eyes, and I felt the magic build.

Ant Eater bowed her head. "We, the witches of the Red Skull, send forth our sister, away from our warmth and into the cold. Away from the light and into the darkness. Apart from us, but always with us. We send her forth so that she may die and be reborn."

I clenched my toes inside my new, kick-ass demon slayer boots. Nobody said anything about dying. What was this portal going to do to me?

It pulsed, sending off bolts of electricity as it grew

to the size of a person. I could still see the hard, sharp paddlewheel below, ready to chop me to bits.

I glanced back at Dimitri, as he glowered in the corner. He didn't deserve to go with me. He'd asked for my trust, my loyalty. And he'd certainly made it clear that he wanted me. I could hardly believe he'd been willing to use me. But, heck, he admitted it. It didn't get plainer than that.

The portal snapped and cracked like a giant bug zapper above the churning river below.

*If this doesn't work, I'm dead. If it does? I'm in hell.*

I snuck another peek at Dimitri, curse him. No getting around it—he lied. He broke every rule I had about how a relationship should be. I knew he never meant for it to get out of hand like it did. Despite what I'd said to him back at the motel, I knew he cared about me.

"Lizzie!" Ant Eater jammed her finger into my shoulder, and I snapped out of my daze. "Do you venture forth freely in the tradition of the great demon slayers of Dalea?"

"I do," I said, fighting to keep my voice steady. I had to trust in my training, follow my instincts. That meant . . . oh heck. I reached back and offered my hand to Dimitri. He didn't deserve it. But I couldn't think of one other person I'd rather go to hell and back with.

Dimitri took my hand, his grasp warm and steady. The circle widened for him, and I could have sworn I saw the corner of Ant Eater's mouth twitch into a shadow of a grin. "We welcome them into our fold just as we send them forth."

"Touch shoulders, grab your possum teeth." Ant Eater said, eyes on her watch. "Okay Bob. Wait for it. Wait for it. Now!"

Bob hurled the liquid nitrogen. It slammed into the portal, sending off a shock wave of blue energy.

"Roadkill!" Ant Eater commanded.

The possum teeth hit the portal, launching flares like fireworks into the river below.

"Both of you. Together!"

I clutched Dimitri's hand and we leaped off the boat.

A frigid wind buffeted me as I struggled to gain a foothold, toehold, anything. We'd plunged into the middle of a giant maze, carved from solid ice. Bitter cold soaked me to the bone and I cursed my ultra sexy, utterly useless miniskirt as a frigid gust blew straight up.

Ahead, the path veered sharply to the left, and the right, and down into a fissure that threatened to swallow us alive. Behind us, a tangle of passageways wound into oblivion.

I braced my hands against slick walls that rose claustrophobically close on each side. Sulfur tinged the air, making it hard to breathe. My heart thumped as I caught a glimpse of hands, faces behind the ice. I yanked my hands to my chest and when that didn't stop the shivers, reached out to Dimitri and let his touch flood me with raw warmth.

"So much for hell freezing over," I told him.

He pulled me close until my chin rested on his bare chest. Poor guy still hadn't changed from our encounter at Motel 6. I hoped his underwear had dried.

"If you think about it," he said, "hell is the absence of affection, love, anything good. It should be the coldest place in any dimension."

He kissed my forehead, my cheeks, my eyes. Each touch warmed me inside and out. We didn't have time for this. Besides, I was pretty sure I was still mad at him. A bead of heat wound its way through my body.

Just one more kiss. After all, I had to keep my temperature up.

He traced his thumb over my lower jaw. "Feel better?"

Damn the man. He was addicting. "You're not getting in my pants on the way to hell."

"This is hell, sweetheart."

I doubted it for a split second, until "What the—?" My voice lodged in my throat as a sharp sting pierced my spine.

Dimitri hissed in surprise. "Don't look back."

# Chapter Twenty

It felt like a thousand biting insects burrowed between my shoulder blades.

A white-scaled lizard lurched out of the ice wall behind us. Its claws sliced at Dimitri as he seized it by the neck and cleaved off its head with his bronze dagger. He tossed the body into the snow at our feet. "Turn around."

His fingers probed my back. I barely felt them over the screaming, eating pain. "It's not bad," he lied.

"Jerk," I said through clenched teeth. He'd promised to stop holding out on me.

"We can't fix it," he said, forcing me to look at him. "Put it out of your mind or you'll never be able to do what you need in order to get out of here."

I'd never been so afraid in my life. I nodded and squeezed his hand, or at least I tried. Cold shock had stolen the feeling from my limbs. "Which way do we go?"

"You tell me," he said, his expression guarded.

I nodded and willed myself to focus on the empty world around us, as the creatures pulsed behind the ice walls towering to our right and left. Past a mass of glowing, red orbs, the path broke sharply and went down to an ice canyon from the feel of it. Straight ahead, I detected a fissure of unknown depth. Behind us, a maze of passageways wound endlessly.

Danger screamed from every direction. I opened my mind, called on my demon slayer instinct to run for trouble and picked our poison.

"Down the hole," I told Dimitri.

"I figured," he said, as a gray, shrouded figure drifted from the abyss. Empty sleeves beckoned. It wanted us. I struggled to see its face, buried in the shadows, as it slammed an arctic blast into us. Now or never.

I braced a hand against my switch stars and jogged straight for it. It beat me to the punch, gulping me down in a single bite. I spun head over tail through ice water. Riptides pitched me deeper, farther. My lungs screamed as I fought to breathe. I clutched for something, anything to pull me out of this hellhole. I dug into my tool belt and released powders, crystals, potions—whatever I could find. One by one, I threw them into the freezing void.

Fresh air rushed me like a wave. I breathed deeply, desperately as I struggled to get my bearings. I pushed myself to my feet, hard to do on a floor made from slush. I sunk down to my ankles in icy muck.

Where was Dimitri?

Frozen walls towered in every direction. I stood in the bottom of a deep chasm. Alone. With no chance of escape and—ohmigod—

"What the hell happened to you?" Grandma. Buried up to her sagging cheekbones in icy quicksand, she crumpled her nose like I'd just blown curfew. Her eyes widened in horror as she gaped at my raw back.

"Dimitri said it wasn't bad."

"He lied."

"Thanks for the reminder."

"Put your hands on your tool belt," Grandma ordered. "Reach for the third pouch on the left."

My fingers clamored for the pouch.

"No!" she ordered as my fingers dipped into the

third pouch to the left. "Sorry. My bad. Third pouch on *my* left, which is your right." She squeezed her eyes shut. "I'm screwed in the head lately."

Yeah, well I think we were both a little stressed.

"Okay, that's it," she said, as I flipped open the third pouch on the right. "Take the crystal. Infuse it with healing."

"What?" Nobody taught me anything about crystals.

"Shut up and do it. The white crystals—holy shit, get your hand away from your back!"

I yanked my hand away. "Hey, this is my first time flinging magical crystals and pixie dust." I needed to know where I was aiming.

She brightened. "You have pixie dust?"

*"No!"*

She rolled her eyes like *I* was the crazy one. "Just grab a crystal. The white ones are like blank slates. Infuse it with health and happiness."

"I don't—"

She glared at me, daring me to ask more questions.

"Excuse me," I snapped. "I'm doing the best I can here." Dimitri had vanished. I was ankle deep in hell, trying to save her sorry butt after some underworld monster took potshots at me. No one wanted to tell me how to infuse a friggin' crystal that I hadn't even known existed an hour ago—Hades standard time—and, for all we knew, Vald would be showing up any second.

"It's not about you, Lizzie," Grandma warned.

"Of course not." I gripped the crystal until it dug ridges in my hand.

*Think*. I took a deep breath and did my best to shove my anger to the side. Think of the one little guy who's always happy, healthy, bounding through a clump of wildflowers as gleefully as he rolls in garbage or—soon after on one occasion—Hillary's white-cushioned deck chairs. Pirate knew who he was and what he wanted.

Even after I chained him to a bench on the *Dixie Queen* he'd still find a way to chase fireflies.

"Impressive," Grandma muttered. "Now stick it on your back."

I felt for the raw wound in my back and *hell's bells.* "I can't reach it," I groaned.

"What?"

"It's too high." I squirmed and stretched. I could almost feel the slippery blood. My blood. I held my breath and reached with all my might, balancing the crystal on the edge of my own personal nightmare. Warmth rushed through me and I about collapsed with relief. Or was that fear? I didn't want to know.

"Grandma?"

"You did it."

I swallowed hard and smoothed my hands over my warm, utterly unmolested spine. Later, I'd have to ask. But right now: "Where's Vald?"

"I don't know," Grandma shook her head, her long gray hair glistening with slush. "He was here an hour ago, waiting for you. Lord, Lizzie. You shouldn't have come." Grandma forced her head up and back, burying the back of her skull in the ice. "He wants you, and your power. I tried to come back and warn you, but some asshole filled my Dumpster with trash."

We had to run. I dropped to my knees in front of her and attacked the slush with my hands. "What do you mean I missed Vald? That's good, right?"

"I can't get out of here unless you can his ass," she said, wriggling her shoulders.

"Yeah, well lucky for us, that's on the agenda anyway." This stuff was impossible. For every scoop I dug, more slid into the hole. I planted switch stars around her to help melt some of it. I was just about to get ahead of it when—*oh no.*

"Grandma are you—" She was. She was starting to

grow transparent, disappear. I shoveled faster, my knees sinking into the ice.

"Behind you," she said, as I detected a whiff of rotten chicken dusted with sulfur.

"Vald?" I asked.

"Xerxes."

"Aw, hell." I could have sworn I'd killed him in my bathroom.

And if that wasn't enough, a griffin swooped over us in a burst of color. Dimitri. It had to be. His wingspan as big as the back deck of the *Dixie Queen* and looked ready to snap some necks. Well, too bad for him—and for me—I was the only one who could kill demons.

I spun to face Xerxes, blocking him from Grandma.

He cackled low in his throat, his blackened lips stretched over rows of serrated teeth. "Lizzie, my pet." His hide, rough and cracked, rubbed like sandpaper as he dug his clawed toes into the slush and readied himself to pounce.

My switch star hit Xerxes square between the eyes, and he exploded into a thousand flecks of light.

"Take that you—ack!" My elation quickly turned to horror as each tiny bit pulsed and grew before my eyes into a demon, just like Xerxes—only pissed.

"Nice going, Lizzie."

"Can it, Grandma."

They roiled upon each other in a mounting wave of demonic bodies. Screeching and belching yellow sulfur, they surrounded me in a chorus of cackles and acrid smoke. I yanked the switch stars from the slush around Grandma. I had five. Make that four. No way could I fight them all.

Dimitri swooped down on us. I grabbed hold of a talon with one hand, slung an arm under Grandma's arm and watched in horror as my fingers sunk almost all of the way through her. She was no more than a wisp of air. I prayed I'd be able to hold on. Dimitri ripped us from the sludge and we soared upward. Wind plastered my hair to my face as we rocketed suicidally high and tight toward the summit of the ice cliff.

He dropped us hard on a narrow landing at the top of the cliff, way too close to the edge. The mass of demons swarmed below like an upset anthill.

"Can they fly?" I asked Grandma.

"Xerxes can, as soon as he assembles himself again." She rubbed the griffin's shoulder. "Attaboy, Dimitri."

She ruffled his lion's body and I could have sworn I heard him purr like a tabby.

"Where do we go?" I asked. I reached for Dimitri, but couldn't quite force myself to touch the short reddish fur on the immense shoulder in front of me. He stretched his powerful lion's body, touching a brightly colored wing to his back paw. And, yes, I'd known what he was. But to actually come face to, erm, beak with my sleek, half-furry, half-feathered, griffin . . . "I hate my life."

"Oh yeah, you've got problems." Grandma tried to climb onto his back, but slipped right through his body and landed hard on the ground. "Good thing my butt's almost gone or that would have hurt."

At this rate, she'd disappear in minutes.

"Just a sec," Grandma said, yanking off her silver cobra ring and placing it over her heart.

I could see through to the ice shelf behind her.

"Oh no," she rolled her eyes. "Goddamned, mother fucking *asshole!*" she screamed at the top of her lungs. "I knew it," she said, kicking the ice shelf, her foot passing through like a ghost. "Fucker stole my mother-fucking essence." She shook her head at my open-mouthed stare. "My goddamned living soul. It's already in the second layer of hell. Fuck!"

"What do we do?"

"Move!" she commanded, her eyes boring into mine. "Get your asses out of here pronto."

"What do you mean?" I asked, desperation clawing at me. "Where are we going?"

"Away," she said.

"Without you?"

"Here's a little bit of trivia. You need two demon slayers to enter the second layer of hell . . . and escape."

Dimitri stomped in surprise.

"Yeah, you didn't know that huh, slick? The slayer always has a twin."

I didn't have a twin. But I wasn't supposed to be a slayer. "Did mom have a twin?"

Grandma nodded. "She did. Serefina. Killed when your mom abandoned us."

Sweet switch stars.

"Your Aunt Serefina rescued the coven, though. Or most of it."

Grandma had faded almost completely away. "I thought if I could hold out until you got here. I don't know when he stole my soul." For the first time, she looked utterly lost. "I didn't even feel it. Leave, Lizzie. There's nothing else you can do for me. Thanks for coming this far, babe. I love you. And I'm sorry."

The griffin let out an agonized wail.

"You too, Dimitri," she said, running her transparent fingers through his feathers. "And for the record, Lizzie, I approve of your boyfriend, okay?"

We'd failed her. We'd also failed Dimitri's sisters. Vald was set to collect them in a matter of minutes.

As Xerxes landed on our ice shelf, whole and royally ticked, I doubted if we could even save ourselves.

# Chapter Twenty-one

"No," I said. Call me emotional, but "we are not leaving here until we axe Vald and save Grandma's immortal soul." Dimitri and Grandma stared at me like I was the one who'd sprouted rainbow wings and a beak. Or maybe it was the immense demon behind me.

"How do we get down to the second layer of hell? I mean it. I'll—incoming!" I hollered as Xerxes launched a barrage of green pointy things from his eyes. I pitched myself onto the frozen ice shelf. Dimitri bolted upward.

The demon's missiles shot right through Grandma and slammed into the ice wall behind her. A large chunk of it cracked from the main body and thundered sideways down the gorge.

"That's just it," she hollered. "You need *two* demon slayers to get to the second layer of hell!"

*Two of me? How were we going to get two of me?*

Dimitri swooped behind Xerxes and knocked the demon back down the ice cliff.

Except there really were two of me—straightlaced Lizzie and kick-butt Lizzie.

"I have an idea," I said, shivering up to my elbows in a patch of slush, realizing I was making this up as I went.

I didn't know if I could do it and it scared me to death and I had no choice unless my nonexistent twin planned on showing up in the next thirty seconds. "What if I split my soul?"

"What?" Grandma squeaked, her entire left half flickering.

"Separate myself," I told her. "Slice my yin from my yang." This was starting to make sense.

"That's the worst idea I've ever heard," Grandma bellowed above the ominously rumbling ice shelf. I wouldn't be surprised if the whole thing went.

"I didn't say it was a good idea," I told her. "But if Xerxes can split into a thousand demons, I'm betting I can cut myself in two."

"I've never heard of it," she insisted.

Evidently there was an advantage to not knowing what the hell I was doing. "What? Do you have any better ideas?"

"Yeah. Get out."

"Not happening," I said. "You said it yourself. This isn't about me."

That was the last thought I had before all of hell swallowed us.

It felt like a freefall from ten thousand feet, only I had no parachute and I was trying to split my soul. I didn't know what my immortal soul looked like, or exactly where it was, but I felt it as sure as I felt my heart pounding like a piston in my chest. I slammed my eyes shut, tore my soul in two, hoping I didn't make it too jaggedy, or rip it forever, or lose any pieces. I didn't know what would happen—or if I'd ever be whole again. I only knew that it was our last best chance to defeat Vald.

I opened my eyes when my knees smacked the ground, hard. "What the—?" The two halves of my soul fluttered inside my throat. I did it. Holy crap.

I straddled Dimitri's crotch. He'd changed back to

his human form and my hands pressed against his naked abs. My knees ached, and my head felt like I'd been pitched off a Boeing 767. This was so not the time to get turned on, except he looked so damned good. Well, the part of him that wasn't frowning at me.

Dimitri lifted me off his—hoo ya—naked body and I felt a familiar tightening between my legs as I took in his clean, male scent. Definitely better than the—whew—natural scent of this place. If I didn't know better, I'd have thought we'd landed in the monkey house at the zoo. I tore my eyes away from Dimitri, lying on the mint green industrial linoleum, his dagger—the ancient bronze one—strapped to his right calf. I squinted against the flickering, overhead lights and struggled to force my legs into working order. The emerald at my throat stung. I slid my hand between the stone and my skin, ready for it to morph into—who knew—I wouldn't have been surprised to be wearing bronze underwear at that point. But, oddly, the stone lost its heaviness and grew cold, *dead* against my hand.

The place reminded me of a high school chemistry lab, if your teacher happened to be Dr. Frankenstein. A web of blue energy crackled above the cluttered dissection tables and industrial countertops. Scattered across it—ohmigod—weasel-faced imps twitched as if they were being broiled alive. They couldn't be. Please. Because they'd each been chopped into bits and reassembled, some more precisely than others. My insides squelched at one pieced-together imp in particular, the right half of its body plump and covered in mottled black fur. The other half, thinner, graying and not quite joined at the head. Brain matter jiggled inside the raw wound, oozing with every tremor of the electric current. I drew my right boot across the floor and felt a slippery squish.

"Step back," a crisp voice commanded.

Vald. I knew it in my demon-slaying gut.

I braced myself at the sight of the fifth-level demon. He looked human—his sandy hair slicked back as he hunched over his notes in the far corner of the room. He'd buried his work nook behind swords in various states of decay, half-assembled switch stars and giant, free-standing aquariums full of creatures like the ones I'd seen behind the ice. Xerxes hissed from on top of an aquarium next to the doctor, spittle clinging to his chin. I reached for my last switch star.

Vald tossed his chart on the counter and eyed me like one of his experiments. "What did I just say?" He wore a pressed white lab coat freckled with burn holes and blood. The slight wrinkles on his forehead deepened as he frowned. "Impatience. The curse of youth."

"Vald?" I demanded.

"Ah, Lizzie. I know you. You know me." He reached into his coat pocket and fed the snarling Xerxes. "And I know you've met my demon," he said, rubbing his fingers over the creature's snout.

My breath caught in my throat as Vald strolled leisurely toward me. "I almost feel sorry for you. You obviously haven't researched or you wouldn't be down here." He stiffened. "And you," he said to Dimitri, who had been silently making his way behind Vald, his ancient bronze dagger in hand. "You need to stop taking everything so personally."

I'd like to see that dagger buried in Vald once and for all. I didn't know how much time we had to save Dimitri's sisters, but it wasn't much. Then we had to find Grandma's soul somewhere among the shelves of chemicals and metal pens carpeted with noxious growths. "Release Grandma and end the curse on Dimitri's family, or I kill you right now."

"You don't have the power."

I cast a switch star straight for Vald's heart. It had to

kill him. Please. If he exploded into a zillion Valds instead . . .

The star sliced the demon's head clean off. Hallelujah . . . holy hell! Xerxes leapt at me and I dove behind a giant aquarium.

The switch star zoomed back to me—too late. Xerxes tackled me and it zipped clear over my head. His weight suffocated me. His sulfuric breath burned me as he reared back to attack. I struggled like an over-turned June bug.

Dimitri hollered somewhere behind Xerxes. *Now!*

The sub-demon buzzed like a defective television and disappeared with a pop. The air sizzled with energy, numbing my fingertips and—as soon as I tried to speak—my tongue. "What the . . . ?"

Dimitri yanked his bronze knife back. He turned and thrust it into Vald's chest. Dimitri twisted the jew-eled handle and shoved hard, burying it to the hilt.

Vald's head lay under an autopsy table several feet away, unblinking and—if I didn't know better— hacked off.

Dimitri stood over the dead demon, his back muscles pulsing like an athlete's after competition. Black sludge bubbled from Vald's chest. I could taste the sulfur in the air.

I moved to stand next to Dimitri, not quite knowing what to say. I wrapped my arm around his bare hip and took comfort in the feel of skin on skin.

"You okay?" He smoothed a tangle of hair back from my face and kissed my forehead.

"Did we get him in time?" I asked, leaning into Dimitri's strong frame as he folded me against him.

Dimitri tucked his chin against the top of my head and nodded. "I think my sisters are going to be all right," he said, as if he could hardly believe his own words.

Dimitri's chest heaved against mine as he reached up to wipe his eyes in relief.

Ding dong the demon was dead.

And that's when I felt a reminder, against my abs, that my delicious griffin was, in fact, naked. My face warmed, perhaps from the adrenaline coursing through my body. "Come on," I told him. "We gotta find Grandma." And maybe an extra lab coat. I had nothing against Dimitri in all of his glory, but I also needed to focus.

Dimitri paused over Vald's ruined body, an unbelieving grin tickling the side of his mouth.

Just when I thought things might actually turn out all right, Vald groaned and sat up.

He located his head, twisted it back into place and yanked the knife out of his chest with a grunt. "I don't think I'll ever understand the human psyche."

"Impossible." Dimitri tensed, every muscle in his body stiff from shock.

"That's just what Lizzie's Great-great-great Aunt Edna said. Before I killed her." Vald eyed us like a couple of annoying houseguests before he strolled over to a plastic tub full of clear liquid. He tossed the knife inside and watched it hiss, bubble and melt into a lump of dissolving metal. "It took you ten years of your life to find that, didn't it?" Vald popped a crick in his neck and contemplated the remains of Dimitri's dagger. "At least ten. There's only one place to get a Slayer Sword and the mistress of Achelios doesn't part with them lightly." He raised a brow. "The last I heard, she was demanding sexual favors," he said, unable to hide a smirk. "I'd be fascinated to learn more. If I thought you'd answer."

"Shut up, Vald." Dimitri pulled me behind him.

"Case in point," Vald said, rifling through his lab coat pocket.

I twisted out of Dimitri's reach. My last switch star lay under the aquarium behind us. I needed to retrieve it quickly, in case the white-scaled creatures could break through glass as easily as they could through ice. "So why isn't he dead?" I asked. "That thing should have killed him, right?"

A timer went off near one of the cages. Vald pulled two vials of boiling acid from his coat pocket and studied them against each other. "Switch stars no longer concern me. I've learned to do many things in the century and a half since your ancestor trapped me down here. Like your mother would have taught you, Lizzie. If she'd been around. If hell gives you lemons, you find a way to suck out their souls."

The creature inside the cage screamed when it saw the vial in the demon's hand. "Excuse me," he said, popping the top with his thumb. "That's the trouble with experimenting on the damned. You wouldn't believe the noise."

I refused to believe my weapons were useless. The alternative was unthinkable. I scrambled under the aquarium, grasped my last switch star and hurled it at Vald's heart, burying it in the exact same place Dimitri stabbed. The vial flew out of Vald's hand, sloshing acid and burning holes in his lab coat. I held my breath. Okay, the switch star didn't zip through the demon, but it did penetrate. If the sword was defective, this could do it. Vald blinked twice and inspected his torn, smoking lab coat.

"Oh now this is rich. You already killed my demon." He yanked the switch star from his chest. "Well, not really. Once he finishes romping through the third dimension, I'll send a trio of imps out for him." He held up the switch star. "In the meantime, I'll keep this." He tucked my switch star into his lab coat.

Dimitri drew his arm around me, breathing like he'd been running sprints.

"Quite touching. I've always wanted a griffin."

"How did you . . . ?" My mind flooded with panic. He'd beaten my switch stars, Dimitri's demon-killing sword, everything that was supposed to work. He couldn't be un-killable.

*Could he?*

Vald eyed me like I was slow. "What else would you suggest I do in here? Knit? Believe me, another hundred and fifty years and I wouldn't have even needed you to break out."

That's right. He still needed my power. Well he wouldn't get it while I lived and breathed. Come to think of it, that wasn't much of a threat.

"If I plan my energy carefully, I'll have enough power to walk the Earth and also revive that great aunt of yours. Evie. I'd like to run some experiments on her. She had extraordinary strength."

"Is that why you took Grandma too?" I watched him closely, hoping he'd betray her location.

"Of course not. She was bait. But she'll be good for experimentation too. I'm always looking for ways to improve my imps. Hybrids, you see. I've never fused an imp with a witch."

My stomach churned. We had to stop this sicko. But how do you kill a creature that can't be killed?

Vald checked his watch. "If you'll excuse me, I have to go collect on a bet." He winked.

*Dimitri's sisters.*

Naked, unarmed and clearly insane—Dimitri shoved me backward and launched himself at Vald. Holy hell. I was about to lose my lover, my grandma, my power and my ever-living soul all in the same day.

# Chapter Twenty-two

Vald moved faster than anything I'd ever seen. He shoved Dimitri into the aquarium and both of them crashed to the floor in a wave of shattered glass, ice water and white-scaled dragon creatures. The monsters bit into Dimitri like a teeming wave of piranhas. I clutched a glass shard in a lab towel and stabbed everything I could, dragging the creatures from Dimitri's body. They hissed and bit at me as I cleaved heads from bodies. Their blood, like hot steam, burned my hands and arms. Dimitri impaled four of them on the leg of an overturned dissection table, their bodies sizzling on the linoleum floor.

Then we both got wise and started hurling them up into the energy web on the ceiling. White-scaled creatures collided with the pulsing imps in an explosion of screams, scales, fur and blood.

"Enough!" Vald yelled. The energy field crackled and died, shrouding the room in shadows. The remaining aquariums glowed, the white-scaled creatures writhing and twisting against the glass.

Dimitri curled sideways from the toxic bites raging through his body. I reached for the crystals in my belt.

Vald stalked straight for me. "That's it. Your soul is mine."

He reached for me and fire shot up my arm as soon as he touched me.

"Son of a—!" Vald retreated, his hands smoking.

My head swam and my knees buckled and I hurled right there on Vald's shoes.

"Impossible," he said, inspecting his blackened hands. "I cured that," he said, as he snagged a towel hanging from one of the U-shaped lab faucets.

Dimitri shook on the cold, hard linoleum. Sweat and blood slickened his entire body. I had to help him. I braced a hand on the overturned dissection table, clutching a handful of crystals, one eye on Vald. I infused the crystals with—*think, Lizzie, what it felt like to be with Dimitri that night at Motel 6.*

The pure wickedness in his eyes as he'd teased me through the boring white button-down he'd found for me because I wanted it. He touched me, moved me, made me feel until I almost combusted with it. He hadn't wanted to change me or improve me; he'd just wanted to be with me. And what we'd done as a result—I couldn't think of anything more happy or healthy.

The crystals radiated in my hand as I fought the remnants of a smile. Just thinking of what that man did to me . . .

I rushed to Dimitri and touched the crystals to the worst of his wounds. The rocks emitted a ghostly yellow light, barely perceptible among the sweat and the blood.

It should have been enough, but it wasn't. He wasn't healing. Something was horribly wrong. I'd felt immediate relief when the crystal touched my back. Dimitri hadn't even opened his eyes. He shivered as I pressed more and more stones to his body.

"Oh my God, Dimitri." Heal, damn it! *Heal.*

A metal clamp seized my neck. What the—? Dimitri's emerald bit into the flesh at the base of my throat.

I twisted my fingers around solid steel as it dragged me backward, away from him.

"Stand up or I make sure he's dead," Vald commanded.

Vald forced me through a tiny back hallway, lined with vats of fetid chemicals. I tried to catch a glimpse back at Dimitri, to see if he was okay, but Vald's grip never let up. He led me into a small room. The faint smell of blood and urine surged the instant a heavy door closed behind us. A closet of a room sprouted from the main chamber and I almost gagged when I looked inside. A pair of bald, tattoo-laden identical twins, very dead, and sewn together at the heart. No question about it, this room was used for torture.

Vald followed my gaze. "Rock stars. Scraggly looking things. They said they'd do anything, so I took them at their word."

In the next room, chains wound around a cafeteria table stained with blood. Cuts and gouges streaked the plastic. Dark scars had settled in the grooves, like cleaves on a cutting board. Hack saws, rusty screwdrivers, pliers and worse hung from Peg-Board on the wall.

I dug in my heels, grabbed hold of the doorjamb and held on with everything I had.

"Come on, now," Vald said, using both hands to pry me inside the room. "I'm not going to torture you. Yet. This is for my imps. I've been finding ways to make them meaner. There's a fine line between piercing an animal enough to make it vicious, but not so much as to harm the muscular or skeletal systems. I've also learned to razor the teeth for maximum sharpness while maintaining core strength."

He kicked open another door and in the hallway outside, Grandma's motionless body lay on a gurney, her silver hair tangled and her eyes staring at the ceiling. I fought back a wave of panic and focused on what I had to do.

Vald dragged me into a soaring room with glass floors, a twisted version of the stacks at City Library. Instead of a patchwork of hardback books, he'd stacked the rows upon rows of shelves with thousands of glass containers. In almost every one, a living soul fluttered near the lid.

"What is it with you people and jars?" I inched my fingers into my belt, the third pouch on the right, and dug out a crystal. I infused it with death, destruction, everything I felt for this evil creature who had stolen Grandma's soul. He'd left Dimitri to writhe and die on the floor while toxins ravaged his body. He'd systematically sucked the life from every woman in Dimitri's family. He'd stolen my grandmother. He'd attacked the Red Skulls, kept them on the run for thirty years. He wanted to suck me dry, kill me and use my powers to go all medieval on thousands of innocents.

I'd kill him first.

I hurled the crystal straight for Vald's forehead. It smacked him right between the eyes and bounced off.

He gave me a sour look. "I really wish you'd quit doing that."

Everyone was depending on me, damn it. I hurled the next crystal straight for his heart. He stepped aside in a blaze of motion and my crystal burst through row after row of glass jars. Souls screeched as they darted, collided and knocked over shelf after shelf. Glass flew, the souls screamed like a thousand fire alarms. In a wave, they bolted for the ceiling like trapped birds. Shit. One of those was Grandma. "Grandma!"

Vald's eyes blazed for a moment, before he stomped down the emotion. "You try a demon's patience," he said, fighting to even the tone of his voice. "You'd better hope she doesn't singe herself on the florescent lights."

I strained to catch a glimpse, any sign of Grandma among the thousands of souls dancing around a series of hot bulbs encased in wide-set metal brackets.

"How about this?" he asked. "I'll retrieve your grandmother and you hand over your power."

I couldn't do it. He was too dangerous.

"Well what if we include the rest of Dimitri's family?" asked the fifth-level demon, far too reasonably.

My eyes had grown dry from staring. I could save Dimitri, his family, Grandma. But I didn't want this monster walking the earth. Or, if I let my mind go there, I didn't want any part of his demon slayer experiments. My mom was right. We should never have come down here. We'd only made things worse.

Vald twisted the clamp around my throat. "What if I do this?"

My body flooded with pain, as if he'd dropped me in a vat of acid. I couldn't breathe, couldn't think.

As soon as it began, it ended. My body tingled, hypersensitive to the static electricity racing up and down my arms.

"Was that effective?"

I didn't know what to do.

"What about this?"

A cramp seized me between the ribs. My breath caught in my throat as Vald drew a spiderweb–thin line of blue energy from my body. He teased it out, unraveling my powers like an old sock. I felt myself grow weak with every pull. My head fuzzed, and my mouth grew dry. When he finished teasing out a length of my shimmering, demon-slaying essence, he dropped the thread to the floor.

"This way takes longer," Vald grunted. "And now I'm going to have to untangle it. An interesting choice you've made."

My rapidly numbing fingers dug into the case at the back of my tool belt. I prayed that the last tool in Great-great-great Aunt Evie's bag of tricks would be enough to cap Vald's ass for good. I inched my finger underneath the lid to find the mysterious creature I'd glimpsed on the deck of the *Dixie Queen*.

Ouch! Damn the thing—it bit me. I shoved my finger deeper. If the little degenerate thought its razor-pointed teeth could stop me at this point, it had underestimated this particular chewed-up, spit-out, not-going-take-it-anymore demon slayer.

It wriggled its sand-papery body far down into the bottom of the pocket until it disappeared completely. Impossible! I wanted to holler as I dug my bloody finger into the bottom of the leather case. Then again, what the hell did I know?

Back to the third pocket from the right. I reached for my last crystal and jerked back in pain as it burned my fingers. Vald's pile of power had grown into a tangle of threads at his feet. I no longer had enough energy to use the few tools I had left.

My stomach sank. I couldn't beat Vald even when I had my powers, much less now. He tossed me a maniacal grin. He was going to kill me and Dimitri—if Dimitri wasn't dead already. Then Vald would walk the earth again.

As if he could read my thoughts, which he probably could given the grip he had on my life force, Vald said, "It will be important to wipe out the coven. And of course any trace of you, just in case you have a twin. I've learned to be meticulous. When I exterminated Edna, I gave in to celebration too soon. Her sister Evie escaped. A very difficult slayer indeed. I've regretted my lack of attention for many, many years."

I felt the two halves of my soul fluttering in my

throat. I wondered what Vald would do to them—to me—after I died.

Vald jolted, shocking me out of my haze. Dimitri stood next to my pile of power, holding up a Transport Spell.

Sweet happy puppies! Ant Eater had shoved that purple noodle of a transport spell in my pocket on board the *Dixie Queen*. I didn't care when or how Dimitri had taken it. God love my crafty, demon-busting boyfriend.

"Cut it, Vald," Dimitri said, holding up the transport spell, "or you're headed for the third layer of hell."

Vald stopped, his face twisted with annoyance and—praised be—doubt. "If you release that spell, you'll also send Lizzie to the third layer of hell," he said, wiggling the thin line of energy that connected me to the fifth-level demon. "I doubt she'd fare as well as I would."

Dimitri drew the spell back like a weapon. "Yeah," he said, his voice colder than the ice cliffs, "but I get rid of you."

I hated it when Dimitri was right. He might be bluffing, but I hoped he wasn't.

Even though I was rapidly losing my powers, I was still a demon slayer. And we lived by the Three Truths. Look to the outside. Accept the universe.

Sacrifice yourself.

"Do it," I told Dimitri.

Vald stiffened. "Don't be premature, griffin," he said quickly. "I'll let you have your sisters if you take them and leave now."

"I think he's telling the truth," I said to Dimitri. "He hasn't had time to kill them yet."

Vald cocked his head toward me. "Lizzie's taken more time than I'd expected."

The demon nodded toward a row of jars at the far

edge of the room. "Open the one with the blue lid. The curse is there."

A bolt of silver danced inside.

"Will you know?" I mouthed to him, lacking the energy for words.

Dimitri nodded. He backed toward the far shelf. Eyeing us, he popped the lid, reached his hand inside and crushed the curse. His eyes blazed with relief for a split second before they hardened again. "Stupid demon," Dimitri said with a smirk. "I still have the transport spell."

Vald launched a switch star at Dimitri. It sliced through his beautiful chest and into the wall behind him. I watched in horror as Dimitri stood for a moment, an awful steaming hole in his chest, disbelief etched on his features, before he pitched forward onto the floor. Blood flowed from him in a sickening, widening pool.

"Stupid griffin," Vald said. "I had a switch star."

It was the single most helpless moment in my life. I couldn't help him. I couldn't even hold him. Vald's pale blue eyes twinkled as he grinned at me. "Ah, switch stars. They're quite useful, you know," he said, returning to the slow task of killing me. "You can't throw a spell from fifty feet."

Numb, hard shock gave way to pure, blind rage. Dimitri could have used the transport spell to save himself. He could have popped it the moment he knew his sisters were safe. But he'd stuck around to help me and I'd be damned if I was going to let him lie there in a pool of blood. I was a demon slayer and I had to start acting like one.

Vald's evil twisted in his heart. I could taste it like I could the black souls as they had twined and pulsed in JR's chest. I leaned forward, pushed toward Vald like I was swimming through water. He yanked me closer, as my essence bled into his hands.

I breathed in pickle relish and seaweed as I laid my hand on his chest. Yeah, well I'd soon smell the sulfuric ting of black, gloopy demon blood. Gritting my teeth, I used every ounce of strength I had left to dig my fingers into his flesh. He hollered and pulled and for a second I thought he was about to fling me away, but I kept burrowing, through muscle and ribs and the goo that jammed under my fingernails and twisted around my wrist, my arm. I grasped his heart in both hands and yanked.

"Enough!" he demanded.

The muscle spasmed in my hand. It curled and pumped, spouting black gore. Alive. Empty. I felt for Vald's essence, his living being.

"Demons don't have souls, you raving lunatic." Vald ground his teeth together, tethered to me by a single thread, my right hand still inside his chest. The two halves of my soul fluttered in my throat. They wanted to be whole again. Tears pushed against the backs of my eyes. I'd give anything to get out of here, to be normal. To leave this entire sick existence behind me.

But it wasn't about me.

*Sacrifice yourself.*

I covered my mouth with my hand and tried not to choke on the acidic tang of Vald's blood. I forced myself to relax, eased my throat open and coaxed the fluttering half of my soul upward.

Vald pulled at the thin thread, unraveling the last bits of my power. His chest healed quickly, the black blood thickening, his skin closing over the wound. I captured the adventurous half of my soul like a butterfly, wound it into my palm and shoved it into the rapidly narrowing hole in Vald's chest.

"You clueless," the demon strained for a breath,

"freak of—" His eyes bugged as he clutched the gaping wound over his heart. Vald fell to his knees as blue fire curled from the gash. He stared at me with pure hatred as the cobalt flame lashed across his body, incinerating him from the inside out.

I should have been relieved, and I was. More than that, I was angry—at Vald for starting this whole mess, at Dimitri for trying to be brave and at myself for not doing more to protect the two people in this world that would have done anything to protect me.

Vald burned hot and fast. I'd heard of spontaneous combustion and this had to be the closest thing to it I'd ever seen. But the blue flame left nothing, not even ashes.

Soul jars burst like popcorn popping. I wrapped my arms around my face and head as souls careened throughout the room. They rushed up, out, in a flurry of beating wings.

My own energy knocked me backward as it rushed back into my body. Heat surged through my veins. On rubbery legs, I started for Dimitri's pale, lifeless body. He wasn't breathing. No. My blood froze. It couldn't end this way. I wouldn't let it.

A familiar presence landed on my shoulder. Grandma.

I pulled my ever-living soul from Vald's chest with a wet glop. It dove back into me, which gave me an idea. "Wait here, Dimitri," I said, hoping he could hear me.

Grandma's soul on my shoulder, I rushed to find Grandma's body on the gurney outside the torture room. With a squeal, her soul belly flopped back into her. I thought I saw her eyes twitch, but we didn't have time to get her off the slab. Not yet. Dimitri could be dying back there. I whipped the table around and drove Grandma back through the broken glass in the soul room, the wheels spattering through Dimitri's blood.

*Don't think about it.*

I clutched Grandma's hand, Dimitri's hand. I squeezed my eyes shut and called to Ant Eater, the coven, anybody else who was listening.

"Get us the hell out of here!"

# Chapter Twenty-three

I didn't even see the portal. It must have snuck up behind us because when the world stopped spinning, we lay crumpled on the floor of a tiny, square-shaped room. The pilothouse. Not that I cared where we were, as long as it didn't involve the second layer of hell. We'd made it back. Now I just had to make sure we all lived.

Which is why I kept my eye on the orb as it stalked us from the edge of a framed Yazoo River map. "Down, portal," I told it. The last thing we needed was to go back to hell. Who knew if demons like Vald stayed dead.

The portal darted sideways and hovered by a decorative brass steering wheel hanging on the wall, honoring a certain Captain Clebius Barnam. It dipped and swayed, gathering courage. I gave it the stink eye and it zipped backward, clanging into a brass bell.

Grandma's eyes fluttered among the mass of long, gray hair tangled in her face. "I'm getting too damned old for this." She pushed her hair back with one shaking hand and braced the other against the wooden wall, slathered in years upon years of white paint.

"Please tell me you know first aid," I said, stuffing Dimitri's borrowed lab coat against his chest wound. The switch star had cauterized part of the wound, but he still bled. Way too much. If he was still bleeding, he was still alive, right? The switch star had cut a hole through the left side of his chest. It had to have hit his heart, his lungs.

The coppery scent of blood hung thick in the humid, night air. Dimitri's skin, drained of color, had gone bluish around his lips. His pulse felt thready, at least it had a few seconds ago. Now? I couldn't feel it. "His heart's stopped."

*No, no, no.*

"Help!" I screamed at the top of my lungs. Grandma hijacked his wrist while I moved north, thrusting both hands against the artery on his neck. No pulse. "Damn it! Tell me you know CPR or magic or *something*!"

She shook her head. "I know he's supposed to die."

I couldn't believe it, even though I held the proof in both hands. "What?"

She looked as helpless and mortified and exasperated as I felt. "Back in the Yardsaver shed. I saw Vald plotting to drag you down into the second layer of hell—look what happened when I tried to stop that. And later, I saw Dimitri dying to save you." She sighed. "It was inevitable." She wiped a spot of blood from his wrist, ignoring the puddle of blood that soaked her jeans from the knees down.

"So he's . . ." I couldn't say it.

"Gone." She helped me ease his head onto my lap. "I'm sorry, Lizzie. I know what he meant to you."

She didn't know jack. Okay, so he'd lied to me and I was mad at him, but he'd had his reason—a good one. And now he'd never know that I needed him too. He'd shown me that I could be strong. I could break a few rules, wear kick-ass black boots and make love until I screamed. And just when I was ready to let go of my past, Vald had stolen my future.

The portal crackled as I sat there with his head in

my lap, unable—no, unwilling—to move. I knew we needed to get out of here. We were free from the second layer of hell, but that orb could send us right back to Vald's laboratory—or somewhere worse.

Maybe there was nothing I could do for Dimitri. But getting up out of the puddle of blood, letting go of him, I'd never get this moment back again. When I stood up, he'd really be gone.

"Lizzie?" Frieda rattled the pilothouse door. "Oh snot. It's stuck. Lizzie?"

"Open the goddamned door," Grandma ordered. "You locked us in with an itchy portal."

"Gertie? Well I'll be a buttercup!" Frieda squealed. "Ant Eater! Get yourself over here! Gertie's back!"

I wanted to smack Frieda for being happy about anything right now. Of course she didn't know Dimitri lay crumpled and—I forced myself to think it—dead in my lap. I didn't know how I thought things would end, but it wasn't supposed to happen like this.

He'd been too alive, too sexy and too stubborn.

"At least he saved his sisters," Grandma said.

I uncrumpled the bloody lab coat from his chest and spread it over his body. He'd have told me it was worth it. But it wasn't. Not to me.

"He wanted to make this thing between us work," I said, running a finger along his strong jaw. "I told him when hell freezes over. Guess we were both wrong." I grazed my fingers over the lips that had kissed away the marks from the black souls, and touched me in ways, well, in many, many ways. Tears crowded my eyes. He'd taught me a thing or two, about switch stars, myself and, heck, what it felt like to be wanted.

"Motherfucking damn it."

"Excuse me?" I said, eyeing Grandma's stormy expression through a squidgy window of tears.

"You're turning me into a pansy-ass," she said,

shoving her hair back from her face with bloody
fingers. She puffed up her cheeks and blew out a breath.
"We can save him, okay. If we act now. It's stupid and
pointless," she harrumphed, "and there's no turning back
from it."

"How?" I asked, hope tickling my stomach. I'd take
any chance we could get.

"You'll be opening yourself to him in ways you
can't imagine."

"No," I told her. "I mean how do we do this?"

Grandma frowned before she shoved her hand inside my top.

"Yow!" Icy fingers. "Some warning first!"

"Like I got time to buy you flowers," she muttered,
her nails scratching the smooth skin under my collar
bone. "Damn it!" A sizzle zipped through her and she
yanked her hand back. "I was hoping I could touch it.
You have to."

"Fine. What am I looking for?"

I lifted my shirt away and almost choked when I
saw it.

"We need to work on your sensing abilities," Grandma
muttered as I stared at the pure white light glowing
from inside my chest. I couldn't feel it, but it was a part
of me.

I reached down and touched it, felt it vibrate against
my fingers. It hummed steady and strong—my living
essence, the thing that Vald had wanted so bad, was
reaching out to Dimitri.

"You do it and there's no turning back," Grandma
warned.

Yes, there'd be consequences, but I didn't care. The
only thing that mattered was having Dimitri back,
alive.

I forced myself to look as my fingers crept into the
sliver of chest above my heart. Blood pulsed in my

ears. The essence clung to me, warm and steady. I took what was mine and slid it into the gaping wound in Dimitri's chest. I tried not to think of how cold he felt. Grandma muttered a series of incantations as I watched my power sizzle inside him.

Freely given, freely taken.

His chest healed before our eyes, muscles knitting together, skin growing whole. I felt for his pulse. Nothing. My hope sank. But still, I had to believe he could do this. *Don't give up. Please, Dimitri.* I did the only thing I could think to do. His head in my hands, I bent down and touched his lips to mine. His lips felt cool. Tears burned my eyes.

He gasped.

Sweet switch stars!

I searched his face. His eyes remained closed, but his chest moved up and down in a beautiful, steady rhythm. I wanted to hug him, Grandma, the portal. He was alive. He'd saved me and I'd saved him right back.

His emerald glowed hot against my neck.

Kick-butt demon slayer that I am, I started crying all over again. "Thanks, Grandma," I said, running my fingers through his thick hair. I couldn't help but think back to the first time I'd given in to the temptation, under very different—and quite toe-curling—circumstances.

"It was dumber for him to go down there than it was for you," Grandma said. "Griffins rule the air, not the underworld."

"He cares about his sisters."

"And you."

I ran my fingers along his broad shoulders. The idea made me smile. I didn't know he was awake until he broke open a weak, but saucy grin of his own. I kissed it right off him. "How do you feel?"

"You don't want to know." He cupped the back of

my head and dragged me down for another kiss. His lips were solid, eager and insistent. I ignored the blood that clung to him and focused on *him*, clean, earthy and masculine. Pure delight threaded through me as he nuzzled his cheek against mine.

"I thought I was dead," he murmured.

"You were," Grandma said.

"Grazed by a switch star," I said, nipping at his delicious lips. "You'll live."

Grandma cleared her throat. I didn't know if she disapproved of the public display of affection or the lie. Frankly, I didn't care. I'd been through enough in the past twenty-four hours that I should be able to kiss this man for a week. In front of a room full of grandmas. And the Pope.

And if she questioned my little white lie, well, I had to do it. If he knew we were somehow connected, he might never let me go. He'd touched me in ways I never knew existed, but I didn't belong in this world any more than he belonged in mine.

But I would take one more kiss.


There were at least a dozen witches and one elated terrier ready to tackle us the minute we walked out of the pilothouse. Pirate dashed for me, his nails skidding on the wooden deck.

"Lizzie! You're here! I didn't know if I'd see you again and I was counting the seconds you were gone. But you know I can only count to four. So I had to count one, two, three, four . . ." He squirmed like a puppy when I picked him up. "And then one, and two and," he said, between licks to my hands, face and wherever else he could reach.

"Ease up, buddy. I'm here," I told him, trying to keep hold of my dog in one hand while my other wrapped around Dimitri's waist. He looked terrible with the bloody lab coat hanging from his frame. But he felt good. And call it wishful thinking, but I could have sworn he grew steadier with each passing minute. I didn't think my nuzzle therapy had hurt, either. Well, except that we had to wait a few minutes before Dimitri wanted to stand up.

"Sorry it took a bit." Frieda patted Dimitri's arm, her bracelets clanging together. "We locked the portal here in the pilothouse so it wouldn't get away again. It likes to ring the bell."

"It's not alive," I told her.

"Okay," she said.

"Step aside!" Sidecar Bob pushed his way through the crowd around us, medical bag balanced between his knees. "I need to get a look at him," he said, nearly running over my toes. "What happened?"

"Grazed by a switch star," I said, yanking my foot back as he spun his wheels sideways for a better look.

"Lizzie! You didn't!"

*Thanks for reminding me about my aim.*

"*No.* I didn't," I said. Which just goes to prove, first impressions die hard.

Witches crowded the main deck. I accepted some congratulations, and a horny toad from Scarlet (I didn't ask). The riverboat's ancient sound system blasted AC/DC's "Highway to Hell" as Pirate and I wandered up to the narrow deck at the front of the boat. Let Grandma have her fun. I wasn't much for loud parties. Besides, it would be hard enough to say good-bye to this life without teasing myself with the revelry outside the pilothouse. Hopefully, Frieda had remembered to lock the door on that portal.

"Watch yourself," I told Pirate as I crushed a Mexican food–craving spell near his tail. Lord knew what that would do to my dog.

I watched the dust from the spell flutter toward the

wooden deck. It would be tough to leave this place, but I'd never made any bones about the real reason I wanted to learn about my powers. I loved my job at Happy Hands. Heck, I wanted kids of my own someday. And while running around with biker witches and griffins had done a lot for my confidence and my love life, this wasn't the place to have a family.

Case in point, as Grandma lumbered up to me with two hands full of steak knives. "For the Beast Feast after the ceremony." She dropped them onto the bench behind me and ignored the ones that missed and clattered to the deck.

"What ceremony?"

"The one for you." She dug her finger into her right ear. "Dang thing's been buzzing ever since, well, I guess I don't have anything to bitch about, do I?"

"Need help getting ready?" Perhaps I could keep the squirrel guts out of the ceremonial goblet.

"Nah. It's a job for the coven. I gotta round them up before they tap the keg." She cast a wry grin my way and hitched up her belt. "I'm not good at this, so shut up and listen. I was blown away by how you handled yourself down there. Don't get me wrong, I always knew you could do it. You're my grandbaby for God's sake. Anyhow, I'm proud. And your mother would be too."

"About my mom," I said, one eye on Pirate, who sniffed at the knives.

"Scarlet told me. I should have warned you except, damn it, I thought I had more time. I saw Vald's plan for you while I was meditating in the Yardsaver shed back at the Red Skull. Unfortunately Vald also saw me."

"It's okay," I told her. "I just wish . . ." What? That my mom cared about me? That she'd been brave or strong or maybe that she'd warned me before she shoved her powers onto me? "I don't have a twin, do I?"

She considered the question. "If you do, I haven't felt her."

"Well that was further from the 'no' I'd been wanting." If I had a twin with the same powers as me, I had to help her. Or . . . my stomach squinched at the thought . . . maybe she was better off *not* knowing.

"I'd suggest you lay off your mom for a while," Grandma said. "It took more than you realize for her to come after you, regardless of what you think about her." She tilted her head and eyed me thoughtfully. "Just know your momma loves you in her own way."

"Okay." I'd choose to believe that, for now.

"I meant what I said back at the Dumpster. I'm looking forward to being your grandma. Not that I'm going to be throwing chocolate-chip cookies at you. Or blowing smoke up your ass." She dug her hands into the pockets of her rhinestone-studded skinny jeans.

"I'm going home," I told her.

She nodded, watching the full moon. "I told Scarlet what you did, ripping your soul in half. You should have seen the look on her face." She cleared her throat. "Here's the thing. She thinks there's a way to rejoin the two halves."

I nodded, relieved. Leave it up to Scarlet.

"According to Scarlet, you have a choice. When we rejoin your soul, we can put it back together and leave your demon-slaying essence behind."

"You're kidding!" I wanted to kiss her. Heck, I'd have been willing to kiss Ant Eater at that moment. Talk about winning the demon slayer lottery. This was even better than learning to control my powers. I could be normal. At last.

"Think about it, Lizzie," Grandma cautioned. "No more switch stars. No more enchanted riverboats. No more throwing giggle spells at Ant Eater."

"No more black souls, death spells, fifth-level demon attacks."

"No more griffins," she said, watching the moon-flecked waves slap against the bow of the *Dixie Queen*.

She would have to mention that.

"Unlike your mom, you won't have to burden any-one else with your powers. 'Course you'll be com-pletely cut off from the magical world." We stood in silence for a moment. "Except that I'll be by to visit from time to time. I mean, you are my grandbaby."

I knew there'd be consequences. I never thought leaving would be easy. Well, maybe I did in the be-ginning.

While I wasn't going to run from this world, like my mom, I knew I wasn't a part of it, like my grandma.

"Let's do it," I told her.

"Think about it. We won't start the ceremony for another," she checked her hog watch, "twenty minutes, depending on how fast it takes to steam the armadillo jowls."

"Of course," I told her.

I didn't need twenty minutes to think. I'd already decided a long time ago. I mean, this is what I wanted, right? It was better than what I wanted, which was to be left alone. For good.

So why did I feel so miserable?

I've never liked good-byes.

Dimitri leaned against the railing on the back deck, one foot propped up on the rust-flecked metal. He would have to look sexy as all get out in worn jeans that hugged his drool-worthy butt and his trademark black T-shirt, drawn tight over his back. Maybe I wasn't the only one feeling a bit tense.

Witches called to each other among the clanking coming from the kitchen and main dining room. Preparations for the Beast Feast were in full swing. I'd left Pirate in the middle of it, riding in Sidecar Bob's lap and sampling everything in reach.

Dimitri's gaze flickered over my dirty purple plaid miniskirt. "Come here, Lizzie."

I wrapped my arms around him, ear to his chest and reveled in the *thwump, tump, tump* of his heart. He'd always have a part of me with him, whether he knew it or not. My chipped pink fingernails traced wicked patterns on his abs. "They send you out here too?"

"Nah. I just got off the phone with my sisters." He burst into a wide grin. "You wouldn't believe it, they're—" He trailed off, lost in his pure rapture. His sisters were alive.

Dimitri shook his head, lit up from head to toe. "Diana has this horse," he said. "She calls it her pony, but don't be fooled—the thing's as big as a Clydesdale. Turns out she's been dreaming of him while she's in her coma. She wakes up, glad as anything to be alive and decides she has to ride the horse, right then and there. Well Dyonne—that's my other sister," he paused, physically unable to wipe the smile off his face. "Dyonne tells Diana to forget about the horse. There's a monster storm brewing off the coast. Lightning, pouring rain, the works. Everybody knows she can't take Zeus out in that. But all Diana can think about is this horse."

He shook his head. "So Diana's out there, soaked, and Dyonne is hollering at her from the window, mad as hell 'Get in here or you're going to get killed—again!' She thinks she has Diana convinced when Diana comes busting through the front door of the house and rides Zeus straight into the dining room." He laughed freely, tears touching the corners of his eyes. "God, I love those two."

He tilted his chin down, still smiling. I was going to

melt into a puddle on the floor if he kept looking at me that way.

He wrapped my hands in his. "I'm flying to Santorini in a few hours to see them," he said. "If the house is still standing—and at this rate, that's a big if." He ran his thumbs in lazy circles over my wrists. Such a small gesture, but I didn't want it to end. "I'd like you to come stay with us."

The two halves of my soul fluttered in my throat. I didn't know what to think. I couldn't.

*I shouldn't.*

Besides, I'd never planned a trip without two guide-books, a typed itinerary and at least three months' no-tice. Well, except for my recent excursion with the Red Skulls and it was safe to say that undertaking hadn't quite turned out like I'd expected.

"Well?" He hitched a brow.

He couldn't be serious. "When would we leave? Now?"

"Ten minutes or so," he said, not half as concerned as he should be. "I was about to come find you."

"Ten minutes?" It would take longer than that to convince Pirate to leave the kitchen. And how would I take a dog to Greece?

*And wasn't I out here to tell Dimitri good-bye?*

"You said yourself school doesn't start for another week," he teased, his lips on mine before I could even think about uttering the word *no.*

He drew me in again and again, his hands trailing down my back, pulling me into him, making me feel . . .

I pulled away. If I wanted to get rid of my powers, the ceremony was tonight. Of course that didn't mean I couldn't see Dimitri later . . . Wait. Yes, it did.

"What do you think?" He kissed the tip of my nose. I could feel every inch of him crushed against me.

I didn't want to think. Just like I hadn't wanted to think when I had him—all of him—on top of me at Motel 6.

It was time to face facts. This was never going to work.

Dang, it was hard to remember that with this utterly hot, raw, sexy griffin standing close enough to touch.

Before I could stop him, he lowered his mouth to mine. He kissed like his life depended on it. It was so easy to wrap myself up in his heat. I circled one of his nipples with a finger and felt him gasp.

"Come to Santorini with me," he murmured against my lips. Delicious. "Black sand beaches, two crazy sisters, my family's old country house." He brushed my hair back from my face and tucked it behind my ears. "I'd ply you with olives and think of many, many ways to entertain you." His lips tasted mine again. Once, twice. "And of course," he said, nipping at the edges of my mouth, "you'd have to skip the Beast Feast."

Yes.

No. My stomach tingled and it wasn't because of the way his fingers trailed down my back. It had to end tonight. I'd always said I wanted to go back, be with my preschool kids, have kids of my own some day.

Dimitri would be better off too, I reminded myself, ignoring the heat pooling between my thighs. He'd spent most of his life trying to save his sisters. Now, for the first time, he could relax and think of his own future. Maybe settle down with a griffin like him. I already hated her.

He nestled his face in the curve of my bare neck. Every nerve ending zinged with the sensation. Oh my fluttering soul, what it would be like to have him again, naked again, inside me.

I had to get out of here.

I pulled at Dimitri's emerald and to my surprise, the bronze chain unwound from my neck. We both watched the teardrop-shaped stone come to rest in my palm. It lay shadowy and thick in the moonlight.

"Here," I said, offering it to him.

*Please take it before I think about this too much.*

"No," he said, as a brief flash of worry crossed his face. "I gave that to you."

"I just think it would be safer with you," I said, dangling it between us.

Disappointment flickered over his features. "You're not coming to Greece."

"No," I said, the stone heavy in my hand.

"Keep it," he said. "We'll talk when I get back."

He captured my head in his hands and kissed me hard. Lips, teeth, tongue. He owned me, and I savored every second of it. I wanted to wrap my legs around him, feel him on top of me. He groaned and pulled me against him. Kissed me like he was never going to stop. Almost like a part of him knew we were kissing good-bye.

# Chapter Twenty-four

*This is the right thing to do*, I reminded myself as I stood inside the mirrored main dining room of the ship. The witches had blacked out the windows and shoved the tables to the corners of the room. We stood in a circle under a wrought iron chandelier, tipped with dozens upon dozens of gaslights.

I'd watched Dimitri climb onto his Harley as we filed into the ceremony room. It was official—he was gone. And when he got back, I wouldn't be here. *Don't think about it.* What's done is done.

Frieda squeezed my hand as peals of laughter rang from somewhere below us. "Giggle spell," she whispered into my ear. "Betty Two-Sticks didn't even see it coming."

"Shut it," Ant Eater growled on my other side.

"I'm just saying." Frieda's bracelets dangled against my wrist. "That woman is slow as pond water."

"Seal the door," Grandma ordered as she wheeled in a squeaky, rumbly dessert cart topped with a heated chafing dish. Flames curled under the dish and something sweet boiled inside. I knew better than to get my hopes up for cherries flambé.

The witches closed their eyes. I felt the magic build. The doors to the dining room slammed shut. No one moved a muscle. The only sound in the room came from bubbles seething over the fire. The air thickened as the gaslights dimmed and cast tall shadows against the mirrors behind us.

I couldn't help remembering the ceremony in the basement of the Red Skull. So much had changed since they'd first offered me their protection.

Grandma bowed her head and the others followed. "We, the witches of the Red Skull, are bound to the magic that has sustained our order for more than twelve hundred years. In it, we find warmth, light and eternal goodness. Without it, we perish. This night, we seek to rejoin the soul of our sister, Elizabeth. May she be one as we are one."

Yeek. Nobody called me Elizabeth unless I was in trouble. I fought back a tangle of nerves. *Let it go, Lizzie. Grandma knows what she's doing.*

Scarlet fiddled with something behind the ceremonial stew.

*Beeeeeeep!* A laptop screeched.

"Sorry," Scarlet muttered.

Oh don't tell me they were getting this spell off the Internet. My soul fluttered in my throat.

Grandma conferred with Scarlet for—not long enough in my book—before she stepped into the circle, holding a chain made from—oh geez—mangled twist ties.

Grandma Gertie was going to fuse my immortal soul with the same stuff I used to wrap bread.

I snuck a glance at Frieda. She seemed to think this made sense. Ant Eater? Riveted. Lovely. The witches observed Grandma with bated breath as she returned to the dessert cart and removed a covered dish. It smelled like chicken. But I knew better. Why couldn't I be related to a coven that drew their magic from plants or, as long as I was dreaming here, chocolate?

Then again, this would be my last ceremony.

Grandma lifted the lid on a plate full of teeny tiny hearts. She held up the twist-tie links and popped a wee ticker into each round hole.

"From death we begin again." She hung the grisly chain around my neck. Bet Dimitri would be glad now that I'd taken off his emerald. It felt gloopy, wet and it smelled like, well, dead animals. Syrupy excess dripped down my collarbone.

"As we join with you now, may the two halves of your soul be joined again."

They darted back and forth inside my throat. Holy heck.

Grandma must have sensed my unease. "Relax," she muttered. "We're not done yet."

I nodded and felt the gloppy necklace shift.

"Are you sure you want to give up your magic?" she asked.

This was it.

Shit.

Yes, I wanted to give up my powers. I was a teacher— and a damn good one. Not a demon slayer. I had to give this up, I told myself, my palms growing slick and sweaty against Frieda's . . . and Ant Eater's. And why did I care about Ant Eater? I didn't even like Ant Eater.

But I loved this life.

Despite everything, I didn't want to leave.

"Lizzie?" Grandma eyed me expectantly.

I hated sudden decisions. And until recently, I'd never been good at trusting my gut. I closed my eyes and searched hard for what I needed to do. I should give up my powers. I should pack up Pirate and head straight home. But . . . "I'm not going to do it." I said. "I'm staying."

I felt the witches exhale in a *whoosh*. Heck, I did the

same thing myself. I couldn't believe it. Me, in all of my over-planning, over-serious, oxford-wearing glory. I wanted to be a demon slayer. And, I thought as I squeezed my toes inside my high-flying, demon-whomping black boots, I might even ditch the oxfords for good.

"Okay!" Grandma said, grinning from ear to ear, not quite sure what to do next. "Uh, Scarlet? What's my next line?"

Scarlet tapped a few keys on the laptop and carried the whole thing over to Grandma.

Grandma placed a hand over my throat and used the other to steady the computer as she read. "As your soul was rended in pieces may it fuse, whole again." She caught my eye and winked. "Stronger for the wound that cut so deep. Wiser for facing the evil that caused it. Braver for having risked so much."

Grandma released my neck and snuffed the fire under the silver chafing dish. Scarlet reached under the cart and held up a large serving platter. On it, she placed a crystal goblet with handles on the sides. I remembered that goblet from the protection ceremony. And if I was lucky, there'd be something in that pot besides mashed squirrel and bakki root.

I felt Frieda dance on her toes. "Ohhh . . . cherried turtles is a delicacy, you know."

Grandma ladled the thick stew into the cup. The top of the crystal goblet clouded with steam.

This time, I'd drink.

Grandma held out the cup to the group. "As we drink, we are one." She inhaled the vapors above the goblet and took the first sip. Frieda went next. The cup made it all around the room and stopped in front of me, with plenty of goo to spare.

*Think of cherry pie filling.* I took it both hands, touched my lips to the sweltering cup and drank. It burned down my throat like a dozen shots of Jack

Daniels, warming me, filling me. The two halves of my soul fused and radiated a sense of completeness and harmony that burst straight through me.

The witches burst into applause. I felt Dimitri's emerald warm in my pocket.

I did it.

Frieda hauled off and hugged me while Ant Eater pounded me on the back.

I squinted as the overhead lights flickered on. "Beast Feast!" the witches hollered, stampeding for the door.

Frieda helped me ease off the goopy necklace and linked her arm in mine. "After that's the dancin'. We captured a ton of dance spells. They take forever to make. Want some?" she asked, digging through her bra. "I've got an Angus Young and a Macarena," she said, stuffing them into my pocket. "Both very big in their time." And wait, she said, fishing below her left boob. "Tango!" She nudged me with her elbow. "I saw you out there heating it up with Dimitri."

Ant Eater shoved her way past. "Wait," she said. "Gertie forgot part of the ceremony." Sure enough, Grandma and Scarlet debated back and forth as they studied the laptop screen. "Quick." Ant Eater popped a salty, jelly beany, bitter-when-I-bit-it *thing* into my mouth.

"Ugh," I said, through three chews and a quick swallow. I felt it every inch of the way down to my stomach. But I completed the ceremony this time. I did it. Come hell or highly unusual witchcraft.

Ant Eater burst out laughing.

"What?" Did I finally break through to that woman?

She grinned, her gold tooth flashing in the lamplight. "You just ate an owl's eye."

Ick. "A magical owl's eye?" I hoped.

"Nope. Just a plain old eye. Sucker!" She thumped me hard on the arm. "That was to get you back for not drinking the protection potion.

"Hey, everybody! Lizzie just ate an owl's eye," she guffawed.

I dug into my pocket, past Dimitri's emerald.

"That'll teach Lizzie not to mess with me," Ant Eater said, her attention on the crowd as I slipped a Macarena spell into her drink.

Too bad I didn't have time to watch Ant Eater star in Dancing with the Red Skulls. I had to go see about a griffin. And I hoped I wasn't too late.

I didn't know how I'd find him. My demon slayer instincts were programmed for danger, not sexy griffins. I'd just have to follow him to the airport, or to Santorini, or hell—wherever I needed to go.

As I dashed over the rumbling gangplank of the *Dixie Queen*, I saw him. Dimitri. I couldn't believe he was still here. "Hold up!" I called like a crazy person.

He sat, back straight, on his Harley. Well, until he heard me yelling at him. I couldn't see the look on his face, but I could tell by the way he hitched his long body off that hog that he was happy to see me. It had been a whole half hour, right?

"You're still here!" I said, plowing straight into him. He caught me and we both lurched sideways. He smelled so good, like sandalwood and pure man.

"Easy now," he said, running his hands along my arms.

I pulled him down to me and kissed him hard. He held me close, even after I broke away. "I had the worst feeling," he said, his breath warm against my cheek. "Like if I drove down that road, I'd never see you again."

I didn't want to think about how close I came. "You knew I'd come back, didn't you?"

"Hoped," he said.

He slid his hand into my pocket and withdrew the emerald. "May I?" I nodded as he slipped the thin bronze chain around my wrist. "You're coming to Greece with me," he said.

Like I could resist. I may not know much about the magical world, but I knew a good thing when I saw it. I'd be crazy to let him go. "Well I figure I've never ridden a Clydesdale up a flight of stairs."

"Diana will be thrilled."

A grin tickled the corners of my mouth. "Me too." I liked the idea of a family whose members watched out for each other. Growing up, I'd have given anything to have that. Now, between Grandma and Dimitri, I could have it two times over.

Dimitri reached into his back pocket and held up my dark blue passport. "A little something JR found in your desk at home."

I couldn't believe it. "You stole my passport?"

He had the nerve to look offended. "You stole my wallet."

"Touché." Ah, the memories lingered long after the underwear had dried. I nipped at his lips. He really was the most stubborn man I'd ever met.

"They're here!" Frieda hollered, wobbling as she scurried down the path on her platform sandals. "Boy oh boy," she told us, "your grandma's hotter than a goat's butt in a pepper patch."

I fought the urge to bury my face against Dimitri's chest. "What now?"

"It's your Uncle Phil. He ran off with a succubus." She patted at her canary yellow bouffant. "Rumor has it, they're in Vegas."

What did she expect us to do? "We're heading to Greece."

"You sure about that? The universe didn't give you

those powers for nothing. You too, buster," she said, flashing a rhinestone-tipped nail at Dimitri. "You owe us one."

Dimitri's necklace pulse, glowed, wound down my body to form a—

Oh no.

I lifted the front of my bustier and peeked down at my chain link bronze showgirl bra, Dimitri's tear drop emerald glowing between my breasts.

Did I really choose this kind of life?

I couldn't help smiling.

Yeah, I did. And I wouldn't have it any other way.

For centuries they have walked among us—vampires, shape-shifters, the Celtic Sidhe, demons, and other magical beings. Their battle to reign supreme is constant, but one force holds them in check, a race of powerful woarriors known as the

# IMMORTALS

The USA Today *Bestselling Series Contuines*

### Immortals: THE REDEEMING
Coming September 2008

### Immortals: THE CROSSING
Coming October 2008

### Immortals: THE HAUNTING
Coming November 2008

### Immortals: THE RECKONING
Coming Spring 2009

---

# Leslie Langtry

"Mixing a deadly sense of humor and plenty of sexy sizzle, Leslie Langtry creates a brilliantly original, laughter-rich mix of contemporary romance and suspense."
—*The Chicago Tribune*

# Stand By Your Hitman

A Greatest Hits romance

Missi Bombay invents things—fatal flowers, Jell-O bullets, stroke-inducing panty hose and other ways to kill a target without leaving any kind of evidence. She's a great asset to her family of assassins. The one thing she can't invent, though, is a love life. Unfortunately, her mom has decided to handle that for her. Next thing Missi knows, she's packed off to Costa Rica for a wild reality show where she's paired with Lex, the hottest contestant on TV. Too bad she also has to scope out a potential victim. But the job becomes tougher when someone starts sabotaging the show...and love-of-her-life Lex thinks she's the culprit!

ISBN 13: 978-0-8439-6037-2

# ❏ **YES!**

Sign me up for the Love Spell Book Club and send my
FREE BOOKS! If I choose to stay in the club, I will pay only
$8.50* each month, a savings of $6.48!

NAME: _____

ADDRESS: _____

TELEPHONE: _____

EMAIL: _____

❏ I want to pay by credit card.

❏ **VISA**       ❏ **MasterCard.**       ❏ **DISCOVER**

ACCOUNT #: _____

EXPIRATION DATE: _____

SIGNATURE: _____

Mail this page along with $2.00 shipping and handling to:
**Love Spell Book Club**
**PO Box 6640**
**Wayne, PA 19087**
Or fax (must include credit card information) to:
**610-995-9274**
You can also sign up online at **www.dorchesterpub.com**.